The Rt Hon Lord Hurd of  educated at Eton and Cambr class degree in history. Follow he became Secretary of State f (1984–85) and Home Secretary (1985–89) before his appointment as Foreign Secretary in 1989. He was MP for Mid-Oxfordshire (later Witney) from 1974 to 1997. Upon his retirement as Foreign Secretary in 1995, Lord Hurd joined the Nat West Group, leaving in 2000 to become Deputy Chairman of Coutts Bank. He is also President of the Prison Reform Trust charity.

Lord Hurd is the author of thirteen books and lives in Oxfordshire with his wife Judy and their son and daughter. He has three grown-up sons from his first marriage.

Also by Douglas Hurd

Fiction
SEND HIM VICTORIOUS
THE SMILE ON THE FACE OF THE TIGER
SCOTCH ON THE ROCKS
WAR WITHOUT FRONTIERS
(all with Andrew Osmond)
TRUTH GAME
THE PALACE OF ENCHANTMENTS
(with Stephen Lamport)
THE SHAPE OF ICE
VOTE TO KILL
TEN MINUTES TO TURN THE DEVIL

Non-fiction
THE ARROW WAR
AN END TO PROMISES
THE SEARCH FOR PEACE

IMAGE
IN THE
WATER

Douglas Hurd

A *Time Warner* Paperback

First published in Great Britain in 2001
by Little, Brown and Company
This edition published in 2002 by Time Warner Paperbacks

Copyright © Douglas Hurd, 2001

The moral right of the author has been asserted.

The author gratefully acknowledges permission to quote from
'Narcissus' by Ted Hughes © 1997, Ted Hughes.
Reprinted by permission of Faber and Faber Ltd.

A CIP catalogue record for this book
is available from the British Library.

ISBN 0 7515 3215 0

Typeset in Goudy by M Rules
Printed and bound in Great Britain
by Clays Ltd, St Ives plc.

Time Warner Paperbacks
An imprint of
Time Warner Books UK
Brettenham House
Lancaster Place
London WC2E 7EN

www.TimeWarnerBooks.co.uk

To the Electors of West Oxfordshire

He lay, like a fallen garden statue,
Gaze fixed on his image in the water . . .
'. . . I never saw beauty
To compare with yours. Oh, why do you always
Dodge away at the last moment
And leave me with my eyes full of nothing
But water and the memory of an image?'

'Narcissus' from *Tales from Ovid*, Ted Hughes

Chapter 1

In paradisum deducant angeli

Roger Courtauld, Home Secretary, shifted his buttocks on the hard seat of the stall. Though the chief constables of police had failed to drink him under the table at last night's dinner he was suffering from a mild hangover. Beside him his wife Hélène peered this way and that from beneath her dark blue hat, rather too large for her trim French figure. Roger guessed that she was calculating whether the Westminster Abbey officials had seated them in the correct order of protocol. Certainly Joan Freetown and her husband Guy were nearer the altar than the Courtaulds, but on the opposite side of the chancel. Was that higher or lower in order of precedence? Nearer to God, certainly, but further from the Prince of Wales. And in any case was the Chancellor of the Exchequer senior in the pecking order to the Home Secretary? For some these were deep waters. Roger neither knew nor cared – though he admitted to himself that he was lucky to have a wife who did both. This ensured, without any effort on his part, that his own carelessness was never flagrantly exploited.

He tried to turn his mind to Simon Russell, the Prime Minister five weeks dead, whom they had come to remember. The poignant melody of the anthem was a greater help than the vague benevolence of the Archbishop in his address. Roger felt that if his mind, despite the hangover, did not seize and pin down Simon Russell, now at the moment of his memorial service, their friendship would dissolve for ever, unclassified and therefore unreal. Had Russell himself (the surname came naturally to the fore despite their twenty years of work together) believed that angels were at all likely to welcome a prime minister into paradise? Perhaps yes, in the same manner, enthusiastic yet decorous, as a Conservative audience welcomed their Prime Minister at the end of a harmonious Party Conference, rejoicing in the grace of a good speech and a ten-point lead in the polls. He supposed that Simon Russell would now be coping with the voice of God in the same patient but not obsequious way as he had always coped with the voice of the people.

Roger shook himself, dissatisfied. That was not the right level of thought for this time and place. Simon Russell had been a conventional Anglican, for sure. Roger had once heard him read the Christmas gospel in the huge gaunt Victorian church at the heart of Russell's North London constituency, St Barnabas, or was it St Matthew? But he was probably a real Christian as well, not exactly fervent but privately praying and communicating with God in a way Roger envied but found impossible.

In any case Russell had been a good prime minister. Roger remembered a joint press conference they had held together at

Central Office during the last election. A young and pretty girl at the back had asked the Prime Minister what he regarded as his major achievement in office. It was a hopeless question, clearly intended to be helpful (perhaps even planted by the Central Office staff) but in fact devilish. Russell had sucked his silver pencil as usual, then begun his answer with a dangerous phrase.

'That's not really the right question.' He had sucked the pencil again. 'You see, being prime minister is not a matter of climbing mountains and planting silly little flags marked Russell on the summit. It is more like navigating a river in a clumsy boat full of passengers, a winding river with sandbanks, white water, rocks, even cataracts at some points, and tidal towards the end. Your aim is to convey your passengers safely to their destination. They are eating, drinking, playing computer games, only occasionally sparing you a glance or a thought. They blame you for the weather as well as for the rubbery soufflé at lunch. Your only reward is the satisfaction of eventually steering their ship safely into harbour. Then you can apply to the company for another voyage, which is what we are doing in this general election.'

The *Guardian* had reported that the Prime Minister dodged the question, but the evening television had taken that excerpt, and several people had commented favourably to Roger on the campaign trail next day.

It had proved an effective low-key philosophy, but Roger had not made it his own. He needed something riskier and more energetic. He shifted again in the stall, knocking a hymn book off the shallow ledge in front of him, earning a glance of reproach from Hélène.

Right, he had done his stint in remembering Simon Russell.

Now he had to concentrate on the big personal decision he faced. To stand or not to stand for the leadership. His mind rehearsed familiar arguments for and against, but in his heart he now knew the answer.

In tuo adventu suscipiant te martyres

Something about martyrs, Julia supposed. Her parents had decided that she should take Latin as a GCSE subject at the age of fourteen. She had outwitted them by simply not turning up at the lessons, and threatening to telephone the *Mirror* if they tried to coerce her. Julia had learned a lot from the speed with which both parents and school had yielded. Her father's position as prime minister, which she hated, could be turned to good effect.

Anyway, her father was not a martyr, or anything like – neither had he or his relationship with her anything to do with this preposterous great church. The Abbey seemed empty of him but filled with irrelevant history and an army of well-dressed hypocrites. She would remember her father her own way. Not the corpse in the coffin which they had shoved miserably through the curtain in the crematorium a month ago. Not even the serene face last seen on the pillow in Joan Freetown's spare room, with the evening sparrows wittering in the yew tree outside the window. Her parents had been staying the weekend with the Chancellor of the Exchequer when Simon Russell had his second and fatal heart-attack. Engaged to join them for Sunday supper, she arrived to find her mother staring into the drawing-room fire while Joan Freetown busied herself with a thousand well-ordered telephone calls about death. Upstairs a red box full of unfinished work sat as a last congenial companion beside her dead father in his bed. Nor would Julia try to find some distant childhood memory, for he had not been prime minister then and being prime minister seemed an inseparable part of him. Julia fixed her mind on a walk with him under the beeches at Chequers, just before tea, the rain coming down hard, the two protection officers muttering ten yards behind and Simon trying to find the right words to re-engage with his daughter after a family row. She had loved him then, tired but turning back to her away from the incomprehensible political commotions that absorbed nine-tenths of his life.

So she did not need to think about him in Westminster Abbey, and could look at the faces around her. Roger Courtauld immediately on her right, the flesh crowding in now on genial eyes and mouth. He had always kept a kind word for her, though she had never known how to receive it. Across the aisle was Peter Makewell, Foreign Secretary and acting Prime Minister, his face old and taut, skin stretched over a cage of bones. Joan Freetown, Chancellor of the Exchequer, elegant as ever in black, harsh hair with a white streak carrying backwards the exceptional pallor of her temples. On the rare occasions when Julia went to a reception at 10 Downing Street or Chequers, Joan Freetown had always given her a glassy smile of recognition, but found no words. Not many words either when she had found Julia weeping in the unlocked bathroom ten yards from her father's body. But the cold water, the towel, the ten-second hug had been kind as well as efficient. Today they were back to the glassy smiles. On the right, the Prince of Wales, himself rather than the usual representative. On the left, the Archbishop and other resplendent clergy – but who was the young man who had caught her eye and lifted his hand in a half-wave? Longish buttery hair, dark suit but an unsuitable bright blue tie, slightly rounded shoulders, even at that range an aggressive expression.

Her mother, too, had seen the gesture, and leaned forward protectively. 'David Alcester,' Louise said, before being asked. 'Best avoided.'

Julia remembered. A year ago this young MP had managed somehow to get himself invited to a reception at No. 10 in honour of adult education. Julia had been cajoled into attending with the promise of a new red dress. David Alcester had backed her against a pillar and told her at length the story of his life. She remembered brown eyes under the blond forelock and a deep political voice. There had been nothing sexual in his advance. His only pleasure, it seemed, was in the rise and fall of his own voice.

For once Julia agreed with her mother. Best avoided.

Had that half-wave to Julia Russell been a mistake? The seats in the south transept were packed close. Though David Alcester was not tall, his knees were jammed against the chair in front. He had met Julia only once, though she had certainly been interested that evening at No. 10 in what he had told her about politics and his career. He sometimes wished that he might look at girls the way most of his friends did, or at least pretended to. But he saw little chance of being swept off his feet by love, or even lust. His fever lay elsewhere. One day soon he would need to think about marriage, or at least a partnership, some good-looking girl who would go down well in his Newbury constituency and help his career forward.

There could be no possible harm in acknowledging Julia, who had been a prime minister's daughter until a few weeks back, and would go on appearing in magazines for years to come. Had there been a glimmer from her in response?

David had applied for a ticket in the Abbey on the general principle that he should be seen at gatherings of the great and good. He had hardly known Simon Russell or particularly approved of his quiet style of politics. David was not stupid and had recognised that from some source he could not analyse his former leader had drawn great strength.. But he preferred his politics clear and rough. The sight of Joan Freetown in her stall resolved him to write to her at once, offering his services in her leadership campaign.

Meanwhile, there were two other matters to be decided. David believed in using every minute of his waking life to the full, and there was nothing to detain his mind in the anthem, the Abbey or any memories of Simon Russell. Begin with his appearance, always important. This was the first time he had worn this new suit. It had been bought off the peg, and was uncomfortably tight under the right armpit. Should he take it back to Austin Reed? Would he have to pay for an alteration? Or would it adapt itself once he had worn it once or twice? He decided to postpone the decision for exactly a fortnight, no more.

Next, he had a question down in the Commons to the Minister for Transport for answer that afternoon about the need for new trees to be planted at the side of the Newbury bypass. In his supplementary question after the minister had answered should he refer to this memorial service and to the late Prime Minister's well-known love of trees? He had read somewhere about Simon Russell's plantings at Chequers and had worked out a phrase. Or would that be in poor taste? David did not trust himself yet as an arbiter of taste. He looked again along the line of distinguished faces in the stalls Yes, this time, certainly there had been a response as he caught Julia's eye. To his earlier half-wave she now returned a half-nod. That was the sign he needed. He would certainly use that supplementary question. There were no votes in taste. 'Would the minister accept that many of us who gathered in the Abbey this morning out of respect for the late Prime Minister remembered in particular his love of our countryside and . . .'

Et perducant te in civitatem sanctam Jerusalem

Peter Makewell liked the lilt of the anthem. He knew nothing of music, but this was a pleasant goodbye tune of which Simon Russell would have approved. Indeed, had probably selected, for Simon had been meticulous, leaving nothing to chance – except, of course, the timing of his death, something outwith the control of even the most painstaking policy unit. Peter Makewell felt that mixture of satisfaction and sadness with which men in their seventies react to the death of younger friends. To this was added a small element of resentment. Simon Russell had failed to spot a gap in the constitutional arrangements of Britain, as a result of which Peter Makewell was for the moment not only Foreign Secretary but acting Prime Minister, a position he had not sought and actively disliked.

The rules of the Conservative Party, endorsed in 1997 under William Hague, provided that an election for the leadership should be triggered either by the resignation of the party leader or as a result of a vote of no confidence by Conservative Members of Parliament. Strangely, indeed arrogantly, there was no mention in the rules of one rather frequent trigger of vacancy, to wit death. It took time to organise a party election, but the country could not wait to have a prime minister. So the ancient wheels of the constitution, which all the experts had banished to the backroom, were produced. The magic circle had operated. The grandees had been consulted on behalf of the monarch. They had worked with traditional speed and secrecy. The Queen had invited Makewell to form a government, it being understood that he would stand down as soon as a new leader was elected under the Hague rules. The grandees had rightly assumed that Makewell would not want to stand in that contest. He therefore found himself temporary Prime Minister because everyone knew that in the long term it was a job he did not want.

Nor was this affectation. Simon Russell, whom he had much respected, had once passed on to him what he had described as the most closely guarded secret of the premiership, that it was not really hard work. The Prime Minister did not face each day the compulsory grind of departmental business. The fixed duties of the office by no means filled the week. Except at times of national crisis there were many hours for the Prime Minister to dispose of as he or she wished. Of course, prime ministers themselves always disputed this. They were likely to be persons of great energy. Not since Baldwin resigned in 1937 had Britain had a really lazy prime minister, though Callaghan had tried. The other had filled the time by constant and often unnecessary intervention in the affairs of departments, then complained of overwork. Prime-ministerial time, Russell had argued, should be better employed in leisurely strategic thought, touring the country to gain first-hand impressions, and consulting wise opinion from outside politics. Makewell had listened, but taken small notice, not least because Russell, during his four years at No. 10, had shown no sign of acting on his own prescription.

Now Makewell was enduring his own experience. An ava-lanche of information daily overwhelmed him. He knew in theory that he had been lucky, in that the one crisis Russell had left behind, the Russian civil war, had been quickly set-tled by negotiation. The British peacekeeping troops would be coming home from St Petersburg next month. But even with-out a crisis Britain seemed impossibly hard to govern. The Scottish Nationalists, feeling robust on a diet of bad history and a high oil price, were pressing again for a referendum on independence. His own party was indignant against the Scots, and also now against the European Central Bank, which had just raised interest rates for the second month running. But he seemed to have no time for these problems of political man-agement. Makewell had never served as a minister in either the Treasury or the Home Office. Now these two great depart-ments, both prolific in problems, daily dumped their mysteries on his desk. Neither of the two responsible ministers, Roger Courtauld and Joan Freetown, nor indeed his own staff at No. 10, seemed to realise how ignorant he was, and it was now too late either to confess or to learn. The details of stop-and-search legislation or the modalities of the withholding tax would always lie beyond his grasp. Once upstairs in his study, soon after his arrival, he had ventured to interrupt a long presentation on a forthcoming Bill: 'Surely these are matters of detail which could be settled elsewhere.'

'As you wish, Prime Minister,' the senior Treasury official had replied, and continued his presentation as if nothing had been said.

Makewell, knowing that, though intellectually limited, he was neither lazy nor stupid, supposed that there must be a way through this thicket. He must abandon dignity and ask for help, either from his main private secretary, Patrick Vaughan, or from his press secretary Artemis Palmer, both inherited from Russell. Could it really be true that Simon Russell had slept with Artemis? Russell's wife Louise seemed to Peter Makewell exactly what a prime minister's wife should be, beautiful, loyal, unpolitical. He could not imagine what spasm of desire or despair might have driven Simon to desert her for the skimpy embraces of his press secretary. But he acknowledged that he himself, long a faithful husband now a sober widower, found it hard to judge stories about the sex life of others. His happiest hours now were snatched at his old desk in the Foreign Office, surrounded by the much loved green and gold wallpaper, coping with the relative simplicities of the Cyprus question or the admission of Balkan states to the European Union.

But he was misusing time. The anthem was moving towards its climax. This was an opportunity to ask advice, not from God, who for Peter Makewell was real enough but dwelt in the Perthshire hills and on Sunday in the Episcopalian Church at Blairgowrie, no, from Simon Russell, who was clearly present with them in Westminster Abbey and able to read minds even more skilfully now than during his life. As so often before Makewell put the problem as clearly as he could to his former leader.

There was no uncertainty about the timing of the election

Douglas Hurd

of the new Conservative leader. Martin Redburn, chairman of the 1922 Committee of Conservative backbenchers, was in effect their group leader. He had the job of fixing the date, and had chosen Thursday, 25 March, for the first stage. Nor was there much doubt about the two likely candidates – Roger Courtauld and Joan Freetown. The problem for Makewell as acting Prime Minister was different. Joan Freetown had told him yesterday that she intended to produce a special Budget on 20 March. She had talked in his study as if this was a decision for her alone, although they both knew that his assent and that of the Cabinet were needed.

'The economy needs stimulating. The country and the Party need encouragement. I have carefully worked out proposals to achieve this. It's all ready. The case for a March Budget is overwhelming.'

She had closed her folder with something approaching a bang. The bracelets on her wrists had clacked vigorously in applause. She had not mentioned the immense impetus a popular Budget would give to her leadership campaign. She had chosen a date five days before MPs would vote on the new leader. She had dared the caretaker Prime Minister to object.

And he had not objected. Nor had he assented. He had muttered, in a way he now admitted was feeble, about wider considerations, about the need to reflect and consult.

'A decision is needed within forty-eight hours,' she had said, closing the interview.

The pros and cons were obvious enough. No point in spelling them out to Simon Russell, who in his present situation somewhere above the altar would see it all clearly. Neither of them, in their hearts, would want Joan Freetown to lead the Party and become Prime Minister. But that was not quite the point. Without actually slipping to his knees he asked Simon Russell for advice.

Chorus angelorum te suscipiat

Joan Freetown had no ear for music, and did not believe in God. She had mixed views about the Church of England. She found its priests and bishops tedious. In her experience few of them had even an elementary understanding of economics, though their ignorance did not deter them from frequent utterance on the subject. But she saw the point of churches, of establishment, and of pulpits if properly used.

Today, however, she was not thinking about these things. She was thinking for the last time about Simon Russell. Her worry was that he had never worried. More than once she had tried to reach him with her concern about the economy, about Europe, about the growing depredations of the Scots. He had always been courteous, but she had felt she never reached him. He had managed the government well, but she could not understand someone for whom that was the main purpose of a political career. She had never detected in him any driving idea. At first she had thought he was simply disguising his hostility to her own ideas, but latterly she judged that at the level of ideas he was genuinely empty.

Now she would be up against the same difficulty, only worse. She supposed, though he had not yet said so, that Roger Courtauld would be her opponent for the leadership. Here again was a man without ideas. At least Simon Russell had had an educated mind, and indeed a natural authority in taking decisions which she respected. Roger Courtauld had none of that. He was shrewd, but that was the only thing to be said for him.

She did not relish the forthcoming contest. She knew that she lacked what Roger Courtauld possessed, the knack of slapping shoulders, exchanging jokes, attracting personal loyalty. She would need help. Not with the Budget: she would spend that afternoon working alone on her proposals, confident that Peter Makewell would let her present them. She must find someone to help her with the in-fighting and the public relations. Her eyes strayed eastward and, like Julia Russell, she fastened on David Alcester, in the pew to the right towards the high altar. Tactically quick, a good grasp of economics, young, ruthless, but not more than was needed, she thought. She allowed her eyes to rest for a moment on the long fair hair, the strong profile, the well-cut suit. Of course he was still a boy. He needed someone to recommend a good barber and would need careful guidance. The blue tie was a mistake. She persuaded herself that it was only his political gifts which attracted her.

By her side her husband Guy was on his knees. He prayed for the soul of Simon Russell, but he did not seriously doubt its well-being. If anyone deserved the approval of his Maker as well as of his country it was the last Prime Minister. But principally he prayed for his own wife, whom he loved. He prayed that she might fail in her ambition to succeed Simon Russell. Partly he was selfish, because he was praying for the safety of his marriage. But he was also praying for his wife's happiness, and for his country's well-being.

Et cum Lazaro quondam paupere aeternam habeas requiem

It was odd, so odd that she could tell it to no one, but that day in the Abbey Louise felt content. Indeed, with the exception of the day of his cremation, she had felt content through the weeks since she had found Simon calm and finally at rest in Joan Freetown's spare bedroom. Contentment might not have been odd had she disliked her husband or wanted him to die. On the contrary she had deeply loved Simon Russell and passionately wanted him to live. But after his first heart-attack last summer she had prepared herself for the second, supposing that when it came it would be fatal. He had died quickly and she hoped without more than a few seconds of pain. He had died before his powers began to crumble, while he was still doing well the job which he enjoyed. That evening in the Cotswolds he had known that his wife was comfortable by the fire downstairs and that his daughter was on her way through the winter evening to see him.

Louise had felt a moment of desolation in the newly built raw, red brick crematorium on Highgate Hill when Simon's body in the impersonal coffin slid through the curtain into the fire. Her own body for a few seconds had seemed torn apart at the knowledge that she would never again quarrel with Simon, organise a week or a holiday with Simon, buy a shirt for Simon, sip morning tea with him in bed, see him patiently waiting for her at the foot of the stairs. But that pain had passed quickly and was replaced by this miraculous crop of memories, which she was still bringing to harvest. Sometimes nowadays she had to force herself away from memories. She made herself go and sculpt in the studio in Wandsworth, which Simon had hardly ever visited. She entertained Julia's friends, whom Simon had never met. She even toyed with the idea of selling the house in Highgate and living somewhere where Simon had never set foot. She knew that he had valued her independent spirit and would have approved of all these acts of recovery through separation.

But today in the Abbey, when the nation was remembering its prime minister, she might indulge herself in memories of the man she had married. Politics had been there all the time. At first she had resented this bitterly. During the first years of marriage she had fought against each evening destroyed by a late vote, each weekend conference, each dull dinner made worse by speeches. Latterly she had continued to fight, but more as a matter of habit than in hope of victory. She no longer expected to drive politics out of Simon's life or even to loosen its grip. Indeed, in these later years she had dreaded the task of living with him once his political career had ended. She could not imagine how either of them would fill the void.

Was the close of the anthem too calm, even sentimental? But that was how she felt that morning. All was well, particularly with her. No one else in the congregation, not even Julia, shared with her the particular heap of small recollections that added up to a sound marriage. When she met him Simon had been short of money. Little habits from that time had stayed with him. He turned off lights when they left a room. He kept the tawdry razors issued by airlines and soap from hotel rooms. He entered a running total on the stub of their joint cheque book, source of many misunderstandings. She had tried to tease him out of some of these habits, and now was glad that she had failed. Hide-and-seek with Julia and her friends in the Highgate garden, the tie she had bought him each year for the Party Conference, a slope of olives in

Tuscany, the exercises he did in the bedroom each morning, walking together through the first sparkle of autumn frost on the lawns at Chequers – this jumble of unrelated snapshots was hers alone. It was useless to explain marriage to the young, for they thought of it only in terms of sex and children. Sex they had without marriage, and often nowadays children too. But they missed the point. Sleeping together and bringing up children were not great matters in themselves. They helped, along with a mass of other events, for better for worse, for richer for poorer, in sickness and in health, to create a familiarity between two human beings that went beyond anything else in life. Familiarity, that was a feeble word. Comradeship, alliance, teamwork, harmony, oneness – none of these was quite right either, but Louise knew exactly what she meant. Now death had parted her from Simon. They had always known that death, and death alone, had that right.

A loss to the nation, to the Party, to this and to that – so everyone told her and, of course, it was true. But death was not a thief, or malevolent: death was simply the stage hand who rang down the curtain on a particular act. That morning Louise felt no loss, just her own happiness.

Chapter 2

Extract from the Budget speech of Rt Hon. Joan Freetown, Chancellor of the Exchequer:

> *Chancellor of the Exchequer*: I turn now to a number of secondary decisions taken in the name of good house-keeping. I propose to move the headquarters of the National Savings Bank from Glasgow to Newcastle. This is estimated to save fifteen million euros in running costs each year.'
>
> *Hon. Members*: Shame!
>
> *Mr Hamish Sandbeg (Hamilton)*: This is appalling news for Scotland. It is an act of obscene vandalism. How many Scottish jobs will be lost?
>
> *Chancellor of the Exchequer*: I have no idea [*Interruption*], of course I have no idea. It will depend on how many of the existing employees are willing to move across the border to Newcastle. The Honourable

Member should put his question to the leader of his party. If the Scottish National Party were not pressing for the break-up of the United Kingdom I might have been willing to leave this United Kingdom institution in Glasgow despite the extra labour costs imposed by the recent lamentable and destructive decision of the Scottish Parliament.

Mr Alexander Mackie (Glasgow Cathcart): Is the Chancellor telling us that this vindictive decision is being taken for purely political reasons?

Chancellor of the Exchequer: It is a matter of common prudence. I cannot ignore the chance of saving fifteen million euros. But I also cannot ignore the growing disquiet among English savers at the prospect of their savings being handled in a city that might, if the SNP have their way, be separated before long from the United Kingdom. If this decision is disliked in Glasgow, its citizens know who to blame. My responsibility is to the prudent savers of the United Kingdom.

Later:

The Chancellor of the Exchequer: . . . I have had to take into account the effect on the English regions of the interest rate rises imposed by the European Central Bank in Frankfurt at their meeting in March . . . Unless counteracting action is taken I am advised that unemployment would probably rise by 1 per cent in Cornwall, 1.5 per cent along the southern coast of England and by up to 2 per cent on both Teesside and

Tyneside. The ECB seems to have taken no account of
these consequences. It will be for the Welsh and
Scottish Executives to assess any similar outcome in
those parts of the United Kingdom. My responsibility
in this matter is for England. I am tonight laying an
order under the Regional Assistance Act 2004 providing for an employment grant of twenty euros per week
for employees to all employers in the regions which I
have just mentioned.

Hon. Members: Brilliant. That will show them.

Mr John Turnbull (Leader of the Opposition): Has the
Chancellor consulted the Attorney General on the
legality under European law of the measure she has just
announced?

Chancellor of the Exchequer: I am shocked that the
Right Honourable Gentleman should take such a legal-
istic line. Those facing the sack as a result of this
European decision on interest rates will note that the
Labour Party is more concerned with legal niceties
than with jobs. Even Lord Blair's government did not
give away the right of government and Parliament in
this country to fix our own expenditure and taxes. I am
exercising that right today. The European Court is the
place where matters of legality could in theory be
tested. Should there be a challenge – I am confident
there will not, but should there be a challenge – it
would not come to court for several years. We would
strenuously contest it – and meanwhile the grant will
be paid.

Hon. Members: Brilliant again.

Extract from political commentary by Miss Alice Thomson in the Daily Telegraph:

> Joan Freetown yesterday produced a highly political Budget. There is no harm in that. It should delight all Conservatives. She used a relatively small administrative decision on the National Savings Bank to highlight her increasing alarm at the loudmouthed vituperation of the SNP. She showed that part of the price of Scottish independence may be paid by the Scots in advance of a referendum if the SNP continue their present campaign.
>
> Her employment subsidy for the English regions may raise greater doubts. The justification was distinctly broad brush. Conservative chancellors have usually supported, not undermined, the general policy of the EU in hacking away at state subsidies. When the Bank of England in the old days raised interest rates and some regions suffered, Conservatives would certainly have argued against compensating state aid. But, that said, the Chancellor received and deserved a loud ovation, even from Conservatives who support Roger Courtauld in the leadership battle. In contrast to the Home Secretary she has shown herself a Conservative of firm ideas and strong will.

'So we either go on or go out,' said Joe Seebright, the editor of *Thunder*, at his daily meeting, with the air of one coining an epigram. These were the words the proprietor, Lord Spitz, had used to him on the telephone just half an hour earlier.

Joe did not repeat the further wisdom of the proprietor,

who had added, 'The truth is, Joe, you yourself don't have a choice. You're too far in. You chose Freetown, so for you she's got to win. Me, I'm different. I'm just a goddamn South African Jew. For me *Thunder*'s in the business of selling newspapers, not choosing prime ministers.' A pause had followed, while across the Atlantic Lord Spitz slurped coffee.

'Remember the *Sun*,' he continued. 'Murdoch changed editors four times before he finally quit. That's not my style.' Another pause. 'One would be ample.'

'Yes, indeed.' Seebright cultivated a monotonous tone in dealing with his proprietor. Either encouragement or dissent led to longer conversation. Anyway, he reminded himself, it was not just a matter of self-interest and survival. He genuinely believed Joan Freetown was right for Britain – brave, experienced, above all definite. Like *Thunder*. The conversation had ended there.

'How's the form book today?'

Seebright's question went to the political editor, Robert Macdowell, who sat as usual in a corner though entitled by seniority to a seat at the table. Two years earlier Macdowell had moved from the broadsheet press to the tabloids. The rewards for his work had thus increased as its quality deteriorated. This did not make him a happy man. Occasionally he exacted small revenges – by slipping words of more than two syllables into his reports, or by prosing away in almost academic vein at meetings such as this.

'As you know there are two stages to the count under the Hague rules of 1997. In the first stage next Thursday Conservative MPs and peers cast their votes. There Courtauld has been edging ahead. Freetown has lost the immediate advantage she gained from the Budget. She made the usual Treasury mistake of supposing that a Budget's immediate popularity will last. Her real difficulty is that MPs know her too well.'

'They only know the silly little weaknesses,' said Seebright. 'They don't like the bracelets and the sharp voice in the tea room. They lose the big picture.'

Macdowell did not comment, but continued, 'By contrast, she's well established in the constituency vote of party members, which follows in a fortnight. She's worked that scene for years, endless supper clubs and annual general meetings, whereas Courtauld has never bothered.'

'Lazy sod,' said Seebright.

'Out there they like her toughness against Europe and the Americans, and now against the Scots. They don't want anything really done about any of that because most of them know it's difficult, but they like to hear the noise of their own resentment. She provides this.'

'If the two votes clash? If the MPs and the constituencies produce different results?'

'The total party membership wins. But they haven't clashed since '97. There's always been a strong deference vote, party members still believing MPs must know best. So her main worry is that the MPs will just tip against her and the membership reluctantly follow suit.'

'We must change tack,' said Seebright unexpectedly. Even the sports team, hitherto inattentive, sat up. This could not mean switching to support Roger Courtauld. Could it mean less space on politics? They sighed wistfully. For a few seconds most of those present nourished a hope of return to the golden days of total concern for football and the sex life of TV personalities. That was how the British press had grown great. But Seebright thrust round copies of a draft leader, and hopes fell. So it was not pulling out of politics, after all, but plunging further in. They read:

> The time for genteel politeness has passed. This morning *Thunder* has to speak its mind. The leadership contest in the Tory Party, always dull, has become a bloody bore. Why? Because we've allowed the politicians to treat it as their own affair. Day after day they've drooled on about the Budget, Europe, devolution, the rest of the political agenda. Excuse us while we yawn. We're about to choose the human being with the most important say of anyone in our lives for years to come – more than the Queen, of course, more than the President of the Internet, more than the editor of *Thunder*, more than, dare we say it?, David Beckham at the head of Man United.'

'Steady,' murmured the chief football editor.

'Circulation down again,' agreed his assistant, but not audibly.

> From tomorrow we are going to change all that. From tomorrow *Thunder* is going to present the two candidates, not as cardboard politicians mouthing speeches but as real three-dimensional human beings. We are going to dig deep into their past. We are not interested in prurient peeping. That is not our way. But we mean to show what kind of personality is going to lead the nation. So wake up, Joan. Wake up, Roger. For tomorrow we're going to wake up Britain.

There was silence. It did not seem to amount to much. Macdowell found the words. 'Good stuff, Joe. But it all depends on the follow-up. You must have something good in the locker.'

Seebright was at his most businesslike. 'For Joan, not difficult. She saved a crippled boy from drowning in the river at Cambridge. A bit of time ago. She was nineteen, the lad five. *Cambridge Evening News* the next day. No one's ever picked it up since.'

'She told you?' It was not like Joan Freetown.

'No. David Alcester came round yesterday. The young MP. He's trying to grip her campaign. He sounded a bit desperate. We've checked with the Cambridgeshire police. It's okay. That'll be in Thursday.' Today was Tuesday.

'And Roger Courtauld?'

'A rather different story, I'm afraid.' Seebright smirked, then handed out one print of a colour photograph, which he carefully collected and replaced in an envelope when it had done the rounds. It showed sea and in the foreground a stretch of white sand. Two young men in swimming trunks were lying side by side on the same blue and white beach towel, eyes shut, apparently asleep, thighs touching. The right hand of one clasped the left hand of the other. No one recognised the fair young man with a magazine lying beside him. Though the photograph might have been forty years old, there could be no doubt about the identification of the second youth. Roger Courtauld's shoulders had been straighter then and his cheeks less chubby, but there was no mistaking the big head, tightly curled dark hair, and slightly crowded features.

'How does this come into it?' asked Macdowell. His

conscience began to stir, always ready to start arguments it never won.

'It depends,' said Seebright.

'Depends?'

'On the way things develop.'

They were friends, that was the odd thing, though five days ago they had hardly known each other. No, that was a slight exaggeration, thought Roger Courtauld, as his campaign committee filed into his room at the top of the Home Office for the morning meeting. Most of them had known each other for a time as political acquaintances, nodding and smiling in corridors and the tea room, forming ephemeral alliances to sign a motion, influence a debate, or exchange current gossip at political dining clubs such as the Bow Group or One Nation. But this was different. After less than a week of the leadership campaign they knew each other under the skin. They were brothers at arms, or rather brothers and sister at arms, for he must never forget Sara Tunstall. Fair and flouncy, she was the most right-wing of his supporters and he still did not know what had brought her into his camp. Was it simply dislike and jealousy of Joan Freetown? Roger feared that quite a lot of his votes in the Commons would come from that unflattering source. One or two other supporters regarded themselves as jockeys who had chosen Roger Courtauld as the horse to take them to their own chosen winning post. That was certainly true of Clive Wilson, the typical ambitious backbencher. He had made himself a name in the Russian civil war by being in the right place at the right time – but not quite enough of a name to propel him into a ministerial job at the Foreign Office without the help of a patron. Roger made a mental note that he must not neglect Wilson just because he did not like him.

But the others – Peter Struther, Raymond Gannet, both MPs, the PR man John Parrott, Simon Cresswick from the Lords – what had brought them to take the risk of identifying themselves with what, at the beginning, seemed like a losing cause? Which led, of course, back to a previous question: what had led him, Roger Courtauld, to put himself forward?

The whole contest was distinctly odd. He and Joan Freetown were colleagues in the same Cabinet. There had been no great rows between them. Each had respected the other's frontiers; they stood on a shared government record; they were both committed to the projects of the late Russell administration. Though he had not much liked Joan's latest Budget he could not attack it because she had bounced it through Cabinet in his presence. Yet if the contest was to interest anyone they had to find something to disagree on. How otherwise were the columnists to find material and their campaign committees something to discuss? So the two rivals were forced back onto the terrain of philosophy and first principles. In their press articles, speeches and interviews they had to argue about the underlying purpose of politics.

Here Joan Freetown had the advantage. Her beliefs were long prepared, well tailored, hanging in the cupboard ready for immediate use. That was not to say that she was consistent, for her philosophy and her practical policies often disagreed. For example, though by nature isolationist, in Simon Russell's last weeks she had joined Roger in forcing on the Prime Minister and the Cabinet British intervention with others in the Russian civil war. But that was in return for Roger's support for her public-expenditure plans, which had been an essential preliminary to her generous Budget, which in turn was a platform for her real beliefs. Luck had been with her on this bargain. The Russian war was petering out, the British troops would soon be home, and she could go back to denouncing the Europeans, the UN, the Scots and anyone who tried to draw Britain into humanitarian wars. She combined a pro-market free-trade approach to economics with a fierce English nationalism. She had plenty of sources to quote in support of both parts of this equation, even if they sometimes hung oddly together. In style she was definite, often abrasive, and clear; on moral matters impeccable.

Against this what had Roger to offer? Day by day he was forced to find answers to this question. At Exeter University his love had been ancient history. In particular he had devoted himself to the Roman empire. Straight roads, legions, eagles, central heating, universal language and law, almost identical cities planted in the Syrian desert and the waste of northern England appealed to an uncomplicated youthful mind depressed by the anarchy of the modern world. *Immensa Romanae pacis maiestas* – the huge majesty of the Roman peace. It was a strong and recurring thought.

But not much use once he had entered the Commons as MP for South Northamptonshire at the age of thirty. There was no huge majesty about the British peace, or indeed anyone else's. He quickly abandoned any scheme of political ideas in favour of Tony Blair's question: 'What works?' The difficulty, he decided, lay not in hatching ideas but in getting through the improvements that observation and common sense showed to be needed. Eventually promoted by Russell to the Home Office, he had found it apt for this approach. Police, probation, criminal justice, asylum and refugees:

plenty of learned folk argued theory on all these matters, but all theory faded when faced with under-recruitment, occasional corruption, relentless pressure groups, press sensations, public expectations. He aimed at and achieved a reputation for cutting knots, for getting things done. The nature of these things seemed of lesser importance. That was the reputation which had brought him so far up the political tree, one leap away from the top. Behind this piled-up work and practical reputation, there was gradually forming a more liberal and humanitarian approach to politics, such as had led him to press for British intervention in Russia. But there was nothing yet that could convincingly be distilled into a thousand words in the *Daily Telegraph* or a cogent address to cynical backbenchers. 'Courtauld keeps his feet on the ground'; 'Courtauld sees things straight, and sees them through'; 'Courtauld gets the best out of the machine.' That was what his friends said in the tea room. For the time being he would have to be content with it.

The Home Secretary's office was shaped and furnished like the lounge of a 1950s transatlantic liner. Large armchairs covered in light tweed were anchored round two large glass tables, designed to carry heavy onyx ashtrays – removed several years ago on public-health grounds. A sinuous rubber plant opposite the main door tried to slither sideways out of its terracotta pot. Both armchairs and plant looked strong against any ocean storm. Under Courtauld's regime the walls were sparsely lined with Dufy and Matisse prints. A cupboard in the Private Office outside contained a set of Boys prints of traditional London, including the old Home Office in Whitehall. These were offered to incoming home secretaries, usually from the Labour Party, who might have less progressive tastes in art. It was not thought likely that any home secretary would wish to move beyond Matisse.

Roger Courtauld, who had been at work an hour already, left his desk at one end of the room and took the armchair that had been left for him.

'Right, press first, as usual.' This was for John Parrott.

'Much of the same, Roger, except for the piece in *Thunder*. You've probably read it already.' But he handed it round. 'Joe Seebright is obviously up to something personal. That's his speciality of course. My contacts at *Thunder* are screwed tight this morning. I can get nothing from them. I don't like the sound of it.'

Nor did any of them. Seebright was an enemy. It was one thing to believe, as they all did, that Roger Courtauld was an intelligent and honourable man who was well fitted to lead the country. It was another to suppose that during his adult life he had done nothing small or great, in private or public, that could be used by *Thunder* to present him in poor light. Against that extreme test, who could be saved?

'Perhaps I should intervene here, Secretary of State. This has just come round by hand.' John Upchurch had been Roger's principal private secretary for three years. He was a meticulous civil servant verging on middle age, who had developed a talent for bureaucratic work and a sound judgement in the rather narrow range of criminal justice decisions that came regularly to be settled in the Home Office. He had been dismayed at first by his new master. By the time he became Home Secretary Roger Courtauld knew that in real life you got the right things done by varying your pace, cutting occasional corners and listening to worthwhile people outside the government machine. Sometimes you had to work appallingly hard; at other times, if you were to keep going as a human being, you had to break away from work and look after your children, your love of music or your bowling average.

These things Upchurch had slowly learned and reluctantly accepted. As an impartial civil servant he had, as a matter of principle, no part to play in the current party contest for the premiership. But in practice he was fascinated, and kept as close to it as possible. He attended the morning campaign meetings to maintain, as he said outside, essential liaison and ensure that the work of the office did not suffer. He did not utter at these meetings except on occasional matters of fact and procedure, of which this was one.

Roger Courtauld read to himself the letter Upchurch handed to him, then read it aloud to the rest of them.

> *Thunder*
> 22 March
>
> Dear Roger (if I may make so bold),
>   I understand that long ago you were for several summers in the habit of taking holidays on the South Devon coast just short of Plymouth. A lovely part of England – you showed better taste than many politicians! In particular you were there during July 1986. It was in that month that the enclosed photograph was taken by a Mr Reynolds, who had rented a cottage on the same estate as yours and who used the same private beach. He formed a habit of taking beach photographs, which he kept. Recently in looking through his collection he came across this particular print, which he has sent to us with the negative. I

should add that Mr Reynolds now holds office in the
South Hams Conservative Association and is a strong
supporter of Joan Freetown. He appears to think that
there is or should be some relationship between this
photograph and your own views on marriage and the
family. At this stage I would not go so far as that. But
as you know we at *Thunder* see it our duty to explore
fully all aspects of the character of the two candidates
for the premiership. I have taken no decision yet on
the publication of this photograph, and should be
grateful for your comments, in particular any details
you may wish to give us about the relationship it
evidently reveals.

   Yours ever,
   Joe (Seebright)

After they had heard the letter, they saw the enclosed print.
It came as an anticlimax. They waited for Roger.

'The print is genuine.'

'You remember the occasion?'

'Vividly.' He paused, looked at them. Yes, he had to treat
them like friends. 'It was like this.'

Shit! Shit! Shit! This absurd disaster was for TV sitcoms, not
for real life, certainly not for lucky, intelligent, twenty-year-
old Roger Courtauld – but now it was happening, and to him.
How did they react in sitcoms? He picked up a plate and
threw it at the door through which the girl with a spotty face
had just left. The plate shattered and fell to the floor. Close-
up to the hero; his good-looking features contorted with anger
and thwarted lust.

Returning to everyday prose, Roger Courtauld read again the note that the girl had brought.

> Roger
>   You will hate me for a bit but I am NOT coming with you to Mothecombe this evening. There is no particular reason. It is just that I have decided better not. By the time Deirdre gives you this I will be miles away from Exeter. I expect we will meet again next term. Perhaps we can be friends, ordinary friends. I have enjoyed our time together, but it leads nowhere.
>   Yours,
>   Sylvia

God, where did she pick up that trashy false/simple style? Rosamunde Pilcher, Joanna Trollope, even Jilly Cooper? And he had been so sure. His aged green Vauxhall outside was packed high with food and drink, sheets for the big bed, plus a TV in case it rained, the set at the cottage being deeply defective. Sylvia was as unlike her spotty flatmate as possible. Her long slender legs were the most beautiful he had ever seen. Only yesterday . . .

'There must be a reason. You must tell me.'

He had tried to coax Deirdre, sitting her down on the only unbroken chair in the kitchen offering a vodka and tonic, boiling the kettle when she said she preferred Nescafé, trying not to notice her spots.

'Is there someone else?'

Now he, too, was drifting into this bogus romantic prose.

'I really can't say. She doesn't talk to me about such things.' Liar. But Deirdre had never been his friend. She had once

almost surprised them in bed together in the university flat
that she and Sylvia shared. Almost, because by the time
Deirdre had entered the bedroom Roger was represented only
by a dent in the bedclothes. Having dressed quickly and
quietly in the loo, he had managed to slip out without con-
fronting her. That incident had been the deciding argument
for jerking the relationship out of its present pattern of hurried
and uncomfortable activity. The expansion of the English
universities meant that someone was always entering or leaving the room where he and Sylvia were together, either in her
flat in Exeter or the farmhouse which he shared with four
others five miles out. So he had organised this end-of-term
weekend at Mothecombe, the holiday cottage near the sea
that his family had bought ten years ago. His parents and
sister would not arrive until Tuesday. He had offered to go four
days earlier 'to get the place ready'. He did not suppose that
his parents, let alone his sister, were deceived, but they were a
broad-minded lot.

Sylvia wore her dark hair long, though this was not the
fashion. It shone as in the shampoo ads. Her eyes were a particularly bright china blue. When those eyes smiled and she
produced her soft, sexy laugh, paradise was near.

Had she been bored by his conversation? She was not interested in politics, though she sat up and paid attention
whenever Margaret Thatcher appeared on television. After
one conversation Roger had bought her a couple of paperbacks about constitutional reform. Had that been an error?
Another time he had tried to talk to her about the Romans,
had even suggested that they go to Rome together in the
spring. She had listened and after a bit smiled and touched his
hand. Nothing had come of that. But surely he had not

overdone the tutorials. They had gone often to the cinema, she had beaten him at tennis, they had walked on Dartmoor in pouring rain, and once made love in a slightly muddy field with buttercups and two cows. All this, Roger had thought when viewing matters from afar, was going reasonably well. The next step was to introduce the most beautiful person he knew to the most beautiful place he knew. In a way it would be a test of both.

And now the test was off, the goal gone, the weekend ruined. Roger read the letter for the third time, and found a straw to clutch at.

'I have enjoyed our time together, but it leads nowhere.'

What if he showed where it could lead? Was she prodding him forward? He found a pen, and scrawled at the foot of her note,

S

Marry me tomorrow.

R

He looked at this for half a minute, then tore the whole lot up. On practical grounds, he told himself. God knows where Sylvia had gone. Her mother was dead, her father wandered round Antibes and St Tropez in the summer. There was no reaching her. Later he did not regret tearing up the letter. Sleeping with a pair of legs, plus long dark hair, even china blue eyes was one thing, marriage quite another.

Roger was still in high frustration, but decisions began to flow from him logically. He swept up the bits of the plate he had broken and finished the glass of vodka he had started while talking to Deirdre. He found space in the car for eight or nine textbooks on the Roman empire, which he had excluded from his main packing as unsuitable for the weekend as planned. He swallowed a hunk of brown bread and Cheddar cheese. He washed up dirty plates in the sink and left a note for his absent house-mates saying he would be back on Monday for the final end-of-term clear up.

As he drove the twenty-five miles to the sea it began to rain. The vodka inside him and the fact that the windscreen wipers of the Vauxhall did not work made it a dangerous journey. The final track down to the cottage was turning to mud. The car slithered and almost hit a tree. Roger wrenched it straight and came to rest outside the back door. Stumbling through the rain he found the key under the third flowerpot to the right.

Inside, the sitting room was musty. The flies on the windowsill were mostly dead, but one or two crawled sluggishly over the flaking paint. It was almost dark. Roger did not unpack the car, not even the sheets or his night things. He did not use the double bedroom, but found a couple of blankets for the truckle bed in the tiny room where he had slept as a small boy. He stripped to his underpants and, with difficulty, opened the skylight window, letting in a trickle of rain. He did not expect to sleep easily, and he was right. After half an hour he went downstairs, and found a can of warm beer. On the late TV news the Prime Minister, Margaret Thatcher, elegant but tired, was denouncing the European Union at a press conference in Rome. Roger switched to a channel in which naked bodies writhed in a murky haze. He thought of going out to get the decent TV from the car, but decided not. He was above murky bodies, could not focus on Margaret Thatcher, and outside it was raining hard. He went upstairs again, tossed and turned, thinking of Sylvia, opened a dog-eared Patrick O'Brian novel, eventually dozed.

When he woke the world had changed. The sun shone; his mind quickly cleared. He was young, and would make a new chapter of his life. He found his father's old woolly dressing-gown on a peg, and a pair of sandals. The muddy path led past the cottage down through thick beeches to the estuary of the Erme. Once at the shore he jumped off the retaining wall on to pebbles and ran to the river's edge. The glittering tide was in full flood, sweeping in over shingle, sand and mudflats, lifting the dinghies, washing against the roots of trees, providing a soft hissing background to the cries of gulls, egrets and oyster-catchers. No other human was present, except for an old man exercising two black Labradors on the opposite shore half a mile away. This was Roger's favourite moment. Would Sylvia have minded the muddy path? Would the water have been too cold for her? Would she have swum naked? Why should these questions now be of any interest? Roger found the deepest, coldest part of the riverbed, shed dressing-gown and sandals and let himself be swept inland, kicking and splashing like a schoolboy, until he came opposite a promontory of rock, where he could haul himself out without too much paddling through mud. He sprinted back along the shore to the dressing-gown and sandals. Minutes later he fried two eggs for breakfast.

The new chapter continued resolutely. Two volumes of history and a notebook were packed with three peaches in a knapsack. He left behind the new novel which he had bought for Sylvia. He meant to work, swim and sunbathe on the main beach at Mothecombe. Paradoxically, because it was a private day for ticket-holders only, the beach was somewhat crowded. Roger swam once, then climbed the steep westerly slope above the beach, passed through a small copse to the summit of the cliff, and emerged on open turf nibbled by sheep. Below him gulls swept and called. Lower still, silvery waves broke on black rocks. It was the second perfect moment of the day. Roger ate a slightly bruised peach and began to read about Augustus. It required some determination to keep Sylvia far away, but he mostly succeeded. How had Augustus managed to revive the ancient disciplines and loyalties of Rome after the murderous mess of the late Republic? Was there a comparison with the early Victorians and their remoralisation of Regency Britain? Roger threw the peach stone over the edge. The sun gained strength. Roger snoozed.

He was woken by someone's presence. The fair young man looking down on him wore white shorts and a scarlet shirt. He, too, carried a knapsack, out of which protruded a German magazine. He spoke perfect English with a slight accent. 'I am sorry. I did not mean to awaken you.'

'That's okay.' Roger sat up.

'Permit me to introduce myself. I am Friedrich Vogl, theological student from Heidelberg. I am walking this coast with my girlfriend Anna, also from Heidelberg. Or, to be exact, I *was* walking. Sadly she has gone away and by bad fortune she has taken the map.'

'Sorry about that – both map and girl.' Damn, the new chapter was being spoiled already.

'So, can you tell me the way to the beach at Mothecombe? We were told that it is particularly scenic.'

'Mothecombe is just a mile beyond that wood, down a steep path.'

But as soon as he spoke Roger saw a decision looming, the

first of his new chapter that involved another human being. He took it quickly. 'But today is a private day. Mothecombe is closed except to those who live there and have tickets for the beach. However I have a ticket and can take you as a guest.'

'I would not want to—'

'It's nothing. I was going back to swim anyway.'

'If you are sure?'

'Sit down and eat this peach while I collect my papers.'

Friedrich stretched long legs on the turf and munched. 'Is it permitted to throw the stone of the peach into the bushes?'

'It is permitted.' Friedrich threw.

'You are already a good friend. A peach, a permit for the swimming . . . Do you mind if I tell you that for me this till now has been a bad day?'

'For me the bad day was yesterday.'

'Ah, really? Perhaps you will tell me. May I tell first? Anna I have already mentioned. I love her and we had the intention to marry. But this morning after breakfast at the hostel she suddenly said she was tired and did not want to walk. I said I would stay with her. She said no, she did not want to walk with me, or marry me, or see me again. She would go back to Plymouth by bus. She paid the reckoning of the hostel and left. It was awful.'

'You had quarrelled?'

'No quarrel, no bad words, even a small kiss the night before when we parted. For me it was – you say thunderclap?'

'Or thunderbolt.'

'Thunderbolt is right.'

Very well. Fate had dealt him this young man: it must be right to ask the next question. 'Tell me, Friedrich, had you slept with her?'

'Made sex with her, you mean? No, that would be against the teaching of the theological college, where she and I study together.' Friedrich paused, and for a second bent his head towards his bare knees. 'But because you are now a friend, we can discuss intimate things. Our moral tutor says that there can be an allowance for moments of exceptionally strong cause. That it may be better to make sex before marriage than to repress it. I had thought that tomorrow, even today, after our walk Anna and I might discuss this.'

The confidence was too great to be ignored, the day unrolled accordingly. For Roger it stopped being the first day of a new chapter of his life. It became instead an interlude, unrelated to past or future. He told Friedrich about Sylvia. They walked to Mothecombe, changed into trunks in the cubicles provided and swam in the bay. It was virtually high tide, and not easy to find a space on the sand for sunbathing among the picnicking families. A path lined by brambles, which somehow found substance in the sandy soil, led up across two stiles and a deep lane to the old one-storey schoolhouse of grey stone. They climbed some steps past two magnificently outpouring fuchsias on to the small terrace of a café. Metal tables were decorated with real cornflowers stuck into patterned mugs. Customers were protected from the sun by umbrellas without commercial emblems, a job lot from a country-house sale, in pleasantly faded blue, pink and yellow. Two lively old ladies had converted the schoolhouse. The young men ate pasties, then homemade treacle tart, and drank cider. Roger talked of his childhood holidays there, of the ponies lent by the big estate, of the August bank-holiday cricket match, of the dangers of the fierce tides in the estuary. Friedrich talked of Heidelberg and the vineyards of the

Neckar valley, of his father the civil servant, of holidays in Dubrovnik, walks in the Black Forest with his theological tutor. They did not talk much further about either Anna or Sylvia.

Back at the beach they sunbathed again on firm clean sand just left by the sea. Children were shrimping in the rock pools, then began to play cricket. A small yacht anchored in the bay and a boat came ashore. Fathers built sand castles. The sun held just the right warmth, the afternoon noises round them were old-fashioned, informal and friendly.

'We lay close together because the sand was wet and we had only my towel. I cannot remember who took the initiative.'

'Initiative?'

'In holding the other's hand.'

'Just that?'

'Only that. It sounds silly. Perhaps it was me. I liked him, he looked like St Sebastian, it was an odd day. I had hardly slept, the cider worked. But then, quite quickly, it changed.'

They swam again. It was the hour when the sun feels hottest, but has passed its full strength. Clouds appeared and a breeze began. One of the families greeted Roger and he introduced Friedrich. His head ached a bit; he felt salty and overcooked.

'Can I ask you something more, Roger?'

'Of course.'

'Can you advise me where to stay tonight? You see, we had planned, Anna and I, to walk all day, and reach the hostel at Salcombe. But that, I fear, is too far for me now.'

There was plenty of space and plenty of food in the cottage, and no reason at all why Roger should not invite his new friend to stay the night. But he held back, not thinking the question through, but because an instinct which he did not analyse imposed a full stop.

'There's a pub at Holbeton. Not far, not bad, not expensive. I'll drive you there if you like.'

A pause. Roger never knew if it included disappointment.

'Yes, please.'

'And that's how it was.'

'And afterwards?'

'I have never seen him again. We exchanged Christmas cards once. Nothing else.'

'Nothing whatever?'

'You are right to ask. Nothing. Not with him, not with any man, any boy. Never.'

'You have heard from Courtauld?'

'Last night, I will read it to you.'

Seebright found the note quickly.

> Dear Seebright,
>   I have received your note and the photograph. I have and will have no comment to make.
>   Yours sincerely,
>   Roger Courtauld

'You should have e-mailed this to me at once. You know I'm following the matter closely.'

'I'm sorry.'

Lord Spitz was indeed hot on the trail, telephoning from

New York or Toronto several times a day. Seebright sometimes felt that he rather than Roger Courtauld was being
hunted.

'So you're stuck.'

'Not at all. We can publish the photograph and make much
of the refusal to comment. Roger's Guilty Secret.'

'Not strong. He has realised that once he begins to explain
and give details he provides a scent for you to follow. He must
be sure that there is no scent which others can provide.'

'So we shall find the young German. That will be stage
two.' Seebright hated being goaded. He was being pushed
beyond reality. The girl he had sent down to Mothecombe
had come back empty-handed. The trail was more than forty
years old. The restaurant on the cliff top had changed hands
and provided no witnesses. Mr Reynolds, who had sent the
photograph, was over eighty, house-bound and surrounded by
the photograph albums that seemed to be the only harvest of
his life. He was kept alive by the vigour of his right-wing
views. He remembered the Courtauld family and their visits to
Mothecombe over the years, but had never known them personally. He was too old to remember and too honest to invent
any particular of the afternoon when he had snapped these
young men on the beach. He had been angry when the girl
reporter had offered him ten thousand pounds to help his
memory.

'You should have gone the whole hog,' Seebright had said.
The girl had been authorised to offer fifty thousand.

'He would have hit me with his stick.'

Sometimes Seebright despaired of England.

He ended the conversation with Lord Spitz as best he
could, and picked up the soon-to-be-famous photograph for

the hundredth time. He disliked Roger Courtauld on political
grounds, but he had come to hate the fair-haired anonymous
German with the closed eyes, faint fatuous smile, and
damnable anonymity. If he ever found that German he would
mercilessly destroy him. He focused on the magazine that lay
half concealed beside the towel. They had checked, of course.
The magazine was an illustrated monthly published by the
Lutheran Church. It gave full and respectable details of youth
conferences, expeditions and aid projects across the world.
Because it was a national publication it gave no clue of the
young man's origin inside Germany.

But, thought Seebright, it gave a clue to his interests. How
would a young Lutheran spend his time in Cornwall in the
mid-eighties? He might or might not make love to a thrusting
young Conservative from Exeter University called Roger
Courtauld. Almost certainly not, but that was no longer the
point. He would certainly have visited churches. Churches,
churches, churches. Churches kept visitors' books. And visitors' books included a space for addresses. Within an hour
the hounds, six of them this time, were back on the trail.
Time was desperately short. Of course it was not easy.

'Visitors' books? What an old-fashioned idea! We threw
them away long ago with the old prayer books.'

'We charge two euros for entry, and of course visitors can e-
mail comments, but we don't take names unless they do.'

'Here you are, but they're falling to bits rather.'

On the second day luck turned. On the sea, surrounded by
caravans, St Peter's harboured in its cemetery a forgotten
minor poet, and dozens of fishermen drowned through the
centuries. Holy Communion was held in the chancel once a
month. Because they could enter by a gap in the boarding that

separated chancel from ruined nave, this service was attended in summer by more swallows than human worshippers. In the vestry, discoloured with damp, was a pile of identical visitors' books, bought in a fleeting moment of parish affluence from W. H. Smith, with the precious space for a visitor's address and another alongside for comments.

> 3 July 1986. Friedrich Vogl, Aventinstrasse 19,
> Heidelberg, Germany

Friedrich had added in the adjoining column 'a peaceful haven for thought and prayer'.

Friedrich Vogl shared with his family a five-room apartment constituting one side of a modern courtyard built across the Neckar from the castle at Heidelberg. He had been glad, though puzzled, to agree to see Jim Scrowl, special personal emissary of the editor of the British newspaper *Thunder*, in connection with a biography planned to honour the distinguished British statesman and Interior Minister Roger Courtauld. Friedrich Vogl had told the editor on the telephone that unfortunately his acquaintance with Mr Courtauld was of the very slightest, only enduring a few hours. But Mr Seebright had said that any recollection from Mr Courtauld's early years would be invaluable. Friedrich agreed to give the interview to the special emissary because he had a happy recollection of those particular hours. He had read in the newspaper that Mr Courtauld was contesting the leadership of the British Conservative Party and was anxious to do anything to help his cause. Moreover, the contribution promised by Seebright to his church funds was substantial.

Jim Scrowl wore his only suit, as befitted a call on a Lutheran pastor. Coffee and sweet cakes were served. But the conversation soon ran dry, as Friedrich had predicted.

'But I never saw him again.'

'You never spoke after that afternoon?'

'Never. He sent me a Christmas card that year and I responded with a New Year greeting from my college.'

'Do you have his Christmas card?'

'Certainly. I found it as preparation for this discussion. I will show it to you now.'

Scrowl took the card, examined it, and at once put it in his folder of papers. Friedrich made to expostulate, but refrained. He did not know the correct procedures in the literary world. He would have liked to keep the card, but if it would help Roger Courtauld by giving it to this journalist, it seemed a small gift in a good cause.

'You are sure you have never seen or heard from Roger Courtauld since?' Scrowl knew from his glance at the Christmas card that it amounted to nothing. Disappointment made his tone abrupt.

'Quite sure.' Why was this man now talking more like a police officer than a biographer?

The conversation petered out. Professional life had given Scrowl a weakish bladder. Time was short, and he did not want to have to stop on the road back to Berlin. He visited Vogl's lavatory before leaving, then thanked Frau Vogl for the coffee, climbed rather awkwardly into his car and was on his way. Suddenly he was in a hurry. He needed a confidential landline to Seebright as soon as possible.

Joe Seebright did not trust Robert Macdowell, knowing him

to be lukewarm in the Freetown cause. But he needed his help on a crucial question. *Thunder* had only one thunderbolt against Courtauld. If the crucial vote of Conservative MPs was on Thursday afternoon, was the thunderbolt best launched that morning, or one or even two days earlier?

'That depends on what you have.'

They were alone in Joe Seebright's editorial cubicle high above Canary Wharf. Seebright hesitated before replying. But he had been particularly specific and reassuring to Lord Spitz on the telephone that morning. There was no point in pulling punches now. And in any case he was proud of the coup which he planned.

He busied himself for a minute at a side table. 'Come and have a look.'

On a piece of cardboard he had assembled what Macdowell at once saw was a plan for the front page of *Thunder*. At the left was the photograph, which he had already seen, of Roger and Friedrich side by side on Mothecombe beach. In the centre was the inner page of a Christmas card dated 1986 from Exeter University. Below the ordinary seasonal greetings Roger Courtauld had written: '*With all good wishes. I enjoyed our day together and I hope everything goes well with you. Roger Courtauld.*'

On the right was another photograph of Friedrich Vogl, this time alone. Once again he was on a beach, wearing swimming trunks, but this time crouched on his heels and holding out his arms in welcome, a broad smile of invitation on his face.

As portrayed in that setting the implication of that smile could not be mistaken. Macdowell was amazed. 'Then he did see Roger again?'

Seebright laughed, delighted that even a seasoned journalist should jump to that conclusion. 'Not exactly.' Again he hesitated, but his pleasure at his own cleverness overcame his caution. He showed Macdowell the original of the second photograph. Cut out from the version displayed on the cardboard was a buxom blonde woman holding a small boy and girl. The happy laughing family group was complete.

'His wife and children?'

'I suppose so. The photograph hung with dozens of others in his lavatory.'

Macdowell gathered round him the tatters of his professional reputation. 'That is utterly wrong and unacceptable. You are creating an insinuation which we know is false.'

'We know no such thing.' Seebright was still reckless. 'Anyway consider what we might have done. You see that in the right-hand picture the German haunches are thicker and the German hair thinner. It was taken several years after the first one. We could easily touch out these differences as if the two pictures had been taken on the same day. We could even strip off these absurd bumbags and show Fritz as God made him. That would remove any doubt. But I, too, have my scruples. It's better if the facts are left to speak for themselves.'

'The facts,' said Macdowell bitterly, and nothing more. He had to think of his family and his bank balance, the two being closely connected. He resigned that night, but without fuss. The severance terms were not bad, and he did not have to take his children away from their private schools.

Chapter 3

Roger told Hélène, his staff at the Home Office, his constituents, journalists and himself that he enjoyed the work. Certainly this had been true in the first year or two at the Home Office. Was it still true? Yes, of course, there could be no doubt about it. He still approached a locked red box full of government work with the zeal of an archaeologist about to force open a sealed tomb. He still relished the canter through each day of meetings. He enjoyed the fierce battles across the floor of the House of Commons or the Cabinet table, each of which revealed something new about the character of those with whom he dealt, and possibly also about himself. Lately, perhaps, had there been some slight cooling of enthusiasm? Yet that surely could not be true, given that so far from dropping off the ladder he was now trying to reach its topmost rung.

In these days Roger found it useful to stick as closely as possible to his usual daily routine. He did not want those around him to regard the leadership contest as extraordinary. He felt that if he changed the structure of his day he would be increasing his own stake on the board. He did not want to do this. When Upchurch had offered to hold back or send junior ministers to attend to less urgent matters of Home Office business until the contest was over he had demurred. 'No, fill the boxes in the usual way. I'll get through them somehow.'

Upchurch had not entirely obeyed. Even so Roger had had to invoke his one o'clock rule two or three times, by which he closed the red boxes of work one hour after midnight, shutting any unread papers out of sight and mind.

On Tuesday, 23 March, Roger left his bed in South Eaton Place at six thirty as usual, and performed ten minutes of bends and stretches on the rug in his dressing room. He put on his clothes to the accompaniment of the seven o'clock news, softly tuned so as not to disturb Hélène next door. The routine was exact; even the exercises admitted no variety, having been prescribed ten years earlier at a time of backache now happily vanished. By seven twenty he was eating half a grapefruit in the dining room. During this process, none of which required thought, his energy gathered for the day. That energy met its first and one of its fiercest challenges in the spread of newspapers across the breakfast table. Here a change had been forced upon him. For the last fortnight all the national papers had been brought early from the Home Office, not just his usual diet of the *Mail* and the *Telegraph*. Though it often made for a fraught breakfast this addition saved time later when his campaign committee met to review tactics.

So there, half hidden beneath the *Telegraph*, was *Thunder*, and the blow that Roger Courtauld had more than half expected ever since the letter from Joe Seebright. Sarah Tunstall and Simon Cresswick, the two optimists on his group, had been sure that Seebright was bluffing and that nothing more would happen. The others had been silent. John Parrott, the PR man who knew the press best, had suggested that they try to get in touch with Friedrich Vogl to warn him of what was afoot. Roger had vetoed this on the grounds that any such approach, if it became known, would smell of an attempted cover-up. More deeply, he did not want to disinter that afternoon in Mothecombe. His own memory contained nothing more than he had revealed to the group; his meeting with young Vogl had happened exactly as he had told them. Those hours had receded from his mind like most past events, until jerked to the front by Seebright. A small silly fraction of his life had fallen into the hands of his enemies. The less it was thought and spoken of the better.

But this would hardly do. Here they were again, a few distant agreeable hours made slimy by the malice of a newspaper. Seebright had followed exactly the plan for his front page revealed to Macdowell: side by side the Mothecombe photograph, the signed Christmas card, and Friedrich alone beckoning his vanished family. He had devised one extra flourish. The thick black headline across the top, MY FRIEND FRITZ, was connected by a pink noose, which dangled down the page until it lassoed the signature at the foot of the Christmas card ROGER COURTAULD.

The leader overleaf addressed any readers for whom the subtleties of the front page might have been excessive.

Thunder promised to bring you the truth behind the premiership contest. Go to other papers for the political promises. At *Thunder* that kind of stuff goes down the drain before you even pull the plug. No, we at

Thunder want to show you the two *characters*. We are tolerant, we respect the rights of private life. But we respect even more the right of the British people to see their leaders straight and clear. You are entitled to know how they've behaved in the past. Isn't that the only way of judging how they'll behave in the future?

Last week we showed you Joan Freetown at Cambridge. Roger Courtauld studied at Exeter University. Nothing wrong with that. He got a good degree. But his life wasn't all study. Not by any means. Our front page tells another story – young Roger holding hands on a Devon beach. Nothing wrong with that either – even though it's a young man he's fondling. Our front page gives proof that this relationship continued. It wasn't a one-day canoodle. At *Thunder* we know who the other man is. We shan't give you his name today. We can tell you that he's German. But there are facts we can't yet know, questions Roger Courtauld has refused to answer. What exactly was the relationship? How far did it go? How long did it last? Have there been other gay chapters in the Home Secretary's life? In short, what the hell went on?

These are fair questions. They are necessary. We don't enjoy digging around in people's lives. There should be no need. One e-mail from the Home Office could settle the whole matter. We promise to print whatever we get.

Over to you, Roger.

For half a minute Roger felt sick. He sat back in his chair. He had been hit on the head. The working of his mind was blocked. Then, groping for the coffee pot, he took a decision. He would quit the leadership contest. The price of entry was too high. He filled the cup and reopened the decision. A modern politician in Britain did not act by instinct. He was tied to friends, and in this case to family. He had to listen before acting if his actions were to be any good. Roger put the question into neutral. He had half a day before he need decide. He would deliberately work at other subjects until he was supplied with the necessary advice. He would add his own views, allow to stew for an hour or so, and serve up a decision.

But from one important quarter advice would only come if requested. There were no staff in South Eaton Place at breakfast time. Roger brought back to the boil the portable kettle from which he had brewed coffee. He created a cup of China tea, added a slice of lemon, then a croissant on a plate, folded *Thunder* carefully, and carried the combination upstairs on a tray. As usual Hélène feigned sleep. Roger drew the curtain, let in the grey-white characterless London light and left her. The only novelty was the paper on the tray. Hélène would need a little time to digest this.

Roger sometimes wondered why Hélène had married him thirty years ago. There was no mystery as to why he had fallen for her – beautiful, intelligent, educated, the daughter of a Frenchman who combined the roles of count, farmer and merchant. The family owned a large fortified farmhouse on a hill above smiling fields, and one of the most profitable Armagnac businesses in Gascony. He had spent a fortnight on holiday nearby with friends, who had taken him over to lunch with the de Landelisse family. The lunch, while delicious, was light and there was no Armagnac from the estate, because tennis was to follow. The count was paired with his estate manager against Roger and Hélène, the countess and other guests watching in the heavy shade of pollarded plane trees. As was proper the count won. In the days that followed there was more tennis, then dinner in a restaurant, then tennis again. Roger, though then only thirty, was plump. He sweated and a small bald patch became more obvious as each game progressed. But he was good-looking in a genial English way, and he let her father win. On the last day of his holiday he picked small ripe figs for her from the tree by the swimming-pool. Side by side on deck-chairs they watched the sun set. Below them a pair of buzzards mewed over a valley yellow and brown with ripening sunflowers. Roger took her hand. 'It is absurd,' he said. They always spoke in English. 'But I am certain, and I cannot know what you think unless I ask: Will you marry me, Hélène?'

There was a silence. Gently she withdrew her hand. 'Of course it is absurd. Two weeks is far too short. But I will come to London to see you. Then we can decide.'

A few weeks later she came, in theory for a course on Cézanne at the Tate. They made love efficiently in his tiny bachelor flat, conveniently close to the Palace of Westminster. He told her about his constituency and the difficulty of opposing the new Labour Government. She listened in silence and he thought he had made a tactical error. But when he proposed again, three days later, she accepted.

'Why did you accept me?' he had asked later.

'First reason, you are a nice man, Second reason, I needed to escape.'

From what? From another suitor? From those smiling French fields? He never found out. He had to be content with that explanation, and it sufficed. Their marriage set quickly into a pattern that hardly altered. Hélène took the minimum necessary interest in politics. She insisted on small matters of respect, appearances and protocol because she knew he neglected them. She went with him to the rented cottage in Northamptonshire. She wore good but not too good clothes at the Mayor's ball and the High Sheriff's cocktail party. She developed a genuine interest in the Daventry art gallery. More important, after a long reluctance she provided Roger with a daughter, then two sons. Beyond that, she led her own life, enjoying London to the full, mostly in a world of artists and writers, French and English, into which she did not expect him to follow. Ignorant, mocking people, seeing them usually apart, supposed that each of the Courtaulds ran their own love affairs. In fact, both were faithful, since for neither was physical love particularly important. Hélène looked after the girl's education at the Lyceé in London; Roger organised the boys at a prep school in Berkshire. They remained fond of each other and shared a bedroom, but in practice there were not many subjects on which they needed to talk. Money might have been one, but Hélène was an only child, the count enjoyed a smattering of political conversation, which Roger provided, and the Armagnac continued to thrive.

Roger's decision to contest the leadership lay on the borderline of their two lives. They had discussed it, but briefly, there being no disagreement. She wanted him to advance himself and would be willing as wife of the Prime Minister to undertake more public work alongside him than came her way as wife to the Home Secretary. He had no idea whatever how she would react to *Thunder*.

'He does not look very intelligent,' she said, sipping tea.

'It amounted to nothing. No more than you see. An afternoon long ago, an hour or so on the beach. Even that makes it sound more than it was.'

She looked at him. 'I understand that. Even if it were more, to me it would be nothing. It is long ago, and anyway,' she shrugged, 'Roger Courtauld and grand passion do not go well together. Mrs Courtauld knows this and does not criticise. But politically for you, I wonder . . .'

She was about to cross their unseen frontier into the heart of his concerns.

'You wonder . . . ?'

But she retreated. 'It is not something for me, Roger. You have good friends who know about these things. You must ask them. I will support you whatever you do.'

He considered pressing her, but the sense of frontier was too well established between them. He shuddered to think of those colleagues whose pillow-talk was politics. Better to have, like himself, a quick kiss, silence, sleep, and in the morning some necessary discussion of the diary or the children.

He moved to the window and opened it. The rough noise of a street market filled the room, but there could be no street market in South Eaton Place. One of the crowd of journalists outside the house looked up and spotted him. 'Are you pulling out, Home Secretary?'

The questions shot in through the window.

'Are you suing?'

'Have you talked to your wife?'

'Have you talked to Fritz?'

He shut the window. For him the immediate escape would be quite easy. In ten minutes his driver would arrive and park immediately outside the front door. The two protection officers would see him through the jostling press, microphones and cameras into the car and away within a few seconds. For Hélène it would be much more difficult.

'You are going out this morning?'

'Of course. I have to chair the parents' meeting at the Lyceé. But do not worry. I must smile when I am photographed, keep moving, and say nothing. I learned this long ago. My smile must be my message, whatever you decide. They will not expect more from me.'

At the same time a similar, though smaller, crowd of journalists was gathered outside Joan Freetown's house off Brook Green. David Alcester, her campaign chief of staff, watched them with satisfaction. 'Brewing nicely,' he said half aloud.

'Come here, David.' Joan Freetown looked up from the sheet of paper on her desk. She preferred to communicate with her friends through David, whom she liked because he was articulate, loyal and good-looking. But she knew there was truth in Guy's description of him as a young man too obviously on the make. She felt uneasy when her husband and her chief of staff were in the room together, and relieved when, as today, Guy was out of London.

'This is not logical, David. You say I have no comment to make, then I make one.' She tapped a silver pencil on the desk. David Alcester sighed inwardly. A fair lock fell across his forehead as he bent over her. He read aloud the text she was studying, knowing that his voice itself could lend arguments to his suggestion: '"Joan Freetown has no comment to make on the main story in *Thunder* today. She herself has answered fully all questions put to her by *Thunder* about the past, recognising the public interest in such openness. She hopes that Roger Courtauld will find a satisfactory way of clearing up the questions in doubt." It reads well, Joan.'

But she remained unhappy. 'Sit down, David.' This was an old device of hers but he had no option. He sat down, she stood up and began to walk about. 'David, you had no hand in gathering this material for Seebright?'

He wondered whether to simulate anger, but decided it would not work. 'None at all, Joan. I told you yesterday. The first photograph came to them direct from an old man in Devon. The rest they dug out for themselves in Germany.'

'You knew about it? You urged them on?'

'They told me what they planned. I neither discouraged nor encouraged. They are professionals.' He changed tune. This was going too far. 'Look, Joan, what is this all about? This story will swing things your way when they were looking bleak. You just have to sit back, smile, poke the story a bit, keep it alive. That's all I'm suggesting.'

'I don't like it, David. I just don't like it. It could work either way. I don't want to be involved.'

Inwardly David Alcester seethed. God, she was a difficult woman to work for. His answer to her first question had been truthful, his second false. Of course he had encouraged Seebright. 'Joan will be delighted.' He had gone as far as that in one conversation. Not for publication, of course, but Seebright would expect a reward – and deserved it.

Joan Freetown returned to the desk, took her silver pencil and crossed out the last sentence of the draft comment. She reread the rest, and crossed out the second, looked at it again. 'I'm sorry, David, we must simply say, "No comment, no comment, no comment."'

'Sorry,' he said to Seebright later, 'she won't play. No comment. I couldn't move her.'

'Damn.' Seebright paused. 'Is that a matter of principle or her judgement of tactics?'

'You never can tell with her.' And in that reply David Alcester was entirely accurate.

'We must hunt down the second photograph. That's our unanimous conclusion.' They had appointed John Parrott to speak for them. Because Roger was half an hour late they had had time to review the situation after the thunderbolt. Parrott had spoken rather formally: it was an important moment.

'The reasoning?' Roger kept his voice flat.

'There was someone else in that picture. The German is communicating with someone we can't see. We know it's not you. If we can find who it is, we can destroy Seebright's story, and show him up as a lying trickster.'

'What do you want me to do?'

'You will have to give us the German's name and the address to which you sent that Christmas card. Then we can find him and get his help.'

Once again Roger felt that deep reluctance to dig up the past, even though it was innocent. 'He will have moved. Anyway, the missing character in the second photograph may be a young man.'

There was a pause.

'You think your German may have been gay?'

'I have no reason at all to believe that.' Another pause. Roger decided to put them to the real test. 'Look. I have to decide whether to continue or quit. The price for continuing may be too high. You accept that nothing wrong happened at Mothecombe. I'm grateful for that. But if I continue it will be on the understanding that we do not touch the *Thunder* story. We say nothing whatever. We let it live or die according to its own strength or weakness. I want to know two things. On that basis would you continue to help me? On that basis do you think I could win?'

Going round the table they all said yes to both questions. But Roger saw that they were not real questions for this particular group. By calculation or by loyalty they were too far in with him to pull back. The most calculating of them, the one he least trusted, made the only interesting remark. 'Virginia Saltoun rang me this morning,' said Clive Wilson. 'She's been on my doubtful list for a fortnight. She said the one thing the Tory Party should not accept was a leader imposed by *Thunder*. So she's jumped. She hates what you stand for, but she'll vote for you. There may be others.'

Later events showed that this might have been a turning point for Roger. Political life is full of anecdotes, thousands a day. Most of them are sterile, disconnected from each other, insignificant. Part of the necessary equipment for successful politicians or political journalists is the power to distinguish between anecdotes. They need to shrug off and forget most of them, while remaining alert to spot the acorn that shoots up to become an oak. This part of Roger's political apparatus was not switched on when Clive Wilson spoke. Even if it had been, the outcome might not have been great, for the telephone rang, and his world changed again. The others could make little of his side of the conversation.

'. . . I see . . . I see . . . Absolutely no trace . . . You were right to ring, I'm grateful . . . I think I'd better come right away, do you agree? . . . I'll be with you in an hour, perhaps an hour and a half.'

He thought for ten seconds after replacing the receiver. There was strain in his voice when he spoke. 'Something personal has come up. Nothing to do with politics. I'll have to leave London for a few hours. It means cancelling today's engagements.'

His colleagues took this bad news on the chin. Roger was not a man to invent little excuses for decisions which inconvenienced others.

'What about the dinner tonight at the Carlton?' Sarah Tunstall was particularly keen on this. She had booked a private room at the club and invited two of his allies and five influential floating voters from the right wing.

Roger paused. 'I'll be back for that, Sarah.' He stood and made for the door. Then the ice broke. He paused again in the doorway. 'You've become my friends,' he said awkwardly. 'You're backing me with all you've got. You're entitled to know my past, my present. But this is something I have to handle before I can talk. Can you all come to the Carlton at seven before the dinner? There'll be no secrets then.' From others it would have sounded artificial. They took it from him, but he went out feeling that there might be a strain even on their loyalty.

His driver had waited in the Home Office courtyard, accustomed in these days to sudden changes of plan.

'We've got to get down to Hillcrest. As quickly as we can make it.'

'Right, sir.'

Mark the driver and Sam the protection officer knew the

road to Hillcrest well. It was the preparatory school in Berkshire attended by the Home Secretary's two sons, young Roger and his brother Tom.

There was little point in hugging his privacy too tightly to himself. Mark and Sam would soon learn the story once they reached the school. Indeed, it might fall before long within Sam's responsibility as a police officer, though strictly speaking his job was to protect the Home Secretary, not the Home Secretary's family.

'Young Roger has disappeared. Not been seen since breakfast. Missed his first class. Probably some simple explanation.'

'Quite so, sir.' But if the Home Secretary really thought that, they would not now be moving fast down the Cromwell Road.

'Excuse my asking, sir, have the school authorities notified the local police?'

'Not yet, Sam. They're hoping the lad will turn up. He's only been missing four hours.'

'Quite so, sir.'

A pause. The traffic thickened through Hammersmith.

'Excuse me again, sir. Would you like us to use the siren?'

Protection officers loved the siren because of the speed and the audible authority it conferred. Drivers liked it because it showed their skill and appeared to raise them above the law. Roger hated it. They slowed down behind a long truck loaded with bright new cars. He was tempted. The siren would cut the journey by fifteen minutes, perhaps thirty. Waiting for bad news could be worse than the bad news itself. But he resisted. At moments of crisis it was better to stick to one's standards in small things. He tried to put himself into young Roger's mind. But soon he was looking into his own mind instead. He cursed the selfishness that he and Hélène had shown a few hours back over the morning tea. They had worried about each other's feelings and forgotten about the children. At the Lyceé Felicity would be all right: she had her mother's tough, rather narrow French realism. Their second son Tom was tough, too, a small English schoolboy devoted to Arsenal. But Roger . . . A politician had no right to have young children.

Rain glistened on the rhododendron leaves as they sped up the school drive. There were tears, too, on the cheeks of the headmaster's wife, who stood to greet them at the top of the steps. Roger's heart stopped as he saw that the woman, virtually a stranger to him, was upset. He could hardly bear to shake hands. He felt a final irrational burst of anger. What right had this pale, scraggy person to shed tears for young Roger? It was the school's job to keep him safe, not to weep over him.

But, thank God, he had misread the signs. Her tears meant nothing mournful. In the Gothic entrance hall, dimly lit by tiny squares of pink and green stained glass, she explained that her husband was teaching the third year, as if that was important. As for young Roger . . .

'He's just come back,' she said. 'That awful newspaper . . . I haven't even had time to clean him up.'

Then Roger was alone with his son. Young Roger was exhausted beyond the point of tears. His bare legs were splashed with mud, where he must have run and fallen. Blood from a small cut was oozing through the dirt on one knee. He ran to his father then, after a brief embrace, turned away.

'Sit down, Roger.'

They were alone together in a bleak sitting room with

chairs back against each wall as if prepared for a seminar. Reproductions of Constable and Turner combined as decoration with photographs of rugby and cricket teams. They conveyed no cheer.

'What's it about, then? You tried to run away?'

Young Roger nodded. 'But it was too far,' he said. And then, worst of all, 'And, anyway, I didn't really want to go home.'

Home, home. The bleak over-protected government home in South Eaton Place was no home for a child. Mothecombe, of course, that was a real home in the holidays, but Devon was unimaginably far for a ten-year-old.

'Why, Roger?' Silence. 'Was it about school? Something you've done? Or we've done?' Silence. 'Was it the story in the newspaper?'

'They laughed at me. Gromson got hold of the maths beak's copy. I didn't understand what it meant.'

Then at last proper tears began to flow.

They had more or less guessed after they had heard of Roger's conversation that morning with the headmaster. Clive Wilson had fewer inhibitions than the rest about other people's privacy. Anyway, hadn't Roger given them, his friends and allies, the right to know? Acting on a hunch Clive had telephoned the headmaster of Hillcrest at lunchtime, describing himself as a close friend of Roger worried about his state of mind and wondering if something was amiss with one of Roger's boys. The headmaster had portentously but understandably declined to give any information to a stranger. 'We at Hillcrest take seriously our responsibility for the privacy of the boys in our care.'

Wilson had seen his opening. 'Then both boys are safe and sound in your care?'

'Yes, indeed. There's no problem with Tom, and Roger came back to school late this morning.'

So the crisis, if there had been a crisis, was over. Clive shared the news with the rest of the campaign committee as they gathered again at seven, as agreed, in the small private room at the Carlton Club. A round table in the centre was laid for the dinner with Roger to which Sarah Tunstall had invited the five influential backbenchers. Clive gazed at the massed ranks of cutlery and glasses. 'I see you like to put plenty of sticky on your fly-paper, Sarah.'

But she was not the sort to enjoy that kind of banter. She would eat some of each dish and sip each wine, knowing that these things were important for the male politicians whom she despised.

'I just hope he's on good form.'

'He bloody well ought to be. He's catching up fast. That poll in the *Standard* . . .'

They had all seen the mid-afternoon edition. It was unreliable, in that few MPs would feel compelled to tell the truth to journalists at this or any stage of the contest. Also, of course, it had been taken before the thunderbolt. It showed a marked swing towards Roger, compared to the week before:

Courtauld	146
Freetown	181
Undecided	40

A separate poll alongside it, of party members in the constituencies, showed a bigger lead for Joan Freetown, but also a majority saying that they would be influenced in their vote by how the MPs had voted the week before.

'One more heave . . .' There was something about political infighting that stimulated platitudes even in intelligent people.

'He should be smiling . . .'

Indeed, coming through the door at that moment, Roger was smiling. For that moment, misunderstanding each other, they were all happy. Then he broke it up. Going to the drinks table at the side of the room he began clumsily to splash cold white wine into glasses from an opened bottle in a refrigerated container.

'Here's yours, Sarah . . . Let's all sit down now. I've something to tell you.'

They sat, untidily, at different angles round the table laid for others.

'I've decided to pull out. You'll understand when I tell you. You've got children, Sarah, so have you . . .'

He told them about Hillcrest and young Roger. They tried to look sympathetic but in their hearts none of them sympathised. The boy was safe, back at school. Some of them had met him, a thin, insignificant lad. There was no reason for Roger to jump out of his groove. They were silent while each considered from which angle to counter-attack.

'Roger, we all understand how you feel. Some of us have children at school, we know how they can worry, and that makes parents worry too.' Clive Wilson came first, the quickest though not the most skilful. His hand tightened on his glass as he got under way. He would write it all up, with advantages as Shakespeare said, in his diary that night. The publishers were nibbling already. He went on, 'There are other factors, Roger, which you simply have to take into account. You won't have seen the poll in the *Standard*. It shows a strong swing in your direction.'

'Yes, I saw it. Sam got it for me. It was taken before the story in *Thunder*.'

'Of course. But the swing has gone on through today. That's the point Sarah was making this morning. I've had several pieces of evidence since then. Seebright and Spitz have miscalculated, as the tabloids sometimes do. The parliamentary Party will not stand being dictated to by the press.'

'It'll be in all the papers tomorrow. They'll wallow in it. The pious broadsheets worst of all. Wiping the smut away with their silk hankies.'

'Then the swing to you will continue. The wiser lobby correspondents know how to sniff the breeze. Before long they'll be writing it in your favour. Particularly *Thunder*'s rivals. In my judgement you've as good as won.'

Roger became irritated. 'That's not the point. They'll all print the story and the picture. They'll make sure their readers get a good wallow in the mud before they tell them how disgracefully muddy it is.'

'That's their way. But on balance—'

Roger tried to cut short the discussion, fortifying himself behind his bulky shoulders and long arms stretched out on the table. 'There's no balance, Clive. Look, I know how hard this is on all of you. I'm sorry, I'm sorry, I'm sorry. I owe you apologies and more. That's at one level, and I don't underestimate it. But it's my life, not anyone else's, which is on the board. I've made a decision to take it off the board. That means the game's over.' He paused. 'Sometimes you hesitate before a decision. I did that all the way back from the bloody school. I

decided at the Chiswick flyover. After that the traffic lights
went green all the way up to the Cromwell Road. The lights
approved all right. I know it was the right choice.' He tried to
push them on to a practical plane. 'So that's it. Thank you all
very much. We need to draft something very simple – personal
reasons, nothing complicated. We'll put it out at once. I'll
dine pleasantly with your guests, Sarah. Then home to bed.
Tomorrow, as they say, will be another day.'

But, of course, they could not let him off like that. Sarah
had meant to tackle him on the same grounds as Clive
Wilson, namely the swing in his favour through the day. That
had not worked. She cast back to her days as a mother of two
young children, one now a merchant banker, the other, a girl,
making forlorn music in Orange County, California. 'What
does Hélène think?' she asked, to gain time while she thought.

'I haven't asked Hélène. She leaves that decision to me.' It
might seem odd to others, but that was the way it was. He had
looked in on South Eaton Place to change his shirt between
Hillcrest and the Carlton Club. If Hélène had been in, he supposed he would have told her. She had been out shopping. It
had not occurred to him to try to reach her on her mobile. He
supposed that he ought to do so fairly soon so that she would
not be surprised by reporters. But Hélène was not part of the
action. Perhaps that was one of the things that was wrong.

Sarah had thought out her line. She moved across the room
and stood over him. In daytime her hair and clothes escaped
all discipline. The disorder in her dress was saved from being
ridiculous by her statuesque figure and the powerful way in
which she moved. She swept through the House of Commons
tea room like a queen who shopped at Oxfam. About six
o'clock most evenings a change occurred. Her unruly grey-

blonde hair was captured by a gold band and imprisoned in a thick tress flowing from the nape of her neck. For the evening she favoured flowing dresses, green, blue or red, the colour always stronger than was fashionable, the material giving off a metallic sheen and a general effect of concentrated power. She was one of Roger's sternest critics at the Home Office, favouring mandatory terms of imprisonment for all serious offences and a national police force. When asked by the press why, despite this, she favoured him for prime minister, she replied, 'He's the best man we've got.'

'You don't favour a woman prime minister then, Mrs Tunstall?'

'Clearly not.' And that was all they could get. She had worked harder than any of them for Roger among the MPs. Heaven knew what arguments she used. This dinner was to be, or was to have been, the climax of her effort.

Without genuine sympathy for Roger but for tactical reasons, trying to remember what it was to have young children, she spoke in a softer voice than usual. With difficulty she had remembered the boy's name. 'Have you really thought this through, Roger?'

He lifted his head out of the fortress of shoulders and arms, and looked up at her. This might be more difficult to deal with. 'What do you mean, Sarah?'

'Young Roger's had an upset.' She had a subdued West Country accent. 'He'll have another tomorrow when the rest of the papers drool over the same story. Your quitting tonight won't change that. Indeed, it'll add to the sensation.'

'For a day or two, Sarah, then it will be over.'

'You know better than that, Roger. The story will be with you and the lad for the rest of your days. Whether it throws a

big shadow or a little shadow on his life will depend on how
you handle it now. If you quit tonight, it'll be a big shadow,
now and for ever. It'll be what people remember you by. They
won't believe you threw away the premiership simply because
one afternoon all those years ago you drank too much scrumpy
in a seaside pub and held hands with a Kraut on a Devon
beach.'

'That's all there was. What I told you was true.'

Sarah had him on the defensive. She touched him gently
on the shoulder. A week ago they had hardly known each
other. 'We know it's true. You told us, and you're not a liar.
But who'll believe it? There's plenty of truth in life that no
one will believe. Usually because it's too small. Particularly in
politics. Politicians have to pretend that whenever there's
smoke there's fire – otherwise what would we live on? The
press even more so. After all, there have to be headlines every
day. Your story is just a tiny wisp of smoke. It was all over by
teatime. If you quit, everyone will believe it was a raging forest
fire.'

For a moment it was as if they were the only people in the
room. From the walls Lord North and Benjamin Disraeli, both
connoisseurs of political drama, looked down with interest.

'You miss the point, Sarah. Only big people cast big shadows. I'm going to cut myself down to size. Not a big chap any
more. So if . . . when I'm out of all this no one will be interested. Page one tomorrow, page eight in a week's time, then
silence. Blessed silence. And the children and I can get back
to normal life.'

Then Sarah made a fatal mistake. Having chaired all day
the Select Committee on the final long-delayed audit of the
Millennium Dome, she was tired. She had drunk two glasses

of Chablis. She could not sustain the uncharacteristic effort that she had made to get into his mind. She fell back into her everyday role as a bit-part politician. She took her hand off his shoulder. Her voice was harsh again. 'Do you really want to see that bitch Joan Freetown in Number Ten?'

So that, as Roger had sometimes supposed, had been her real motive in supporting him. He won back control of the discussion by throwing a question to John Parrott, the PR man. 'John, is there any evidence that Joan Freetown was in any way behind the *Thunder* story?'

John Parrott hesitated.

'Well? Come on, you must know.'

'No evidence. She's been at home all day, refusing comment. Her people say it came as a complete surprise to her. They're firm that she won't touch it.'

'Why did you hesitate? Let's get this straight.'

'It's just that David Alcester's been going round with a grin on his face dropping hints of more to come. He's close to Seebright. But that doesn't implicate her.'

'That man's a snake – she'll find him out in good time. She's the one who's standing, not bloody Alcester.'

'She'd be a disaster,' said Sarah.

'Not a disaster,' said Roger. 'We mustn't believe our own propaganda. Or, at least, not the wilder bits of it. You dislike her because she bangs about and has no sense of humour. Both things are true. They're not hanging offences.'

Sarah was not having this. 'You dislike her too. And think of that populist Budget. It was all wrong and went sour very quickly.'

'I'd never go on holiday with Joan – or tell her about my love life, let her buy my shirts. But I did a deal with her on

Russia the other day, remember? She's straight and she's strong. The Budget was a mistake. She'll learn. And you'll all learn to live with her.'

It was not a cheerful evening. For the most part the dinner guests and the support committee steered away from the subject that had brought them together. The argument was over; the statement had been quickly drafted. It said simply that for personal reasons Mr Roger Courtauld was withdrawing from the leadership contest, and would give no interviews. The chairman of the Foreign Affairs Committee talked at some length about the collapse of the revolt in Russia. They argued whether the Scottish Parliament was entitled to hold its own referendum on Scottish independence. Sarah explained why the Crown Prosecution Service was not taking action against the accountants who had concealed for several years the financial problems of the Dome. Roger left early, though courteously, and with thanks to them all. There was no port.

Letter from Joe Seebright, editor of *Thunder*, to Herr Friedrich Vogl:

> Thank you so much for your letter. I can quite understand your concern, and am glad that you wrote so that I can clear it up.
>
> My colleagues and I are deeply appreciative of the help which you have given us in our project. It is true that some of the material which our representative Mr Scrowl discussed with you has been caught up in the present political contest for the leadership of the Conservative Party. We regret any difficulty this may have caused you, but we considered that the public,

indeed the democratic, interest in this matter should prevail.

You raise in particular the question of the framed photograph of your family on holiday. There must, I think, have been a linguistic misunderstanding here (in our work these difficulties occur from time to time). My colleague Mr Scrowl believed that you were making available all relevant material, and does not recall your making any specific exception. Here again I apologise for any embarrassment, and have pleasure in returning the photograph which he removed from the lavatory, together with a voucher entitling you to four tickets to the forthcoming friendly match at Nuremberg on 10 April between Bayern and Newcastle United, a football company owned by this newspaper. I hope you and your family have a pleasant afternoon.

One of the austere cupboards at South Eaton Place was just wide enough to contain Hélène's array of dresses. At the end of the row were two silk dressing-gowns, but occasionally she preferred to borrow Roger's only such garment, large, scarlet and woollen. It made her look twenty years younger.

'So you are leaving the battle?'

There was no reproach in her voice, either for the substance of the decision or for his failure to consult her in advance. Nevertheless it was a decision whose ripples definitely crossed the frontier within their marriage into Hélène's zone, and he felt apologetic. 'I had to decide quickly. I would have asked you if you'd been here.'

She said nothing, but lit a cigarette from a silver case on the table beside her. She smoked rarely, as a sign of independence, making it an action of elegant authority. The case, the long matches and the Limoges ashtray were more important than the nicotine.

'Have you talked to Felicity?'

Their daughter would be upstairs in her own room, doing her homework.

'Yes, I told her.'

'How did she react?'

'She said that when Joan Freetown came to the Lycée to talk about monetary policy she held the headmistress's hand for at least ten seconds.'

Roger laughed for the first time that day. 'But I doubt if they lay together on a towel. There would hardly be room.'

Another pause.

'What do you think, Hélène?'

'What should I think? In England, as in France, you erect mysteries round the political process, like fences to guard some prehistoric encampment. For many years I have not tried to enter or to understand more than I need. It is now too late to commence my education.'

A spurt of resentment ran through him. Usually he was content with the freedom of thought and action that their relationship gave him. Every now and then he longed for close understanding and mutual dependence. Under the fig tree long ago in Gascony she had been ready enough to listen to him talking about politics. 'That's rubbish, Hélène. There was no political mystery about this. I did it for young Roger.' He told her about his visit to Hillcrest that afternoon.

Hélène stared at him. For once she did not treat what he said as something expected and discounted in advance. She stubbed out her cigarette, half smoked. When she spoke her tone showed that a similar resentment was running through her. 'Sometimes I have to decide whether you are a hypocrite or blind. On the whole it is more comfortable to be married to a hypocrite. On this you are blind, only blind.'

'You mean?'

'You did this for yourself, not young Roger at all, just yourself. You are not old for a politician, but . . .'

'But what?'

'For myself I am content with your decision. Also for little Felicity. But I remark that fatigue makes men weak before they know it. Even when they are still young. I saw it in my father. I see it now in you.'

'That's nonsense too, Hélène. I have never felt so full of energy.'

It was as if he had not spoken.

'I, too, am tired, and will now go to bed. *Bonne nuit.*'

She did not kiss him, but smiled at him as she left the room, her resentment purged by the pleasure of having the last word.

Letter to the Home Secretary:

> Dear Daddy,
> My knee is better and the blood has gone but I am not allowed to play football today. The first XI beat Ludgrove 3–0. Tom has a cold so he is off games too. I have not run away again.
>
> I am looking forward to the holidays. A man called Jim will look after the school guinea pigs till we come back. There are six of them. We have not been allowed to see the newspapers today. But Gromson says you are

not going to be prime minister. Does that mean we can live in the country and have a pony?

Love to Mummy and Felicity,

Roger

Chapter 4

At Peter Makewell's prep school, St Martin's, by a long and cheerful tradition, the boys had manufactured at the beginning of term a mock Advent calendar in the shape of a huge green cardboard tree with paper panels set in the branches. Each panel opened to reveal a number. The number recorded the days still remaining till the beginning of the next holidays. The tree, called Happy Harry for reasons too remote to remember, had been at first discouraged and once destroyed by the masters; but by the time Peter Makewell reached the school, authority had relented, and even allowed each panel to include friendly caricatures of themselves and of leaving boys embracing the magic number. Happy Harry stood at the side of the stage in the school hall, behind the grand piano on which the school song was played at the close of each concert.

One Lent term the school had been invaded by floodwater from the Thames. Peter Makewell remembered how the headmaster, a theatrical young man, had announced that the school would have to close the next day, then strode across the stage in his gown and ripped open Happy Harry's panels in succession until he unveiled the number one. Peter Makewell could hear the cheers even now. He had recently received and responded generously to a financial appeal from St Martin's; among the projects to be financed were a new grand piano and certain necessary repairs to Happy Harry.

Peter had secretly adopted the Happy Harry principle in his own life as prime minister. Each night he received at the top of the papers in his top box a stiff white card listing his engagements for the next day. Each night he wrote a number on the top right corner of the card. His private secretary Patrick Vaughan had guessed what it meant, but did not think it right to comment. The number was the Prime Minister's best estimate of the remaining days he would have to stay in office. On the latest card the number was twenty-eight. The 1922 Committee, to which all Conservative backbenchers belonged, had fixed 25 March as the date for the first round of voting in the leadership election. If a third candidate emerged in addition to Joan Freetown and Roger Courtauld there might have to be a second ballot four days later. A fortnight after that, party members in the constituencies would vote. Unless, as seemed to Peter Makewell highly unlikely, the constituencies disagreed with the choice of the MPs, the new leader would be announced by mid-April. Then events would accelerate: Peter would go at once to the Palace to resign, the Queen would send for Joan Freetown or Roger Courtauld the same day, and he would be on the sleeper to Perth, as a backbench MP on, he thought, the evening of Friday, 9 April.

That had been his calculation last night, before Roger Courtauld had rung to say that he was pulling out. There had been no serious conversation. Roger had spoken quickly, almost curtly, as if he had a dozen urgent calls to make, of which the call to the Prime Minister was not the most important. Peter Makewell guessed that Roger wanted to head off an attempt to persuade him to think again. Certainly, given time and a congenial atmosphere, he would have had a go. He thought the story of the photograph on the beach puerile in all senses of the word, and he disliked the idea of Joan Freetown as his successor. But he was given no time to mobilise his thoughts, and in any case he was handicapped by a prejudice against interfering in other people's private decisions.

So how would that affect his personal arithmetic? Probably not by much. Some maverick backbench MP might try to gain personal publicity by putting up at the last minute against Joan Freetown and denying her a walkover. The wheels of the Party's election machinery would have to turn as meticulously for a farce of that kind as for an evenly matched race.

Peter Makewell opened one of the packets of oatcakes that the Russells had left in the larder of the Prime Minister's flat at the top of No. 10. The cupboard had been almost full – cereals, oatmeal for porridge, honey, marmalade, coffee beans and a host of different biscuits. Peter suspected that these were not Russell leftovers at all, but that Louise had sallied forth to Sainsbury's in those hectic days after Simon's death to buy provisions for the incoming widower. The preponderance of Scottish products for a Scot to eat strengthened the suspicion: so far as he could recall from their rare working breakfasts Simon had been a man for croissants rather than oatcakes. If so, it had been an odd act of kindness by his widow at a time when Louise had been fraught and very busy. The thought prompted Peter to look at the bottom of the engagement card propped in front of him against the jug of coffee. Yes, that was satisfactory: 8.30 p.m. Private dinner.

No restaurant name, no name of guest. But the protection officer would insist on knowing in advance and would book a table. Il Gran Paradiso behind Victoria, he thought. The Russells had taken regular holidays in Tuscany, so he assumed that Louise would like Italian food, which, at Il Gran Paradiso, was succulent and pleasantly served. He had hesitated before writing to ask her to dine with him. He had a shadow of a reason. The Chequers trustees, who ran the country home which every prime minister was entitled to occupy, had put forward a plan for reorganising the garden in front of the house. They wanted to replace the present regiments of red roses with a miscellany of colours on either side of a new stone path flanked with lavender. This would lead down steps to a statue of Norma Major, the historian of Chequers, conversing with Lord Lloyd Webber, composer of the hugely successful musical that took the story of the house as its central theme. Peter Makewell had found this scheme, warmly recommended by the trustees, in the red box for his first weekend as Prime Minister. Under cross-examination, Patrick Vaughan had admitted that Louise Russell had expressed, as he put it, 'certain rather substantial reservations' about it, which was why, uncharacteristically, Simon Russell had left it lying around, neither approved nor condemned. The trustees were still keen, the money for the whole scheme had been set aside and the statue commissioned. But as a matter of good manners and prudence Peter Makewell thought it right to consult Louise, even though she had no status in the matter now that Chequers had passed to him as the new Prime Minister. He would also like her advice about the cook at

Chequers and what the local reaction would be if the trustees reversed Lord Blair's decision and allowed the local hunt to draw a wood at the edge of the estate. Also, he had to admit, he liked Louise and was bored with official dinners or evenings spent alone in the company of his work.

Peter Makewell looked down the rest of the engagement card. It seemed only the other day that he had complained so bitterly about the avalanche of paper from departments. This was no longer so oppressive, partly because he had mastered the substance of the main government policies, partly because the volume of business had contracted. At a time of political uncertainty senior civil servants hoard submissions, giving their immediate masters the false impression as their workload decreases that all is settled and calm. Out of sight and earshot a pile of intractable policy conundrums wait for the reshuffle or the election, after which they will be quickly deployed for decision by the new Prime Minister and his colleagues. The Chequers scheme was the sort of second-rank non-political project that a skilled private secretary would try to slip past a caretaker prime minister during such a period.

The Prime Minister of Dominica was second on Peter Makewell's card of engagements. She would worry him again about the genetically modified bananas she wanted her island to grow but which the EU scientists would not permit. The President of the European Central Bank came next. He would certainly protest about Joan Freetown's Budget speech. He would be even more cross this morning after reading over his breakfast at Claridges that Joan was now bound to become Prime Minister.

The director of the National Portrait Gallery – the man wanted to arrange for the painting of Peter's portrait, or the sculpting of a bust. An honour, of course, but Peter planned to dither until after day zero, confident that the tiresome project would lapse with his own premiership. But first of all . . . The phone rang.

'Sir Martin Redburn is here, Prime Minister.'

Sir Martin was chairman of the 1922 Committee.

'Ask him to come up to the study, would you?'

A few minutes later: 'Martin, come and sit down. Coffee?'

'Yes, please, Prime Minister. Milk, no sugar.'

Peter Makewell had nothing against the chairman of the 1922 Committee, but he did not like the man, and was not sure why. Peter knew himself to be an anachronism – tweedy, nearly seventy, a Scottish laird with English manners, holding no particularly strong beliefs, following a tradition of service. While constantly complaining about them, he privately enjoyed the TV jokes and the press cartoons that, in one way or another, treated him as a dinosaur and the last of his kind. He relished the assumption that there would never be another prime minister so gentlemanly and out of date. Yet here was Martin Redburn. Not that Martin would ever, short of some earthquake, become Prime Minister, or a minister of any kind. Martin Redburn had been among the first to embrace the new career structure of the House of Commons. After entering the Commons he had quickly earned an extra salary as member of the Home Affairs Select Committee, then after five years had earned rapid promotion and a substantial salary as chairman of the Transport Committee. Peter Makewell preferred running a department to criticising it, but he approved the transformation of the Commons that this reform had brought about, and could welcome Martin Redburn as one of the first to make a success of climbing the new parliamentary ladder. Nor did he quarrel with Redburn's views which, in so far as they could be discerned, were close to his own. Probably Redburn stood a few yards to the right of the acting Prime Minister. He had recently made no secret in private of his personal support for Joan Freetown, while in public preserving his neutrality as organiser and arbiter of the election process. But both men were pragmatists, sharing a definition of the Conservatives as a party of sound administrators rather than political ideologues.

And yet Makewell did not like the man. He admitted to himself that this was partly snobbery. Redburn looked like a traditional Tory, had been educated at Radley and was often described by foolish journalists as patrician. But this was not right. He often wore tweeds, but preferred them lightweight and new, whereas Makewell's were old, indestructible and heavy. The creases on Redburn's tweeds were straight and precise; the Prime Minister's creases wandered hither and thither and occasionally disappeared. The Prime Minister's shoes were clean, cracked and English; Redburn's more highly polished, smooth and Italian. In the argument that seemed unending both men supported fox-hunting without hunting themselves, Makewell from Scotland because his children and most of his friends hunted, Redburn from Kensington because most of his constituents there thought a ban would be illiberal. The capital assets of the two men were of similar size, but Redburn's dividends and capital gains yielded twice as much as Makewell's income from agricultural and sporting assets. Makewell belonged to Boodles Club, Redburn to the Carlton. Makewell spent Christmas in Perthshire, Redburn in the Seychelles.

Makewell preferred to work in the Prime Minister's study

on the first floor of No. 10, for the uncomplicated reason that this was the room designed for that purpose. He had none of the political hang-ups that had led John Major to work in the Cabinet Room or Lord Blair in the room designed for the Prime Minister's private secretary. The authoritative spirit of Margaret Thatcher no longer hovered in the study. It was where Simon Russell had worked, where he and Peter Makewell had often talked informally and in confidence, as is necessary between Prime Minister and Foreign Secretary. However long he remained in office it would not occur to Makewell to change pictures or move furniture.

Because he did not like Martin Redburn he had thought of returning to his desk after they shook hands and letting Redburn take the hard chair in front of the desk. But Redburn headed straight towards the deep armchairs by the fireplace, and the Prime Minister followed, hoping that his bad-mannered plan had not been spotted.

'Prime Minister, I am grateful for your time.'

In his day Simon Russell had always expected to be addressed as 'Prime Minister'. Though a mild and essentially modest man, he had believed in and used the authority of the office. Makewell was ill at ease with the title, but had never been on first-name terms with Redburn and did not want to start now. He nodded silently.

'The leadership contest has taken an unexpected turn.'

'Yes, indeed.'

'You have heard, then?'

Makewell was puzzled at the question. The story had led the news in every morning paper.

'Roger's decision will, I suppose, give Joan Freetown a free run, give or take some stray no-hope maverick.'

'I think not, Prime Minister.' Redburn straightened his tie, which was already straight, and crossed his legs. Makewell could see that the man was preparing to enjoy himself. 'I think not,' he repeated.

'What do you mean?'

'The 1922 executive met last night. I called a special meeting as soon as I heard that the Home Secretary had withdrawn from the contest.'

Makewell stayed silent. He suspected that Redburn was going to ask him to persuade Roger to change his mind and continue to stand. He could not imagine why, unless that story of Redburn's support for Joan Freetown had been wrong.

'I have to tell you, Prime Minister, that after a short discussion, a strong majority of the executive concluded that, despite her many talents, Joan Freetown should not be allowed to succeed in the circumstances.'

Makewell was genuinely amazed.

'This comes as a surprise to you, Prime Minister?' said Redburn, obviously pleased.

'It certainly does.'

'If I may say so, the sooner you appoint a parliamentary private secretary the better.' This was patronising, but well founded. The main job of a PPS was to keep the Prime Minister abreast of waves of opinion in the Commons. Makewell had not got round to choosing one.

He tried to retrieve the initiative. 'Joan Freetown is admirably qualified, and I had understood that you—'

'Yes, indeed, Prime Minister, but the situation has changed. Up till a few days ago this was a contest between two admirably qualified candidates, as you say, of whom I on balance gave a slight preference to the Chancellor of the Exchequer.'

God, the man was irritating.

'But you must see that if she became leader of the Party in the new circumstances the real winner would not be Joan Freetown but Lord Spitz. The press, by a disreputable device, would have asserted control over Parliament and the Conservative Party. This must not be allowed to happen.'

'It was certainly a disreputable trick. But are you suggesting that Joan—'

'Not at all, Prime Minister. Whether all of her supporters were equally scrupulous I do not know but according to my information the Chancellor of the Exchequer refused to have any part in the device.'

'Then . . . ?'

'That point is not really relevant, Prime Minister.'

Martin Redburn rose, and stood in front of the empty fireplace, as if he was in his own home. Behind him was a painting of the younger Pitt, the subject slender and determined, sharp nose in the air. To his surprise Peter Makewell saw that Redburn was about to abandon his elaborate manner and speak his mind.

'You must understand this, Prime Minister. It is the heart of the matter. My only surprise is that so many of my colleagues felt as I did. During the twenty-five years I have been in politics the power of the media has grown. Press, radio, television, I make no distinction. So far as we politicians are concerned they began as the means by which we communicate with the people. In those days they carried columns and columns of our speeches, produced word for word, hecklers and all. Fine and good, a necessary part of the growth of democracy. Then the editors began to take a hand in advising us what we ought to do. Well and good, we had to accept that – though, God knows, they have no qualifications, no relevant experience, no mandate from anyone except whichever prejudiced millionaire happens to have bought them. But they were not content with our public affairs. They began to pry into private matters, who slept with whom, whose son was on drugs, who paid for a good meal at the Ritz. The public laps up all this stuff as entertainment, they buy the papers, listen to the programmes, and the hypocrites who write it up think that it gives them power.'

'So it does, so it does,' said the Prime Minister. This was a weary discourse, the stuff of many smoking-room grumbles. He tried to remember if there was some small murky episode in Sir Martin Redburn's past that might have fathered this outburst. The Prime Minister of Dominica would soon be upon them.

'But it's not real power. It's bluff. No one really cares a damn if you have a mistress or a couple of bastards hidden away in Blairgowrie.' This was really most un-Redburn-like. 'But if they discovered them the media would start to bay at you. And you'd run. That's the point. You'd run, just as Courtauld has. Once you've started to run, they chase you, the hunt is up, the horns sound, and they chase you to death. Everyone enjoys it, and it's all unnecessary. If you'd stood your ground, you'd see them off.'

'No bastards, I fear, not even in Blairgowrie.' Makewell tried to lighten the atmosphere, and failed.

'Nor had Courtauld down in Devon. Just an afternoon on the beach with a boyfriend. Hand in hand for an hour or two, for God's sake. I don't care if they buggered each other senseless in the bushes. It would not in the least affect his ability to lead the Party. He failed us, failed us all, not there on the beach but yesterday when he copped out.'

Martin Redburn sat down as abruptly as he had stood up. The passion had not gone out of him but there was a pause.

'I agree with you. But I doubt if I could get him to change his mind.' Makewell had no intention of trying.

'Of course you couldn't. He's run into some thicket now to hide. There's nothing so stubborn as a coward. He's a lost man. We have to find another candidate. Not against Joan, against the media.'

'Ah, I see now. Have you found someone?' There was no one of any substance. The Prime Minister did not need a parliamentary private secretary to know that. No doubt they'd found some exhibitionist who'd make a show of it.

'Yes, we have. Three of us had the same idea separately. All except two of the executive endorsed it.'

'May I know the name?'

'You may. It is Peter Makewell.'

'But . . .' Then Makewell paused. The idea was so preposterous, so foreign to his character, his position in life, his wishes, that he could not immediately find words to reject it. 'You must all know how reluctant I was to come here, even for a few weeks, how I hate the hassle of it all, how keen I am to get out.'

'Of course we know that. It's part of the attraction. You belong to a different world, a different generation from the rest of us. A world before spin-doctors and focus groups, a serious world. For the moment, that's what we need.'

Peter Makewell stayed silent. His main wish was to kill this absurdity once and for all, but he did not know how.

'The people against the press, the people against the press.'
Redburn was relentless. His voice began to rise again. 'It
would win you this leadership election. Indeed, Joan Freetown
might pull out and wait for another day. It might even win us
the next general election. You'd scrap all this rubbish about a
new Freedom of Information Bill. Straw was right about that
in the old days. That's just a piece of media greed tricked out
as a service to democracy. You'd need a good Privacy Bill and
a stronger Press Commission between now and then. None of
that would be difficult – once we realise how fed up our constituents are with being patronised and demeaned by the
media slobs. All right, they've been amused, bewitched, led
astray – and now they've had enough. This Courtauld thing is
the last straw. The e-mails are pouring in. And you're the
man to prove it.'

Peter Makewell had found time to collect his words and
make them formal. 'I am flattered,' he said, 'but even more I
am amazed. I fear I don't have time to discuss it all now. But I
must ask you to thank your executive and tell them that on
both personal and political grounds I regard this proposal as
completely out of the question. They should dismiss it totally
and immediately from their minds.'

'They will not do that, Prime Minister . . .' As if on cue
Patrick Vaughan appeared in the doorway.

'The Prime Minister of Dominica, Prime Minister.'

Sir Martin Redburn rose. For the first time in the interview
he was irresolute. He had expected more time. 'Please think of
what—'

'I really have nothing more to add.' Peter Makewell was
moving to the door to greet his next visitor who wore bright
green. 'Prime Minister, I'm delighted to see you again . . . Not

since the Commonwealth summit in Kingston. I expect you
know Sir Martin Redburn?'

Now that the burden of work had somewhat lifted, Peter
Makewell had reverted to his old habit of taking a bath before
dinner. In the Foreign Office there was no bath. Some mean-
minded predecessor had installed a flimsy plastic shower in
the annex to his office. The dials, hard to manipulate, had
often subjected the Foreign Secretary to jets of unwanted cold
or scalding water. One small advantage of his promotion to
No. 10 had been easy access to a deep, old-fashioned bath in
the flat. He missed the soft brown water of the Highlands, the
occasional tickle of peat against the toes, but in public life one
had to make sacrifices. Peter was in a good mood as, with the
water temperature just right, he reviewed the day and looked
forward to the evening. He really felt extraordinarily well,
and at seventy that was increasingly important. He was
pleased that Martin Redburn had offered him the crown, and
pleased that he had turned it down. It was all nonsense, of
course. It was not surprising that the 1922 executive should
feel a spasm of annoyance against the press and against
Courtauld for giving in to them, but you could not build a
leadership bid, let alone a government programme, on such a
flimsy foundation.

There were several reasons for good humour. The Prime
Minister of Dominica had been brief on bananas. The man
from the Portrait Gallery in arguing for a bust had been particularly flattering about Peter's chin and the line of his jaw.
But, above all, he was looking forward to his dinner with
Louise. She had seemed distant and somewhat formidable as
the Prime Minister's wife. He could see now that she had

been struggling to keep for herself and her daughter some thin slices of Simon Russell's life. She had been devoted to him, there had been no conceivable doubt of that. But now that he was gone she seemed more relaxed and friendly. She was also remarkably handsome and well turned-out. Peter's own wife had turned somewhat mousy in her last years, to his secret regret. She had stopped buying clothes, even in Perth, and never looked at herself in a mirror. Modest himself in dress, he liked a woman who could carry with conviction a dress that swept the ground and wore diamonds at her throat.

Not that Louise would be carrying diamonds tonight at Il Gran Paradiso, which was one reason why he had chosen the place. At the Savoy or Claridges they would be fawned on and gaped at; by the time they left the restaurant there would be a photographer in the foyer. There was a risk, too, at Il Gran Paradiso, indeed it would be strange if nothing appeared in any of the gossip columns. Somehow that risk seemed less obvious and vulgar. The food, he knew, was good and the price modest. He did not believe in spending large sums on meals, and persuaded himself that Louise would feel the same. Il Gran Paradiso had offered him their private room, but this would look as if he had something to hide, and he had turned it down. The protection officer on duty had booked a table at the back of the restaurant. He and his colleague would sit at the table nearest to the Prime Minister, and he had arranged for a third table close by to be kept vacant. Peter Makewell chose his blue suit by Hardy Amies with four buttons down the jacket. For years he had felt, without much justification, that this particular suit conveyed a slight dandyish impression. He kept it for the small number of unusual private occasions in his life.

He prided himself on punctuality, and was irritated to be
held up as he left No. 10. Ladies, and in particular perhaps
prime ministers' widows, should not be kept waiting. But the
First Minister of Scotland wanted to speak to him on the telephone. The FMS, formerly a Labour Lord Provost of Glasgow,
commanded a truly municipal flow of words. There was a tradition – new, like so many in British life – that the First
Minister had direct access to No. 10. Peter Makewell knew the
man to be worthy, but was irritated by his continuous unwill-
ingness to grasp the depth of the irritation that the Scots were
arousing by their voluble demands on Whitehall and at
Westminster. As he took the mobile phone in the outer hall of
No. 10 he guessed that Mackay would be complaining in some
form or other about Joan Freetown, and so it proved. She had
refused to see him to discuss compensation for the move of the
National Savings Bank from Glasgow to Newcastle.

'She'll not even speak with me on the telephone. As you
know, Prime Minister, we Scots are slow to anger, and for
myself I'm told I have a reputation as a man of few words. But
you'll understand that the dignity of my office may compel me
to break silence if the Chancellor continues this discourtesy.'

There had never been any question of silence. The First
Minister had been voluble on the subject of the National
Savings Bank ever since Budget Day. But the way he phrased
the complaint showed Peter Makewell that there was a personal edge to it, which could perhaps be softened. He did not
want a great row with Scotland at this moment. He beck-
oned to Patrick Vaughan who, after six years as a private
secretary, was good at hovering at the right time and the right
place. 'Tell the Chancellor's office, would you, that I hope she
will telephone the First Minister personally about the Savings

Bank? She can say that as a concession to himself there will be some job compensation for Glasgow, and then tell him in strict confidence what was agreed at EDX yesterday.'

Patrick mounted a mild protest, so that he could tell the Cabinet secretary later that he had done so. 'There would be a risk of a leak in the Scottish press, Prime Minister, before the announcement is made in the Commons.'

'Not a risk, Patrick, a certainty.' The Prime Minister put on a heavy black London overcoat against the cold March night. 'But that will not, I think, be the first time . . . or the end of the world.'

As the door of No. 10 closed, the Prime Minister climbed into his car, and the principal private secretary retreated to his lair. Both had the same thought, which both found new and agreeable. Peter Makewell was picking up the job fast – just as he was about to give it up. If he had allowed himself to continue like this, he would come within range of Simon Russell's formidable reputation for subtle traffic control. But, of course, within a few weeks he would be gone.

Patrick Vaughan knew nothing of Sir Martin Redburn's mad suggestion that morning. Mad indeed, thought Peter, as his car edged out through the gates into Whitehall. So mad that he had genuinely forgotten about it all day. No need to give it further thought. He resolved in particular not to mention it to Louise Russell that evening.

The Scottish kerfuffle and red traffic lights at the foot of Whitehall, by the Abbey, and again in Victoria Street made him five minutes late. The proprietor of Il Gran Paradiso was at the door, smiling in the Italian manner, warm but not obsequious.

'The *signora* is already here,' he said, with a touch of pleased intrigue in his voice. But as soon as Peter Makewell entered the restaurant it was clear that all was not well. Louise was there, certainly, standing not far from the entrance talking to the protection officer who had gone to the restaurant in advance. Her cheeks were flushed.

'The Prime Minister thought . . .' said the protection officer.

Louise knew him well because for six months he had protected Simon Russell. 'I'm sorry, George, it just won't do.'

What on earth could be the matter? Looking through the restaurant, Peter Makewell could see at the far end the triangle of unoccupied tables as planned. To him they looked crisp and inviting. The rest of the room was fairly full and, of course, knowing eyes began to turn towards Louise and himself.

'I'm sorry, Peter, I'm really sorry, but it won't do,' she repeated, as soon as he reached her. He withdrew his plan for a light kiss on the cheek. By now the whole world seemed to be looking at them. Damn.

'It's that young man.' She did not actually point, but nodded to a table adjoining the empty white triangle. 'I'll explain later, but I'm afraid I can't sit as close as that to David Alcester.'

Peter Makewell had not recognised Alcester from the back, but now he turned his head towards them. Sweep of fair hair too low across the forehead, orthodox English face of the charming variety, now lit with genuine surprise turning to insincere welcome. He was entertaining, or more likely being entertained by, a lady journalist from the *Daily Mail* gossip column.

'This is a pleasant surprise. Come and join us,' said Alcester, getting up and moving to join Louise and the Prime Minister in the centre of the restaurant. His legs were rather too short for his torso, which already carried a few pounds of excess weight. Even at this early stage of his political career he preferred to be photographed behind a desk or cross-legged in a chair. He spoke as if he were host in charge of the entire restaurant. But he was addressing a void. Louise had already bustled the Prime Minister and the two protection officers out into the street. A cold drizzle had set in, which matched Peter Makewell's gloom. A well-prepared evening was collapsing in ruins. He silently cursed his protection officers for not having investigated the other diners at Il Gran Paradiso. Unfairly, since they were not employed as his political or social chaperons. Where to go now? It would be tactless to take Louise back to No. 10 only weeks after she had left it, and anyway that would mean rushed scrambled eggs from an indignant housekeeper. The Savoy, he supposed, though . . .

But Louise took control. 'I know the steak house at the top of the street. The manager worked for Government Hospitality long ago.'

Within minutes they were seated round a scarlet plastic tablecloth drinking the steak house Rioja, and contemplating a menu that consisted entirely of different weights (eight, twelve and sixteen ounces) of rump, sirloin or fillet of beef. Every helping was supplied automatically with chips.

'Just the place,' said Louise. 'The young love it.'

Not at all the place for Peter Makewell, who was not young. He examined the pop stars on the walls, trying to regain calm. He was uneasy because there was no table free for the two protection officers – they had been forced to retreat into the March drizzle. He had thought of asking them to share the table with Louise and himself, but that was not compatible with the style of the occasion and in any case she might object. And having been a protected person only for these few weeks, he still felt awkward with his protectors, particularly at the thought of upsetting them.

'He wasn't wearing his trousers, that was the point,' said Louise, examining the menu.

Peter Makewell, thinking of protection officers, was baffled, as she no doubt intended.

'That young man. His name is Alcester. He's an MP, you ought to know him. I do not think he has actually seduced Julia, but when I came home early from the studio he was about to try. This was ten days ago. Bad legs, too, podgy.'

Peter Makewell remained baffled. He was childless.

'It played like an old-fashioned farce. I was shouting. He must get out and never come to Highgate again. He had trouble with the zip of his trousers. I think I'll have eight ounces of fillet. He was in such a hurry, he left in his socks. He thought I was going to hit him. I still have the shoes. Cheaper than they look from a distance.'

'And Julia?' This was not at all as he had expected or wanted, but he had to follow along her track.

'She was giggling at the other end of the sofa. She had all her clothes on. Whether she was laughing at him or at me I couldn't tell. Probably both. After he had gone, she clapped for a couple of seconds, she said, "Oh, Mummy," kissed me, and went up to bed as if nothing had happened. Since then I've asked no questions. I might get bad answers. I don't think she's seen him since. Girls don't like men they've seen in ridiculous positions, particularly if they helped them get there.'

Louise paused, and for the first time he could look at her

properly. The simple dark grey dress without jewellery contrasted with the flamboyance of her dark auburn hair and heavy makeup. He did not know her well enough to be sure if the simplicity of dress resulted from natural taste or recent widowhood. In either case it was right for the steak-house, while he felt pompously overdressed. He undid the jacket buttons of his dark blue suit.

Louise continued to talk to him as if he were an old friend. 'I miss Simon, you know, but for the little things mainly: the cup of tea he brought me in the morning, the way he remembered my birthday three days late. Why not for the big things? I often ask myself that. We had a long life together full of travel, crises, grand occasions, big hotels, country cottages, talk and love. It was a long good chapter, and it came to a natural close. There was not much more to be said or done.'

'But you are still young, and . . .'

But 'beautiful' could not come out. The harsh house Rioja was carrying him some distance but not that far.

'Now there is just an unexciting epilogue, a dim page or two to wrap things up. A trip to my studio every day, perhaps even an exhibition of sculptures next year, a few parties, an occasional photograph in the glossies, gradually more days in our Somerset cottage, the horizon comfortably narrowing down to the village fête and work on kneelers for the church . . . or could there be a whole new chapter?'

'A new chapter, surely.' This was more than gallantry.

'But the new chapter would be called Julia. I begin to think that's a book of its own, her book and not mine.' She paused. 'Physically speaking, Julia lives in Highgate. She sleeps there most nights, and manages a good breakfast. But since Simon died her real life's elsewhere, and I'm not part of it any more.

I provide the washing machine and the scrambled eggs, with toast.'

The steaks arrived, with seven different kinds of mustard on a tray. In his bath an hour ago Peter Makewell had imagined a conversation that started with the trustees' proposals for Chequers and moved, slowly – say, over the coffee – to more personal matters. He was inadequate to cope with this reversal of the natural order.

Unexpectedly Louise guided him on to his own track. 'Tell me, why did you ask me to this delicious dinner?'

He had to admit that his fillet steak was worthy, though not to be compared with the creamy risotto he would have been eating in Il Gran Paradiso had David Alcester kept his trousers on. 'You may remember that the Chequers trustees have a scheme—'

She laughed, having taken two full glasses of the Rioja. 'Prime Minister, Prime Minister, what are you saying? A new rose garden in exchange for a medium-rare steak? You'd be getting a bargain.'

He could only plough on. 'I was told that you had objected – or, rather, that Simon had objected on your behalf.'

'Objected, objected . . . of course I objected. But I objected to the trustees, not the scheme. They're a dreary lot of bankers and lawyers pretending to understand gardens, trees and the countryside. It was my duty to twist their tails.'

'Then as regards the scheme . . .'

'I've no objection at all. Norma Major deserves a statue – she did an excellent job with that book of hers. And that wilderness of dull red roses certainly needs breaking up. Tell the trustees I fought like a tiger, called them all sorts of evil names, but by sheer charm you won me over.'

'You're laughing at me.'

'Certainly. Prime ministers are there to be teased. Do you like Chequers?'

'To be honest, no. I hardly go there.'

'But you can't go back to Perthshire every weekend. And Downing Street is hardly . . . But, I forgot, you're still Foreign Secretary, you still have Chevening.'

Yes, indeed – Chevening, elegant Queen Anne brick, soft in the light of a summer evening, or bright with the hillside frosty white on a Boxing Day morning, his study looking over the lake and a crowd of geese promenading like ambassadors on the lawn. Since his wife had died Chevening had gained over Perthshire in his affection. By comparison Chequers was dark, cluttered, dull and oversupplied with history.

'Do you enjoy being Prime Minister?'

There was a connection between the houses and the jobs that went with them, but it was a bit too abrupt for Peter's taste. 'Not at all. The work is hard, endless and often uncongenial. I can't think how Simon put up with it for so long.'

'He loved it. It became his life. He went on for too many years, but you've only just begun. You ought to stay.'

'Stay? What do you mean? I only took it on as a—'

'A caretaker? Yes. But sometimes the caretaker inherits the house. You'd be better than either lazy Roger Courtauld or that shrill Chancellor of yours.'

Obviously Louise did not bother with news bulletins, or indeed newspapers. He told her of Roger's withdrawal from the leadership contest.

'Well, even more so . . . What are people like me to do faced with Joan Freetown?' Her voice softened. 'She was good to us, very good to Julia and me, when Simon died in her spare bedroom – but that's different from welcoming her as Prime Minister. You should stand. You've no good reason not to.'

'You're the second person today to say that.'

'Who was the first?' She was surprised. Later, much later, she told him that up to that point she had been merely teasing him.

'Martin Redburn.' And, contrary to his clear resolution at bathtime, he told her of his morning meeting.

The story changed her mood to serious. 'You must take it,' she said.

He expostulated, over the *crème brûlé*, which was leathery, then over the double espresso coffee, but he could not shake her. Nor, he assured himself, could *she* shake *him*. He wrote a cheque for the dinner because the steak house would not accept a credit card even from a prime minister. By now just about everyone in the restaurant had recognised them and was staring, some openly, others pretending not to.

'I'd like to go back to not being recognised,' he said to Louise, helping her on with her coat, trying to wrap up the argument. 'But I expect most of them are looking at you.'

'Don't deceive yourself. You're talking as you might have talked ten years ago, when we first met. I'd have believed your modesty then, but it rings false now. Like Simon you're hooked on the work and you relish the publicity, though you keep that last a close secret even from yourself.'

'Nonsense,' but he was pleased. The car dropped him in Downing Street before taking her north to Highgate. This time there was no plan, but he kissed her, lightly, on just one cheek.

'Nonsense,' he said again to himself, very pleasantly, as he waited for the lift inside No. 10. 'Nonsense,' again, as he climbed into bed.

Guy Freetown had left the hotel in Tokyo to walk round the Imperial Moat, which he said would take him an hour. Joan was thus free to dance a jig in front of the largest mirror of the Royal Suite. None of the friends and allies of the harsh, handsome, humourless Chancellor of the Exchequer would for one minute have thought her capable of such a silly gesture. Guy would have remembered it from the happy days of their early marriage, but even he would have been amazed to find it still in his wife's repertoire.

But then the news from London was amazing, fantastic, absurdly splendid. The flood of press cuttings had just stopped flowing from the fax machine. Joan had stacked them neatly on the ornate little desk alongside; even in triumph she was neat.

HAND IN HAND ON BEACH — ROGER QUITS

HOME SECRETARY QUITS BUT — 'I WAS NEVER GAY'

GAY PHOTO CLINCHES JOAN'S TRIUMPH

NOW IT MUST BE JOAN

It had been hard to decide whether to come to Tokyo for the board meeting of the International Monetary Fund. David Alcester, as her campaign manager, had been against it. She should stay at home, he thought, chat in the Commons' tea room, smile at wobbly backbenchers, give another interview to the *Evening Standard*, appear yet again on *Newsnight*. But David, though brilliant and utterly loyal, knew only the partisan part of Joan's life. She might be running for the Tory leadership, but she was still in charge of Britain's finances. This IMF meeting was not routine. The European Commission was angling to replace Britain and France on the board of the fund with a single European representative. The French had been staunch up to now, but it was rumoured that they might change if a Frenchman were chosen to represent Europe. There would be a tussle, mostly behind the scenes, and Joan must be at the heart of it. Guy had been clear that she should stick to her commitment.

'How will it look,' she had asked David Alcester, just before she left for the airport, 'if I stay at home chasing votes and there's an ambush in Tokyo and we lose our seat?'

David, sitting on the sofa in the Treasury, had chewed his handkerchief and looked cross. He had not yet learned a gracious way of admitting that he was wrong. This was an art of which Joan was ignorant herself, but which she valued in others.

ROGER'S BEACH SHAME
THE HOLIDAY SNAP WENT WRONG
'YES, I GUESSED' SAYS ROGER'S EX
THERE WAS ALWAYS SOMETHING ODD ABOUT HIS KISSES

Joan disliked these secondary headlines. She had no time for Roger Courtauld, grudging the success that, up to yesterday, he had achieved with so little apparent effort. Certainly she would much rather have beaten him in a fair fight without the benefit of the beach photograph. But the excitement was that she had won, she was going to be Prime Minister. Was it too early to ring David Alcester and get the latest feel? Nine hours' difference, so it would be seven in the morning in London.

The telephone rang; the bouncy voice did not wait for her greeting. 'Marvellous press, Joan. I made sure they sent you all of it.'

'Many thanks, David. For that and for everything. Are you still in bed?' She brushed aside and quickly buried her wish to visualise David Alcester in bed.

'No, just back from the gym in the basement. Twenty lengths in the Olympic pool. Joan, we need to seize the moment. I've rung Redburn already to say you think the uncertainty is damaging to everyone. Now Roger Courtauld's out they should telescope the timetable, and get you elected within a couple of days.'

The young man took too much on himself, but Joan forgave him since the cause was so good.

'What did Sir Martin say?'

'Hummed and hawed, said, not easy, he'd think about it.'

'Any sign of another candidate?'

'None, though he said he'd have to leave a day or two in case one came forward. But it would only be a maverick.'

'You're sure, David?' There had been something in his tone that suggested he was reassuring himself.

A moment's silence.

'David, you must tell me if there's anything on your mind. There must be no secrets between us.'

'It's just something Redburn said. And it's confirmed in the *Telegraph*, page two, I think. He said a good many people were cross with the press. Didn't like the photograph ploy. Didn't think Roger should have given in to it.'

'But I had nothing to do with it.'

'Everyone knows that. Redburn said it himself. You're in the clear.'

'The danger is that these people will get at Roger Courtauld this morning and that the foolish man will change his mind and come back in.'

'Yes, I agree that's the danger.'

But it wasn't.

Statement by Sir Martin Redburn on behalf of the Conservative 1922 Committee:

Tuesday, 23 March

In view of some erratic misreporting I have been authorised by the Committee to explain why I yesterday approached the Prime Minister, Sir Peter Makewell, on behalf of the Committee and invited him to enter the contest for the leadership of the Conservative Party. We did not take this exceptional action because we underrate the claim of the Chancellor of the Exchequer, Joan Freetown, to the leadership. On the contrary some of us would in normal circumstances have supported Joan Freetown in this contest. But the circumstances are not normal. The *Thunder* newspaper has attempted to destroy the candidature of the Home Secretary, Roger Courtauld, by a device that is at once obscene and absurd. Other newspapers have shared this tactic while appearing to condemn it, by giving extensive publicity to the story and to the insinuations that surround it. The growing unease with which most of us have for years regarded the sleazy influence of the press on British politics has come to a head. Others who have not hitherto shared this unease can now see its justification. The press claims to cleanse the body politic but in fact pollutes it. Self-regulation has failed.

The time has come to protect the public from a growing evil.

The Conservative government under its new leadership will now need to put forward proposals for an effective law on privacy. We are familiar with the reasons why this measure, often condemned, has always in the past been shelved. Behind the excuses the underlying reason is lack of courage. When it came to the crunch, politicians of all parties have declined to challenge forces in the media that might cripple or destroy them. There should be a much more stringent measure preventing the abuse of ownership of newspapers, television and radio. The government should abandon its plans for a more generous Freedom of Information Bill. The clamour for greater freedom of information masks the greed of the media for greater power. But they are not elected by the people and have no right to speak on behalf of the people. The culture of sleaze in the British media is now more damaging to the public than any culture of secrecy in Whitehall.

Meanwhile there is a case for emphatic public protest. We endorse the suggestion that on every Wednesday for the next six weeks, beginning tomorrow 24 March, individual citizens should refrain from buying any newspaper from any shop or news-stand.

More immediately, we welcome the Prime Minister's decision to accept our invitation to stand for the leadership. We believe that in the new situation he will receive overwhelming support from Members of Parliament and from our supporters in the constituencies, whatever their previous intentions. We believe

that Peter Makewell can restore the unity of the Party
and equip us to confront successfully the many challenges (including the challenge of the media) which
confront us.

Joan Freetown read this text standing up beside her desk in
the Royal Suite. Up to now she had had a good day. She had
intimidated the Japanese chairman of the IMF meeting by
threatening to walk out if there was any discussion of any
proposal to replace the British, French and German seats on
the board with a single European seat. She had told the
French that she would veto any French candidate for such a
seat who might put his head above the parapet. She had no
right to bully the Japanese and no veto to scupper the French,
but in her career Joan Freetown had often found that the
confident assertion of a right you did not possess was almost as
good as acquiring it.

All the more vexing, therefore, to find this setback at
home.

'Rather well written,' said Guy, 'in a traditional sort of
style.' He, too, had spent a happy day, visiting temples and
gardens in the company of an old Japanese business friend. He
was entirely relaxed, wearing a rather too heavy suit that had
seen faithful service in the Cotswolds.

'Nonsense, it's rubbish from beginning to end. A total
meaningless rant. We all know the press at home is destructive. But what's that got to do with the leadership contest? Let
me ring Peter Makewell at once before he makes an ass of
himself.'

'Why don't you ring David Alcester first, to check the facts
and get the background?'

This was unusual: Guy hardly ever spoke of David Alcester, as if by silence he could conjure the young man away from his place at Joan's side as her political henchman.

Joan was already dialling. 'David?'

'I was just going to ring you.'

'What the hell is going on?'

'You've heard, then. I warned you last night that—'

'You said nothing about Peter Makewell.'

'I knew nothing about Peter Makewell. Redburn leaned on him hard. They've all gone mad over the press.'

'So?' A silence. 'So? David, I'm asking you.' Still silence. 'David, I rely on you.'

Joan sat down rather abruptly. Guy could imagine the young man wrestling with his calculations of his own self-interest, mixed with scraps of loyalty to Joan. Complicated men are not at their best, he thought, on complicated occasions. He had noticed and feared the note of attraction in his wife's voice, not because David Alcester was capable of threatening his marriage or had any interest in trying but because he knew from the past that when Joan became fond of young men she tended to follow their advice even when, or particularly when, it was bad. He held his breath, so that David could not know he was listening on the extension on the sofa by the mini-bar.

David Alcester spoke slowly as he turned a page in his own career. He decided to tell the truth. 'The PM will get all Courtauld's support and add maybe a dozen of his own. That should still leave you with a winning hand among the MPs, if you hold your own pledges. And once you have won with them you'd romp home in the constituencies. At least, that's what I would have said two days ago, but I'm not sure of even

that now. It sounds as if the constituency chairmen are
whooping the Party up against the press more loudly than
anyone. Anyway it all depends on your holding those pledges
in the Commons, and I'm afraid you won't. They're shifting
already. I've had three calls since breakfast . . .'

'Who?'

'Suffling, Lerwick, Andrew Jones – all much the same,
undying admiration for you, your turn will come, but this is
rather a special occasion.'

'Skunks.'

'Indeed, Joan.' A long pause. 'I'll stick by you if you decide
to go on . . .' This was said slowly. Guy sensed that it was a
gamble. In having said this David Alcester had added weight
to the advice that came next: '. . . but on balance you should
pull out now and declare for Makewell.'

'You're sure? I could fly back at once. You're sure there's no
hope?' Her hand clenched round the receiver and she pressed
her lips tight together as she did during difficult moments in
the House of Commons.

'Quite sure, Joan.'

'Thank you, David.' The conversation ended. She turned
furiously on Guy. 'How did you know what David Alcester
would say?'

'I had no idea. I just knew you would want his advice.'

'You didn't talk to him before I came back?'

'Certainly not.'

'What would you have done if he had said I should fight
on?'

'I should have persuaded you otherwise.'

'Tried to persuade me.'

Guy suppressed a smile. He knew he would have won. He

would have played the highest card of all: their marriage. Because he had only played that card once or perhaps twice in thirty years it had never looked like failing.

Joan went to her husband and kissed him. The tears of anger in her eyes were replaced by others. As she kissed him he held her tight. Her black hair with the silver streak was soft against his shoulder.

Later they slipped out of the back door of the hotel, dodging the two Japanese protection officers. Guy knew of a tiny restaurant nearby, with just eight stools against a curved bar. The proprietor boasted that a famous wrestler had once eaten five hundred shrimps in quick succession at that bar. The shrimps came sizzling, small, tasty, expensive. Warm sake and the sense of refinding companionship turned the evening into a success.

'You don't mind my using David Alcester like this?' she asked, on the way back to the hotel.

'Provided you use him rather than let him use you. And provided he gives you the right advice.'

'Does he?'

'Usually not. Tonight yes.'

She kissed her husband again in the hotel foyer as they waited to go up to bed.

As in many Japanese institutions the modern lift was manned, quite unnecessarily, by a pretty girl in geisha costume. She was shocked into giggles by this public embrace of elderly Europeans.

Chapter 5

Two Years Later

'You're the only person I can say it to. We're not going to win.'

Before replying Louise placed the Prime Minister's early-morning cup of tea alongside the Conservative election manifesto on his bedside table. 'Of course we're not going to win. The odd thing is, you don't seem to care.'

'You don't find that odd at all.'

Peter Makewell sipped as his wife rejoined him in bed. But in truth she did find it odd. Newspapers were constantly asking Louise to write articles on the only woman in history to have married two prime ministers in succession. She always refused, but after two years the differences and the similarities were clear in her mind. She had never made morning tea for Simon Russell because he used to make it for her. She would not have joined in political conversation with him, except when provoked by rage, for in those days she had regarded politics as a destructive force that must be prevented from occupying all her husband's life. Now, three years later, everything seemed quieter, less intense, less important.

Marriage, or at least marriage to Louise, encouraged Peter Makewell to clear his mind honestly on matters that would otherwise have stayed opaque.

'I am doing my best to hold the Party together. Why? So that Labour don't get too big a majority and both your husbands can go down in history as having done a reasonable job. Particularly the first, of course.' He meant it. His respect for Simon Russell was one reason why she had married him.

'Is that what you're going to say at the Central Office press conference this morning?'

'Of course not.' He scrabbled for the speaking notes interleaved with the manifesto. 'Our latest private indications from the constituencies show a marked swing away from Labour as the huge importance of the campaign issues sinks in. We are on course for a third successive election victory on Thursday week.'

'That's interesting.' Louise was at her dressing-table now, organising her face. 'What are those huge issues?'

'Ask the Young Demon.'

It was a dangerous suggestion. Louise was only recently reconciled to her daughter Julia's decision.

The Young Demon was Julia's partner David Alcester. They had lived together for nearly two years. By the vagaries of politics he was now Chancellor of the Exchequer. This had seemed extraordinary to begin with, but the shape and balance of the Conservative Party had made him the only viable successor to Joan Freetown. In accordance with British political tradition the loving couple lived next door to Peter and Louise Makewell at No. 11 Downing Street. The Young

Demon, they supposed, relished the embarrassment this caused.

'Where's he off to today?' asked Louise.

'Scotland, I think. I thought of telling him he could stay the night at Craigarran. But I didn't.'

'Why is he always up there? Precious few marginals. He just seems to enrage them by telling them they can't have more money than the rest of us.'

'That's his job as Chancellor of the Exchequer. It plays splendidly here in England. That's why we're gaining ground on Tyneside and in the North West. He's on to something with his New England Movement.'

'Politics,' said Louise, as if the word was itself a verdict.

'You made me do all this.' The Prime Minister headed for the bathroom. She blew a kiss to his retreating back. 'When it's over, can we eat again at that steak house?'

'It has a lot to answer for.'

'You've enjoyed every minute.'

'Why the hell are you going to Scotland again? You were there for a day last week, and the week before. General elections aren't won in Scotland. And you hate the place.'

'It's staying with a certain couple in Perthshire that I hate.'

'Don't worry, Mummy's stopped asking us – she told me so.'

Julia's eyes followed David Alcester round the room as he quickly packed his overnight bag. Razor, pyjamas, excessively strong aftershave. He tended to gamble with timetables, and she knew he would have to be out of the house in ten minutes. He had been angry after their argument last night. Up to then they had followed what she called the Tangier rule, after the city where they had spent their first weekend together.

Under the Tangier rule Julia and David made love after an argument and did not return to the subject for a week. But last night he had slept in the dressing room and this morning he spoke without looking at her.

She noticed that he was packing all the clean shirts from the drawer, four at least. 'When are you coming back?'

He turned to face her for the first time that morning. 'I don't know. I'm in different cities every day between now and polling day. The Treasury work can follow me round. I've done my meetings and press conference in London. There's no need to come back here till the election's over.'

'No need?' Julia's voice rose.

David cut in. 'And, as things stand, nothing much to draw me back.'

Suddenly this became intolerable. She could not bear to let him drive away to Heathrow with this barrier of ice between them. She returned quickly to last night's argument. 'You only want me to marry you because it looks good politically.'

Last night he had fiercely denied this. This morning he just looked at his watch. 'I don't have time to go into all that now. You turned me down last night. For, I think, the fourth time. I shall not ask again. We must both think what should happen next.'

The ice was growing thicker by the second. He would leave her, perhaps for ever. The internal telephone rang. 'Car here? Thank you. I'll be down in a minute.'

Of course she did not want to marry David. She wanted to sleep with him, even to have a baby by him. Both these things were possible nowadays without a wedding. Marriage was different, it meant a promise for life. And David was already married, to his politics. He wanted to commit bigamy. She knew that where politics were involved David made no distinction between truth and falsehood. Would he draw a line anywhere? Was there anything in his life that was not political? She had steadily refused so far to be drawn into that cage. After all, was she not Julia, famous as the Prime Minister's daughter who had been noisy, flamboyant, a pain to her parents, Julia who danced all night with unsuitable men, Julia who was arrested for possessing cannabis, and later for demonstrating violently in Whitehall? Above all, she had been free. It had been part of that freedom to encourage David to make love to her on the sofa at home in Highgate. She had thought it was she who was making the capture. His lovemaking had improved greatly since then, but she still took the lead. Each time, momentarily after the climax, when his eyes closed and the fair hair flopped over his forehead, she felt in charge. But within minutes he was again the ringmaster. She could see the cage now; she knew exactly what was in store. It was acceptable for a rising young politician to live with a beautiful girl. It was exciting when that girl was the daughter of one prime minister and the step-daughter of another. It proved something significant about modern politics. But the show moved on, and when the next image was viewed on the screen, it must be of the same girl transformed into a sober and godly matron, on the arm of the new party leader. She would still be beautiful no doubt, but with a settled beauty compatible with tradition, the family, the Party Conference and a firm line against all forms of moral deviation. In short, the Chancellor of the Exchequer wanted to be Prime Minister, and this meant marrying his mistress.

In the light of day Julia's spirit revolted against entering the cage. But even so . . . David was still in the same room, but would soon be gone. The prospect was intolerable. His voice, his mind, his body, the thrust of him in bed, his habits good and bad, all the bits of him would disappear. Yet they were now part of her life. She could not cut herself in two.

'Come here,' she said.

'There's no point.'

'Come here, David. I'll think about it.'

He looked at her carefully, made a calculation, picked up his case, kissed her lightly on the cheek. 'Think well,' he said, and was gone.

Clive Wilson was waiting in the car outside No. 11 Downing Street. David Alcester treated him as a private secretary rather than as a Member of Parliament of some standing.

'Can you ring them in Edinburgh and tell them to cancel that first briefing session?'

'Why's that, David? We'll be there in good time if we catch the ten o'clock shuttle.'

'We're going somewhere else first.' Then, to the driver, 'Do you know the Glebe Hospital in Roehampton? Past Barnes station and up Roehampton Lane.'

'I know it, sir.'

'Right, that's the first call.'

'Joan Freetown?'

'Yes.'

Clive Wilson busied himself with the call to Edinburgh. He was content to be a man of exceptional usefulness and was well proven in the role. First to Peter Makewell during the Russian crisis, then as one of Roger Courtauld's campaign team, and now attached to Alcester the rising star. Having no particular ideas of his own, he found no difficulty in giving

faithful service to politicians occupying widely different philo-
sophical positions. Each time he managed to shift his loyalty
without doing himself fatal damage. He knew that he lacked
the bite and the forcefulness to reach the top himself. He also
lacked the gift of attracting the affection or respect of others.
But, being shrewd and hardworking he traded these assets for
a share of the action, for a place close to whatever was happening. That was why he was going with the Chancellor of
the Exchequer to Scotland.

'Have a look at this.' David Alcester thrust at Wilson the
final text of the speech he was to make that evening in Leith
Town Hall.

> We have one last chance at this election to point out
> to the Scottish people the dangerous choice they have
> to make. One fact is for sure – we cannot go on as we
> are. We cannot any longer accept the twisted statistics
> by which the Scots accountants in Charlotte Square
> yearly justify the extraction of extravagant subsidy for
> Scotland from the British Exchequer. We cannot any
> longer allow the so-called Scottish Parliament to bog us
> down in endless petty arguments about what happens
> on which side of a border that should long ago have
> been relegated to the history books. Above all, we
> cannot continue to receive at Westminster an exces-
> sive number of Scottish MPs. Too many Scottish
> Members represent mountains and sheep rather than
> human electors. It is no longer acceptable that these
> invading Scots should vote on English matters at
> Westminster, when we English MPs cannot vote on the
> equivalent Scots matters. Devolution, ladies and

gentlemen, has become delirium. Cold water is needed. Either the Scots must accept fair play within the United Kingdom, a kingdom four-fifths of whose inhabitants happen to be English, or – sadly indeed but firmly – we should say that if the Scots want to rule their own affairs then they should do so plainly and openly, bearing the cost of separation, shouldering their own burden without English subsidy or special benevolence, competing with other foreigners for English investment. The choice is theirs; we ask simply that it be made quickly, and without the blather which has marked Scottish discourse at the Holyrood Parliament over these last years.

'Good stuff,' said Clive Wilson, a hesitant note in his voice. 'But?'

'The audience won't like it. The Scots Tories try to dodge the main question. You're rubbing their noses in it.'

'It is not meant for the audience in Leith Town Hall. It's meant for these people.' David waved to shoppers in Kensington High Street. 'Even more for the North of England, the old enemies of Scotland. They've got to be woken up.'

Clive Wilson took courage.

'Tell me, David, you've got the two main Alcester themes – against the EU and against the Scots – both running pretty well. Which is the more important to you?'

'The Scots, of course.' Alcester paused, unused to sharing anything approaching a confidence. 'Europe is always with us as a punch-bag. There will always be foolish decisions and bizarre speeches out of Brussels for us to grumble at. But there's a limit. Most people know that it makes no sense to ditch the euro or leave the EU. It's settled now. But nothing is settled about Scotland. There's room for a real upheaval there.'

'Which you want? You want the Union to disintegrate?'

'If that meant the Tory Party could rule England for ever.' Alcester saw that he had gone too far. 'Of course that's putting it too crudely. I've always been a Unionist. But if the price of the Union is too high? That's why I've formed the New England Movement. At least, let us show the Scots that the price of their behaviour could be too high. That way they'll behave better.'

'That doesn't seem to be what's happening. The more we bang on about the price, the stronger these extremists in the Central Belt become. It's Labour and the moderate Nationalists who suffer.'

'Precisely, Clive, precisely. The extremists, the Scottish Liberation people, aren't going to win any seats. But if they frighten enough people, then it's we who can gain, north and south of the border. We can show how frightening they are.'

They were crossing Hammersmith Bridge.

'Isn't this your constituency?' asked David. But of course he must have known all the time that this was Clive's patch. It would have been quicker to get to the hospital over Putney Bridge. 'We've got ten minutes in hand. Is there anywhere we could do a quick walkabout?'

Alcester had made a virtue of traditional electioneering. He believed in walkabouts, in town meetings with real people, in the soap-box oratory reinvented in 1992 by John Major. He disdained studios and TV debates. That way the publicity followed him, not the other way round. It did not matter that there were no journalists around the shops in Barnes through which they bustled shaking hands. David Alcester was already well known and a small crowd gathered. All the London media would know by lunchtime. The story would be that there was no 'story', nothing prepared, nothing artificial, just a man of the people among the people.

'But it's Clive Wilson you've come to see – of course you know him and how hard he works for you in Barnes. I'm just his helper today.'

Ten minutes well spent, not least because it buttoned Wilson closer to him.

'Thanks for that.' They were back in the car.

'Not at all. It was fun . . . Look, have you a copy of our manifesto on you? Can you find the Scottish paragraph?'

Clive Wilson read it out: ' "The Conservative Party remains devoted to the Union of Scotland with the rest of the United Kingdom. Within that Union we shall work to correct the present unfairness thrown up by crude Nationalist pressures within Scotland. We shall work with the elected Scottish Executive and the Parliament in Edinburgh to achieve a better constitutional and financial balance." '

'Good Central Office prose,' said Alcester. 'Nice and vague, but does it fit what I'm going to say at Leith? Can we argue, you and I, that I'm just filling in a few gaps in official policy?'

Clive Wilson liked the 'we' and the 'you and I'. He was also grateful for that small crowd in Barnes. His majority was not entirely safe. He put his own judgement to sleep.

'Yes, of course. The two fit together very neatly.'

'I thought so. Thanks.'

David Alcester paused, then took a decision. Clive Wilson would never be a great man, but from David's point of view this was an advantage. Clive was a shrewd organiser, and worth keeping alongside.

'If we lose – or rather, when we lose – I'm going to change things.'

'You'll become leader.'

'I hope so. I think so. Then we'll have to do what we're failing to do in this campaign. Reach out to people who take no interest. Frighten them, excite them, get them into the streets. That's what the New England Movement is about – up to now it's just small groups here and there, and I've had to keep it within the framework of the Party. But if I lead the Party, that will change.'

'How exactly?'

But David Alcester was not yet ready to trust Wilson further. 'You'll see. But I want you to be part of it.'

'Gladly.' But for the first time in his dealings with David Alcester, Clive felt a twinge of caution. He was a man for the back stairs and the smoke-filled room, not for violent shouting and shoving in the streets.

The car turned through laurels into the hospital drive.

Spring had turned back to winter. In the streets of Barnes this had not been apparent; they were blowy and bleak, as usual. But as the car moved through the gardens of the hospital a soft flurry of white across Clive's windscreen might have been either snow or falling blossom. The stucco battlements of the Glebe stood out a shade paler than the March sky. Their Strawberry Hill Gothic seemed to stretch for ever along the flanking lawn. Within this fortress were fought innumerable battles against death, battles unfair in their balance of power, for success was measured in decay rather than cure. Clive knew the place well, for it lay near the southern end of his constituency. He was accustomed to canvass patients and staff during each general-election campaign. The results were satisfactory on the whole. He usually timed this election visit as close as possible to polling day. If he came too early the dramatic clarity of the Conservative candidate's visit would become confused with other influences in the minds of some patients as the days of the campaign passed. A small proportion of the effort was bound to go to waste, since several dozen electors left the Glebe each week, either back to their homes in other constituencies or into the disenfranchisement of the crematorium. Despite its electoral assets, the Glebe filled Clive Wilson with gloom.

It was not easy for the two politicians to reach their objective. The approach drive was too narrow for cars to pass each other without driving in and out of the ranks of vehicles parked irregularly on either side.

'Do you mind staying here?' said David Alcester when the Peugeot finally found a gap big enough to nest in within a hundred yards of the main portico.

The relationship between the two men made this an order rather than a question. Clive was still grateful for the chilly but successful walkabout in Barnes ten minutes ago. The greengrocer, an elderly man of pronounced liberal views, had actually welcomed David Alcester into his shop and loudly complained of the absence from the market of the usual crop of new potatoes from Egypt. David and Clive had joined him in refusing to blame the weather and fastening instead on absurd health restrictions from Brussels and a greedy Scots wholesaler called Mackie. A small but satisfactory crowd had gathered. David had bought a bag of Cox's Orange Pippins.

'Just helping my old friend, Clive Wilson,' he had said, pushing the change into a cardboard lifeboat on the counter.

'We need every vote this time to keep those greedy Scots at bay.'

'And those interfering Eurocrats,' Clive had butted in.

'But particularly the Scots. Did you hear the Bank of Scotland closed another thirty branches last week? All in England, of course.'

On parting David had shaken the greengrocer and his wife warmly by the hand. 'We must be off now to pay our respects to Joan Freetown. She's not too well, but I'm sure she's properly looked after up the road at the Glebe.'

Clive had supposed that they would both join the pilgrimage into the hospital. He had never felt close to Joan Freetown – she had always been too definite in her views to suit his own sinuous approach to politics – but he collected personalities as in youth he had collected postage stamps, and she would have been a notable addition. However David Alcester was already out of the car. 'About half an hour, I should think,' he said, closing the door with just enough authority to forestall any discussion without actually falling into rudeness.

The automatic doors of the hospital fitted awkwardly into the pretended Gothic of the entrance. They hissed slightly as they opened, and then closed, excluding the cold spring. David Alcester was ushered into a different world, warm, bureaucratic, smelling of past meals and the carbolic used to remove their memory.

A woman greeted him at the reception desk, her voluminous garments overflowing somewhat the cubicle in which she sat. She radiated a kind but rule-based authority. This was the National Health section of the Glebe, about four-fifths of the whole, depending for its survival on the private wing in which Joan Freetown was lodged.

'The Milburn Wing?' asked Alcester. He knew the way, having visited once before, but with a politician's instinct judged that the woman in the cubicle would like to be asked.

'Down there to the right and straight on through four fire doors. Turn left when the paint becomes mauve, and straight on for another two hundred yards till you see the Milburn plaque.'

She spoke by rote but, as he had guessed, she was pleased.

'Is there a shop nearby? I need some flowers.'

'Yes, indeed, that way, just past the disabled toilets . . . but can I ask if the patient you're visiting is having cancer treatment?'

'She is.' He wondered whether to mention Joan's name. He was slightly irked that he had not been recognised.

'I'm afraid they won't allow flowers near her. Because of the risk of infection.' The lady was not by nature uncharitable but her day had been changed for the better by the opportunity of instructing a fellow human in something he could not do. 'I'm really sorry,' she added. 'Of course there is no objection to artificial flowers.'

David Alcester found the shop, crowded into a corner not much bigger than the receptionist's cubicle. Paracetamol, magazines, cheap perfume, get-well cards, boxes of soap, and a huge variety of chocolates. The previous exchange about flowers was otiose since there were none. He looked around impatiently. There was nothing there that Joan would welcome. He bought last week's *Economist* from the volunteer in charge, and started off down the long walk to the Milburn Wing. David Alcester spared a thought for his recent argument with Julia. He had failed to get his way, but there would be other opportunities. He moved his mind to another subject, reflecting that while a second or two was enough for him to think of Julia, she would be spending hours thinking of him.

David had banished from his mind an awkward question that was likely to confront him soon after the colour of the walls turned to mauve. Joan Freetown would be expecting him because he had telephoned the night before, and established that this would be a convenient time. He had done this direct to the wing. He wished now that he had made contact with Guy Freetown. If Joan was as ill as he suspected, Guy would almost certainly be there. Everyone admired Guy for his absolute devotion to his wife despite his dislike of politics. He was credited with keeping some sparks of generous humanity alive in Joan regardless of the shifting weight of Cabinet work and political ambition. David knew from past episodes that this was broadly true.

David had been Joan's political disciple and political friend. He had suspected that from time to time she had felt sexually attracted to him. Sometimes a change in her voice, sometimes her hand on his shoulder, or a long touch of their fingers as she passed him a document – these had been sufficient signs for a man acutely aware of his own physical drawing power. But he had never tried to displace Guy. That would lead nowhere and, anyway, he doubted he could succeed. Guy was quiet in manner and insignificant in appearance but he held over his wife a power the greater for being rarely exercised. David did not join in the general admiration of Guy. He resented the man who had prevented Joan Freetown from using her natural cutting power to best effect. She had been too subservient to Simon Russell, too restrained in her struggle against Roger Courtauld, too ready to let Peter Makewell outwit her with his show of old-fashioned integrity. At the crunch each time she had patted David's knee and done what pleased Guy. But now he supposed that their interests were converging. Both were genuinely devoted to Joan, and would wish her last days to hold as much happiness as possible. They would still differ as to how such happiness might be composed.

The nurse on duty recognised him. 'Hi, David, we're expecting you. How's the election going?' She was dressed in bright blue; none of the nurses wore uniforms at the Glebe. Her dreadlocks helped to convey informal jollity to the world. He had never met her before, but her name badge introduced her.

'Is Mr Freetown here?' The approaching moment was serious for David Alcester, and he felt in no mood to deploy his usual political charm with strangers.

'Oh, you hadn't heard?' For a moment Nurse Wendy allowed the world to dampen her good cheer. 'But he's out of danger this morning. We'll soon have him skipping about again.' She had brought this nursery phrase from a traditional hospital in the Caribbean.

'He? What do you mean "he"? What has happened?'

Guy Freetown's car had been rammed from behind by a truck the night before on the Headington roundabout just east of Oxford. He had been driving to see Joan after a snatched few hours of opening post and paying bills at their Cotswold home. He had been wearing his safety-belt but the forward jolt had dislocated his neck.

'Broken it, you mean?'

Nurse Wendy laughed. 'Dislocated, we say nowadays. He's

still unconscious. I rang just now because Joan was worrying. They'll put him in a collar for a few months, then he'll be fine.'

Although David Alcester had found Guy a hindrance whose processes of thought he could not understand, he could not imagine Joan without him. The three of them had worked as a triangle of which two sides were now disintegrating.

David was genuinely moved that morning at the thought of Joan's illness, which was why he had insisted on leaving Clive in the car park. But in a general election campaign only limited time was available for personal emotion. He looked at his watch. If the day was not to be wasted he must catch the one o'clock shuttle to Edinburgh from Heathrow. 'Can I go in now?' he asked.

'Don't forget Nanny's rules.' Nurse Wendy pointed to a notice. 'Shall I help you on with your little apron?'

David washed his hands in disinfectant squeezed from a bottle in the basin in the corridor. Wendy tied a plastic apron round his back. He did not know what he was going to find beyond the door. It carried Joan's name slotted into a metal holder.

Joan Freetown sat upright in bed, propped by three pillows. The room was in half-darkness, but David could see that her face was heavily rouged. There was another change he did not immediately identify. The thick white streak of hair running back from her forehead just above the parting had been her political trademark for as long as he could remember. It had gone. Her hair was black and lustrous without interruption. He realised, with a shock, that this was a wig. In giving her some months of extra life, the chemotherapy had exacted its price. 'David, my dear.' She stretched out; his plastic apron crackled as her shrunken arms embraced it.

'Nurse Wendy says you're doing fine.' She had not said this, but certainly would have done so if asked. Joan did not answer, but lay back on her pillows. By the side of the bed a flask of colourless liquid was suspended on a stand. A pipe, plastic again, carried the liquid drop by drop until it disappeared at the top of Joan's blue nightdress. Every minute or so the apparatus produced a musical note, sad but peaceful, as if recording an apology from modern medicine to Joan Freetown for its earlier ravages.

'How's the campaign?' The words came from a dry mouth through cracked lips.

David, moving newspapers from a cane chair, sat down and told her. The sluggishness of Makewell and Central Office, the lamentable inactivity of Roger Courtauld and all other party chieftains except himself, their continuing failure to narrow Labour's lead in the polls, the neglect of the two issues that could really stir the English electorate, namely the interfering Europeans and the grasping Scots, the birth of his New England Movement. He could see her face and neck strain as she exerted herself to follow what he said.

There was silence when he finished, punctuated by the measured note of the drip.

David Alcester was suddenly impatient with Joan's passivity. Her natural energy was being destroyed by the futility of this darkened room. He rose abruptly to open the half-closed curtains and let in some winter light. The cord snagged in his hand; the curtain moved an inch, then stuck.

'Leave it,' Joan said, with strain in her voice.

He sat down again, and forced himself back into courtesy. 'Sorry to hear about Guy.'

'Yes,' she said. 'He will be all right.'

David recalled the moments over the last five years when he had judged that he could take Guy's place. He had listed one or two incidents in his memory, knowing that each was trivial, even silly, in case they might one day be turned to good effect. He did not find Joan sexually attractive but would have slept with her had it been necessary. Somehow the moment had never come for a political takeover of Joan Freetown in the interests of his career. Guy occupied a compartment of her life into which she invited no other and which she was not prepared to discuss with him.

David gazed at the fox-hunting prints, bizarre and tasteless against a chintzy wall. Red paper peonies glared at him from an alcove opposite Joan's bed. Dozens of get-well cards were pinned to a green felt noticeboard around the fire safety instructions. Nurse Wendy came in with a large cardboard menu and invited Joan to choose her lunch.

His frustration returned and he got up to go. He believed that he would never see Joan Freetown again. He had not wanted a sentimental farewell, which would have been out of character for both of them. He had hoped, he now realised, for one last great rumbustious political discussion. She should have torn into his description of the lacklustre election campaign, attacked the faint-hearts, told him to pull himself together, and generally been her bossy, intolerable, irresistible self. But he had come too late. She was drifting back, perhaps, into older memories of Guy and the Cotswold farmhouse, then forward into death and whatever happened next.

'My meeting is in Edinburgh at five,' he said. 'Goodbye, Joan.'

Again she stretched out a skeletal arm on top of the

blankets. He came to the bed, crackling the absurd apron, lifted the hand and kissed it, as she in turn said, 'Goodbye,' and then, without explanation, 'Sorry.'

He left the room without a word of thanks to Nurse Wendy, tore off the apron and threw it on to a chair in the lounge. David Alcester had strong self-control. He had not wept for thirty years. The indoor walk back to the main door was just long enough for him to dominate the sharp stabs of sadness and frustration. But he never forgot them.

'How was she?' asked Clive, back in the car.

'Pretty good. She sent her regards.'

They drove to Heathrow in silence.

'IS THIS THE DULLEST ELECTION CAMPAIGN ON RECORD?'
   By Alice Thomson

As we approach the last weekend of the election campaign the loudest noise to be heard is the light snoring of the electorate. The two elderly party leaders tiptoe up and down the kingdom as if anxious not to wake anyone. If you listen carefully you can just catch the impression that the Leader of the Opposition might tinker with the tax system – of course, in a way from which everyone would benefit. He might be a little more co-operative with our European partners while, of course, preserving the British veto on everything that matters. He might be a little frosty with the right-wing governments in Poland and Austria, but would maintain our traditional friendship with both peoples. He might increase the fines on farmers who grow GM crops or clone farm animals without bureaucratic authorisation while, of course, encouraging the

scientific community to press on with yet further exper-
iments on both subjects. All this from a man who has
been trying to be Prime Minister for fifteen years. If he
asks the bookmakers he will hear that the job will be
his in a week's time. Will John Turnbull have the will
to grasp the prize?

Not that much grasping will be needed. The Prime
Minister, Peter Makewell, goes through the motions of
modern campaigning. His website is crowded, there is
no pause between his e-mail shots, his computers con-
duct their telephone canvass with silken efficiency.
Once upon a time there was a man behind all this
apparatus, a steady Scottish laird, who became the natural choice for moderate Tories when Roger Courtauld
stumbled over that beach towel. Not that Peter
Makewell has been a bad prime minister – the way in
which he had clamped down the Tory fury against the
press two years ago had been masterly. But he must be
the only holder of the office less well known at the end
of his term (we must surely be there now) than at the
beginning.

Only one leading politician is giving the election
campaign a taste of the noise and colour that used to be
traditional. David Alcester is not a nice man, but he
has chosen a style of politics in which niceness is unim-
portant. To an amazing extent he has managed to
detach himself from the record of the government, of
which he is a senior member. No one asks David
Alcester about the rather dull Budget he produced soon
after taking over from Joan Freetown. No one asks him
how he would pay for the manifesto commitment to

abolish capital-gains tax in the life of the next
Parliament. Perhaps this is because no one expects the
Tories to win again. But there is no doubt that David
Alcester, a modern politician, using the old-fashioned
techniques of public meeting and radio broadcast, has
seized the initiative on his two brutal issues, Europe
and the Scots. His New England Movement is still in
its early days, but its slashing attacks on both targets
are already scoring hits. There is a difference between
the two. Europe is an old target full of holes, punctured
by generations of critics having their fun. The
European Union will never be popular, but everyone
knows that nothing much will change. The fear of a
superstate has gone, as one dreary meeting of ministers
follows another. No party is going to disrupt the economy by rerunning the referendum on the euro. That
reluctant and honourable change of tack has gone into
political history alongside Peel's repeal of the Corn
Laws. We are left with a large, awkward, often quarrel-
some union of states, vaguely right-minded in big
matters and bureaucratic in small, easy to criticise, hard
to reform and impossible to abandon.

David Alcester understands this well. That is why he
reserves his sharpest barbs and subtlest tactics for the
Scots. The issue has been brewing since the Scots
achieved their Parliament in 1999. David Alcester has
brought it to the boil. While claiming to be a Unionist
he and his New England Movement are in effect incit-
ing the English against the Union. His speech last
night in Leith Town Hall foreshadowed a tough assault
on Scotland's fiscal arrangements and on the number of

Scots MPs at Westminster. I understand that he went well beyond anything approved by the Prime Minister at the Manifesto Committee of the Cabinet. He aims to make the Scots more unpopular in England than they have been since the days of Lord Bute and Dr Johnson. He means to ride this wave into the next Parliament, with what result neither he nor anyone else can predict.

I have found in recent days that everyone is talking about David Alcester. Few people like him; even fewer despise him. This is not a bad foundation for political advancement. So, as the election campaign drones to its close, watch this space.

Chapter 6

'That's generous of you. I talked to Louise about it in case you made the offer. Yes, we would like to spend the weekend at Chequers, to pack up our things and say goodbye to the staff. You'll find them excellent.'

'Stay a week, if you like. Or two. Florence is not exactly used to country life. It'll take her a bit of time to realise the pleasure of it. She's in no hurry.'

'She'll love Chequers, I'm sure.'

The telephone crackled. Neither man was quite sure if any of their staff were listening in. There was a pause. Then the next Prime Minister said rather awkwardly to the present Prime Minister, 'Do I wait for the Palace to ring? Sorry to ask you, but no one at Millbank has the faintest idea. It's so long since we were in power.'

'Don't worry. I'll go out into Downing Street now, and concede. The Queen will drive up from Windsor, send for me, send for you. You don't actually have to kiss hands. You'll be installed at No. 10 here by teatime. The staff will line up in the entrance, and clap you warmly as you come in. Don't take that too seriously. It's a tradition, they do it for everyone. Louise will make sure there's something up here in the flat for you to eat.'

'Thanks. That's very kind.' Another pause. The two men had known each other for a quarter of a century, but always in a political context. It seemed natural to revert to this. Turnbull, as the winner, led the way. 'It all went pretty much as expected, I think. You got a dozen more seats than we forecast, but no harm in that. If he'd lived Simon Russell would have done no better for the Tories, maybe worse. I just wanted to say that to you. The country wanted a change.'

'I agree about the dozen seats. Carlisle, for example. Berwick-on-Tweed from the Liberal Democrats. We did relatively well in the North. Why was that, do you think?'

'No mystery. Alcester stirred them up with all that nonsense against the Scots. That's my only complaint about the campaign. You should have reined him in.'

'Not possible.'

'Now he'll be pain and grief to both of us. I know he's your son-in-law, but . . .'

'Not quite.' Peter Makewell had a thought. 'I haven't checked – does it look as if you'll depend on Scottish Labour votes for your majority?'

'Yes, thanks to these dozen extra seats of yours.'

'Pity.' He did not need to spell out the trouble ahead.

'Can you keep that lad out of the way? Shadow Foreign Secretary would do. On home matters he's a pain in the arse.'

'You're assuming I'm going to keep the leadership of the Party.'

'You've done better than expected. No one will challenge you.'

'Except myself. Aided and abetted by my wife.' Another pause. Then the conversation changed from polite exchange to hard business.

'Are you seriously considering standing down?'

'I am.'

'All I can say is it's your duty to carry on and keep your Party in shape.'

'That's balls."

Turnbull was by nature phlegmatic. A generation earlier he would have smoked a pipe. But every now and then a more forceful character broke out.

He spoke firmly. 'Being Leader of the Opposition is the worst job in politics. I'm bloody glad to be shot of it. You'll have that job by teatime and you can't run away. It's public service, and you know it.'

'Public service, indeed. You're an old-fashioned Tory at heart. I always guessed it.' But Peter Makewell, uneasy in his own mind, was not prepared to argue the point further. 'Anyway, congratulations again. You must get on with your Cabinet-making.'

'And a right shower they are, when you see the names on paper. Who's to be Chancellor of the Exchequer? Never a one of them can count.'

Peter Makewell knew that Turnbull would have prepared the Cabinet list in his own mind months ago. But both men ended the conversation liking the other the better for it.

Tynemouth flickered on to the screen: a big increase in the Conservative majority, a beaming middle-aged woman with a blue rosette and ample display of teeth. 'A high turnout compared to others, and another northern result against the Labour trend,' shouted the commentator. He shouted because he thought this was the best way to hold the election-night audience after a campaign which, everyone said, had been the dullest in history.

'Silly woman, fabulous result,' said David Alcester.

They had returned from his own count in Newbury Corn Exchange to the tiny cottage which they rented just north of the bypass.

'She's done better than you,' said Julia. David's majority had been quite sharply reduced.

'You don't understand anything.' The tiny bedroom under the eaves had been chilly when they reached it an hour earlier. David had turned on both bars of an old electric fire. Now he sprawled in the only armchair, wearing only the old yellow wool dressing-gown that he kept at the cottage. Julia, still in her constituency tweed suit, lay on her side of the double bed. Watching David follow the election results was like watching him make love to a mistress. Julia was amazed to remember that, not long ago, as a Conservative prime minister's radical daughter, she too had been interested in politics.

She listened without understanding to David's exposition of his own cleverness in raising the cry against the Scots. It had played well in the north. It would play well everywhere, even in Newbury, now that the electorate had landed itself with a Labour government dependent on the votes of Scottish MPs at Westminster.

'You'll see tomorrow,' he ended.

'What's happening tomorrow?'

'I told you. Rally of our supporters in the Market Square. I thank them for their efforts.' He paused. 'There'll be a few people from outside, I expect.' He smiled to himself. 'Just to make the point.'

What point? Julia did not care. Since their row on the day of his Leith speech they had hardly communicated. He had stayed away, returned to London. They had come down to the count in Newbury, without either fresh quarrel or reconciliation. She found this intolerable.

The television moved away from announcing results to a discussion between experts. She saw a chance. 'David,' she said. 'Come here.' To her great relief he left the pundits and lay beside her slipping his hand under her shoulder. She raised herself from the pillow. He began to undo the large buttons at the back of her suit.

'Tangier?' she said, half in question.

'Tangier,' he said, in affirmation.

She undressed slowly. David was patient now. He let Julia take control. It was the only act of power on her side of their relationship. In all other matters he dominated, even bullied, her in a way to which she could not get accustomed. But in these rare moments it was she who guided and David who submitted, until she had brought their bodies together and he lay exhausted beside her. For a fleeting moment they were both happy, and he looked about fifteen.

The telephone rang. There was no extension in the bedroom. David swore, pulled on his dressing-gown and hurried down the steep straight stairs. She could hear him pick up the receiver in the sitting room. He said nothing for a while, then, 'Ah. That's very sad. I'm sorry.' A pause while his calculating mind resumed control. 'You've told Mr Freetown . . . What do you mean you can't find him? I see, I see. Yes. No, I've no idea where he can have gone.' Then, very firmly, 'Look, Doctor, I have some experience with the press and handling these matters. It is essential that *no one* gives this sad news to the media before you have found Mr Freetown. If he finds out from radio or television there will be great pain for him and embarrassment to you. Obviously you will go on looking for him. Meanwhile, I strongly advise you to keep silent. Please ring me if you have any difficulty.'

David climbed into bed, expressionless. He still wore his dressing-gown. There would be no more lovemaking that night.

'Joan is dead?' asked Julia. She had nothing in common with Joan, but remembered her kindness at the time of Simon Russell's death.

'Yes.'

'Sad. You are sad. You were really fond of her.'

'Yes, Julia, I was.' He turned away his face. She kissed his shoulder. 'I said goodbye. And the world must go on.'

'Will you now become leader of the Conservative Party?'

Roger Courtauld had just returned from his count in South Northamptonshire. This year Hélène had declined to accompany him. In recompense she had prepared a late-night supper of pâté, herb omelette and goat's cheese with a Chablis at the right degree of chill. She had characteristically and accurately assumed that nothing Roger might have been offered when outside her jurisdiction had been worth eating. She had turned off the television and lit the fire. The two of them sat, as they had so often sat before, in armchairs at either side of the flickering logs, a picture of married harmony. Yet her question showed how far apart they were.

'What do you mean, lead the Party?'

'It is logical. You withdrew from that contest two years ago because of the stupid photograph, which no one now remembers. Peter Makewell was the winner, but he was never intelligent and has now lost the election. So there will be a new leader. No one is better placed than you.' She refilled his glass, and for the first time he noticed she was wearing a smart jacket of brown Indian silk over cream linen trousers.

'The thought is absurd, Hélène. Indeed, it horrifies me.' He spoke more sharply than he intended.

'Why absurd? Why horrific?'

How could he explain, weary, in need of a bath, disappointed by his own sharply reduced majority? They had so few conversations of any substance, he and Hélène, that each seemed to become more difficult than the last.

He put aside his tray, and softened his voice. But he knew he would never be a diplomat.

'Look, *ma petite*. I will try to explain. First, I could not become leader. Not because of the photograph. That is not forgotten, but lingers below the surface. There are wider reasons. Time has moved on. I have deliberately stayed out of the public gaze. That has helped us as a family. Which is why I did it. But it means I am no longer in the first rank. Our friends in Daventry were talking about it even during the count. Chattering away – there was nothing else to do tonight. Either Makewell will stay for a bit, or David Alcester will take his place – that was their thought. They discussed it quite happily in front of me. No one supposed for a moment that I might again be a candidate. People like John Wilson and Eileen Hodge from the town branch. As you know, no one likes me more than those two.'

Hélène leaned forward to put a log on the fire. 'If you knew all this already, why in heaven did you stand again?'

Roger hesitated. He knew he could not explain this to her convincingly. He had lost all appetite for the political battle, and in particular for the media-ridden noise of the House of Commons. In his day he had enjoyed it all, and jousted as sturdily as any. But that day had passed; now he wanted to plan the evening. He wanted his horizons to narrow slowly and happily, so that there was more time for the boys and Felicity, for the garden, for village interests and the village church, for the committees and causes of Northamptonshire. All that was compatible with four or five years as the back-bench Member of Parliament for South Northamptonshire. He would be diligent at his surgeries. He would unveil plaques at the opening of hospital wards and school computer centres. He would become less of a partisan figure, more of an elderly uncle to all his constituents. In opposition the whipping should be quite relaxed; in any case he was senior enough to ignore summonses to Westminster that did not suit him. The party whip had no more hold over him. He enjoyed the feeling that a pleasant corner of England belonged to him, that in every village street or shopping precinct he knew someone or could remember some anecdote from its past.

But he saw suddenly that none of this was for Hélène. It was incomprehensible to her. Hélène's idea of politics was strictly centralised, as became a Frenchwoman. The local constituency for her was simply a necessary condition of power at Westminster. He had somehow supposed that when the time came she would acquiesce in his plan for their gradual retirement. Because he was now a coward in their joint relationship he had also supposed that the practical questions would be more easily resolved if he did not discuss them with her in advance. He began to realise his mistake. But he could not summon up the energy needed to convince her. A part of him, he was surprised to find, did not really want to try.

So he simply said, lamely, 'I stood again because that fits into our life down here.'

'Your life, Roger, your life. Not mine. Not mine any more.' Hélène went to the table in half-darkness at the end of the sitting room and poured herself a whisky. This was unusual. 'Listen, Roger. This poor little French girl was not interested in politics when you found her. She did not ask you to bury yourself in that dirty ridiculous career. But when you decided, I decided also – to help you, to push, to entertain, to organise on your behalf. But it is still a man's world. My contribution in your eyes was as nothing. So, gradually, I did less. It did not matter to you. Perhaps you did not notice. At the time of the photograph affair I was already apathetic, as you remember. Since then, even more so. But today I decided that if you wanted to make one more political effort, once again I would be at your side.'

She paused, and he understood the elegant supper, the exceptional wine, the Indian tunic. But this conversation had come at least three months too late.

Hélène went on, 'What I cannot accept is a rural prison down here. Mud and puddles for nine months of the year, dull people for twelve. It suits you as you grow old, lazy, sentimental. The ambition has left you. It suits the boys because you have taught them it is better to shoot rabbits than to go to the theatre. But for Felicity and myself, it is nothing. The house is cold, the garden a burden. You cannot expect us to make our lives a void simply to please your English rusticity.'

Once again he summoned his troops to turn her round. Once again they failed to appear. 'What do you propose?' he asked, after a pause.

'It is simple. Felicity and I will stay in the flat in London. That will be our home while she is still at the Lycée. You will make this house your base. I will not come here. The boys will come to me for part of the holidays in order to become civilised, and for the rest they will come here to shoot more rabbits. When Felicity leaves the Lycée she and I will return to Normandy.'

'You've certainly thought it through.'

'Of course. What else was I supposed to think about during these last weeks, months, years?'

'You actually wanted it that way? It sounds like it.'

'No, Roger, no. This is, as you say, my plan B. My plan A would have made you Prime Minister, or at least now Leader of the Party.'

'That is impossible.'

'So you tell me.'

His marriage was slipping away, and still he could not stir himself to save it. He sat in his chair, no longer sipping the Chablis, inert, tired, unsure.

Her mood changed again as she came back to the fireside and touched his cheek with a hand cold from the whisky glass. 'Roger, you are preparing to be miserable. I can read your face. That is the English way. Perhaps you will telephone tomorrow for some social worker with untidy hair and big breasts to come and counsel you.'

'Don't laugh at me.'

'It is too late for tears, at least for us. We French regard these things less tragically, perhaps because we are at heart more serious. Reflect a little, my dear. Behind your pretences you know that my plan B will suit you quite well.'

There was truth in this, thought Roger, as he climbed the stairs to bed. He would sleep apart in his dressing room without drama. He hated to feel that he was losing something happy from the past. But when he thought of the future, the Northamptonshire future, perhaps it would be better for him to live without Hélène, and better for Hélène to divide herself between Notting Hill and Normandy. He knew enough about his children to understand that the key for them was not where they lived but how their parents treated each other.

'We will be friends,' he said to Hélène through the door, as he undressed. She already lay in the four-poster bed, which was rather too large for the long narrow bedroom. It was half a question.

'Good friends, better friends,' came the answer.

As so often, what happened when David Alcester was around differed from the expected. Julia drove him to the Market Square in Newbury the day after the election. She expected a sedate gathering of Conservative supporters from the constituency. David would thank them for their efforts. He would argue despite the disappointing figures that it had been a triumph to hold back the enemy assault on the South Berkshire constituency. He would encourage them to continue loyal and energetic support for the Conservative Party, by which he and they meant himself.

There indeed they were, about sixty of them, the nicest people on earth. Julia knew most of them by now. She suspected that some of the women and perhaps one or two lads of his local Young England Movement were drawn to David by his fleshy good looks and that helpless lock of fair hair. She often found it difficult to join in the chorus of praise that they heaped on him for integrity, courage and straightforward patriotism, but she had learned by now to keep her mouth shut. She looked back persistently on her loud, colourful teenage views, which had embarrassed her father, the Prime Minister. Her views now were not so colourful, and she reserved them for David and occasionally for her mother.

The local supporters deserved this half-hour of thanks, and Julia did not grudge it. This group, to their surprise, were being kept out of the Corn Exchange where they had expected the party to be held. It was sunny at last, but not all of them had come dressed to cope with the chill wind that was tossing the daffodils deployed in rectangular terracotta containers round a dais erected outside the main door. Something else was afoot; they did not have to wait long to discover it. Julia could hear coaches driving into the bus station between the square and the river beyond, then the noise of ragged cheering as they discharged the passengers. A procession of contingents entered the square, each comprising three or four dozen men and women of all shapes and ages, some carrying banners of the red and white cross of St George, others the name of their city or county. Carlisle, Newcastle, Berwick, Lancaster, Manchester. The Leeds contingent included a brass band, which stationed itself behind the South Berkshire supporters in the centre of the square. There was nothing military about the occasion, and no attempt to march in step.

David and Julia stood concealed at the entrance to a newsagent's shop until the square was almost full. Then David led her forward towards the daffodils. The couple were recognised with a cheer that gained strength as it travelled round the square. They climbed on to the dais. Julia noticed that the constituency agent had distributed St George's flags to the somewhat baffled local supporters. Three television vans had positioned themselves to the side of the dais. David, without a coat, looking ten years younger than his age, waited for the remaining busloads. Bradford, Liverpool, Halifax – the square was almost full. To her surprise his expression was solemn. He was doing nothing to milk the crowd. She found herself composing her own features accordingly. The band was still silent.

So David had put together a national rally as a gesture of defiance, snatching a personal success out of the Party's defeat. They must have started from Carlisle round about dawn. But Julia could see he had something else in store.

David lifted his hand until the square fell silent. The click of press camera shutters became the loudest sound. 'Thank you, my friends, for being with me here in my home town this morning. We have things to say to each other. But first I have news for you. Sad news. Joan Freetown died in hospital last night.'

A murmur of surprise and dismay ran through the crowd, tinged with pleasure at being present for a dramatic announcement.

'She was a friend of mine. She was a friend of us all. But, more than that, she was a friend of England. She was our inspiration.' A murmur of approval. 'It was she who first warned of the dangers that beset us. You and I in this have been her followers. On your behalf . . . I visited her in hospital last week, I thanked her. I thanked her, and said goodbye.'

David paused, drew a black armband from his coat pocket and slid it up his left sleeve to a point above his elbow.

Instinctively, though she had not seen him do it, Julia knew that he would have practised this gesture before the mirror in the cottage bathroom. She wondered where on earth he had got the armband.

'When the drum beats once I ask you all to lower St George's flag to the ground in memory of Joan Freetown, to do her honour, to give her our final thanks. After two minutes when the drum sounds again I want you to raise your flag and hold it proudly aloft. That will be your pledge. We promise that together we will continue her work for England until we save our country from the dangers that threaten us.'

The three Leeds drummers did their work. The banners fell, silence was observed, the banners rose. David interrupted the beginnings of applause. 'I had come with a long speech, but I find I have already said all that I wanted. So now I ask you to walk with me behind the band through the streets of this town. Let us show the people of Newbury, and the people of England, that today is for us not a day of defeat, but a new beginning.' The applause was not loud but prolonged and heartfelt. Standing next to Julia, the chairman of the South Berkshire Conservative Association blew his nose emotionally.

The parade – David was anxious not to call it a march – took an hour. Then they went back. This time the élite of his local supporters was inside the Corn Exchange, munching sandwiches while the contingents from the north trooped back to the bus station.

David sought out Julia and manoeuvred her into a corner, beneath a varnished brass panel recording the mayors of Newbury under the town crest. 'It went well,' he said, half a question, half a challenge.

'"Aloft" won't do,' said Julia.

'Aloft?'

'"Hold your banners aloft." It's bogus – pseudo-Churchillian.'

A year or two ago he might have been amused, and argued back at the same time. Now he stared at her. 'There's a lot you'll have to understand,' he said.

Yes, she thought, you're turning yourself into a humourless Fascist, and you want me to follow you. Encouraged by her own anger, Julia tackled him with a thought that had just come into her mind.

'No one knew of Joan's death until you announced it just now.'

'That's right. That way we'll lead every TV bulletin tonight.'

Julia spoke more slowly. 'I heard you telling the hospital not to announce it last night.'

'Not till they'd told Guy. That's common decency. They couldn't find him last night.'

'Do you know that they found him this morning?'

'They're sure to have. He'll be at Little Stourton.'

'Why didn't they ring there last night?'

'They didn't have the number. Only the number of the London flat. The doctor told me they rang Number Ten, but there they had instructions only to give the London number. Guy always insisted on their privacy at Little Stourton. But I'm sure they'll have found him by now.'

'You can't be sure. And, anyway, you could have given them the Little Stourton number yourself.'

'I could have, Julia, but I didn't.' For a moment she had penetrated his armour. 'Anyway, what is this – an inquisition? What possible harm have I done?'

'You should have rung Guy yourself. Last night, as soon as you knew.'

'My dear Julia, I would have been the very worst person to tell Guy that particular item of news. I'm sure he suspected for many years that I was her lover.'

Suddenly shaken to rage, Julia moved to hit him, but hesitated. He caught her hand. 'Everyone's watching. Behave yourself.'

'You're a shit above all shits. You organised it all to give yourself a scoop.'

'I organised nothing. Joan died when she died. I tweaked the timing of the announcement a bit, that's all. Anyway, who suffered? Not Joan, poor woman. Not Guy – he slept quiet last night. Not the media – they have two stories for the price of one, Joan's death, my rally.'

'You don't understand . . .' She knew this was lame, but they were in different worlds, side by side under a pillar in the Newbury Corn Exchange, he half-way through a ham and cheese sandwich, she grasping a glass of Argentine red in the hand that had almost struck him.

'No, I don't understand. Luckily I don't have to. We must go home now. I want to watch the two o'clock news.'

She followed him out in silence, thinking of her father, Simon Russell, and then, by a sideways leap, of Louise.

'So everyone in the village is thinking of you. And of course you mustn't dream of looking after the churchyard today. I'll get Bert to do it. I'm sure he won't mind.'

The churchwarden had rung as soon as she heard the news on the two o'clock bulletin. Guy left the receiver off the hook, knowing that it would soon start a whine of complaint, but badly needing a few silent minutes. He had forgotten that it was his weekend to tidy the churchyard. The call from the hospital had obliterated, for the moment, all outstanding business from the rest of his life.

When he had been discharged the day before from the John Radcliffe Hospital in Oxford, Guy might have asked the taxi to drive him to London, to the flat, or indeed straight to Joan in the Glebe. That was what most people would have expected. Instead they had driven him here, at his request, and left him, having satisfied themselves that he was fit to look after himself until the daily help came on Monday. They were busy people and could not be expected to probe further.

But Joan in the Glebe Hospital was to him like Joan in the Treasury, Joan in the House of Commons or at the Party Conference – belonging to a world in which he had no lasting part. For years he had inserted himself into that alien world at moments of critical decision. He had tried to make sure that Joan did not unbalance her life by sacrificing everything, and in particular her own standards, to political success. After her resignation that danger had gone. What he now loved was Joan at Little Stourton, in the past and, he had hoped, the future.

The Joan of politics, even the Joan sick in the Glebe, the Joan for which a big memorial service would now be held in London, was no longer part of him.

As a result he had not been there when she died. Would she have wanted him? Perhaps. As the Frenchman once said, for those who did not believe in God, death was a solitary business. Joan would have died alone, even if he, David Alcester, Peter Makewell, the whole Parliamentary Party and the media had been gathered in sympathy at her bedside.

He had visited the hospital the day before his accident. They had talked about protecting the pear blossom at Little Stourton from frost and whether he should divide up the daffodil bulbs, which had had a disappointing year, on the slope leading up from the back door to the stables. This had been their farewell talk, calm, practical, unpolitical. He was content with that.

After the telephone call they had faxed him a form from the Glebe Hospital with little boxes to tick. Cremation? Certainly not, he had written over the box. Did he need counselling? He had thrown the form into the wastepaper basket.

Slowly Guy gathered the implements necessary for tidying the churchyard. The grass was not yet growing, so he would not need the mower. It was not true that Bert would be quite glad to take Guy's turn. Bert was set in his ways and would grumble for weeks. The doctor had said that a little gentle exercise would do Guy's neck good; it was now encased in a collar. Some clipping and weeding round the graves was necessary. It could be done quietly, almost without effort. His first visit was to the empty plot of grass, just south of the porch, that would welcome Joan when finally she came home.

'Too wet to walk before tea?'

Of course it was too wet. The rain alternately dribbled and spat at the window-panes of Chequers. The hint of spring in the last few days before polling day had disappeared, its place taken by the return of a characterless English winter.

But Julia knew that her mother's question was only superficially related to the weather. For four, nearly five years the Russell family had spent most weekends at Chequers. The spirit of Simon, husband, father, prime minister, was more vivid for both of them at that time in that place than any recollection of the men with whom they now lived and, in a funny way, loved. Simon had never played tennis at Chequers and rarely swum, but he had walked in all weathers, taking his womenfolk with him when he could persuade them. They knew where the boots were stored and where the rain jackets hung.

'Of course we must walk,' said Julia.

But once they were out under the dripping beeches there was nothing particular to say about the past. Neither was in the mood for amiable reminiscence. Julia was there because she needed to consult her mother, but it was an unaccustomed activity and she did not know how to set about it. So she advanced sideways via the election result. 'He'll miss it all? Peter, I mean.'

'Of course,' said Louise. 'He'll pretend not to. He has been telling me for months that he expected to lose and how splendid it will be to go back to Scotland. But I know that in his heart he hoped for a miracle that would keep him here, and the red boxes flowing.'

'And you?'

'What do you mean, and me?'

'I can't see you settling down in Perthshire.'

'Can't you?' Louise quickened her pace as if to get away from the question.

'You'll be bored to tears.'

'You're wrong, Julia. Boredom is the curse of the young. I can sculpt in Scotland as well as in Wandsworth. Anyway, I expect we'll find a flat in Pimlico or Chelsea.'

'Peter will stay as Leader of the Opposition?'

'I suppose so,' said Louise. 'I'm not sure. There was a time when I asked all these questions myself and was impatient for an answer – or rather for the answer I thought was right. That seems long ago. Now I am with a lesser man, but a good man. I shall wait and follow.'

'That can't be right. Peter Makewell married you so that you could give him the answer. He told me so once. He wanted to borrow your force.'

'No, Julia, no. And even if he did I cannot deliver force any more. It is running down inside me. Quietly and slowly, not suddenly like Joan Freetown. Soon the battery will be quite flat. I am content.'

They had passed out of the wood through a swing gate on to a path bordered by iron railings on one side and primroses on the other.

Suddenly Julia burst into tears. For the first seconds she was crying for the loss of the fierce energy that had made her mother so exceptional – and so maddening. Then she began to cry for herself, and that went on longer. Louise had never been good at physical caresses, but she awkwardly caught hold of her daughter and held her head against the wet, shiny, green outside of her coat. 'Is it David?' she said.

'What am I to do?'

Julia extricated herself. The two women walked back towards the house. Julia told the story of Joan's death and the display at Newbury. Louise knew most of this from television.

'You've discovered that the man you live with is a shit,' she said, without recrimination, like a doctor declaring a medical fact. 'It happens to a lot of people.'

'Do I leave him?' Julia was still in tears.

'Do you love him?' There was no answer. 'I don't mean, do

you enjoy David making love to you because obviously you do, though God knows how and why. He used to have a certain cubbish charm, but now he's putting on weight. I mean, can you imagine life without him? Living by yourself in London? You can write and speak well enough. Being who you are you could easily get a media job. Julia Russell, it sounds well. And enough drama in your past to make you interesting. Think about it.'

'I think about it all the time.'

Louise's words had been harsh, as usual, but Julia was now inside the fence with which her mother protected herself from the outside world.

Once back inside the Hawtry Room, with the curtains drawn against the dusk, the fire lit and a teapot as companion, she began the whole story again from the beginning. The memorial service for Simon in the Abbey, her sense of belonging nowhere and to no one, David on the sofa at Highgate. His clumsiness, at the moment of lovemaking, her sense of power over a powerful man, the sense of loss when they quarrelled or he went away. She described his awfulness too, the combination of brutal political ideas with subtle tactical skill, the cynicism, the contempt for truth and gentleness. He was pressing now to marry her. She could not hold him off much longer.

'Does he believe in anything? Anything except himself.'

'Deep down, I think, yes. And it's not just himself. Indeed he's unsure about himself. Deep down I think he has a belief in England that drives him on. I may be wrong. It's well hidden in all the rubbish. Often he's so bogus and rhetorical that I think that's all there is. But it can't really be so. There's something more.'

Julia sipped her tea and took a second biscuit. A beech log lost its position in the fire and fell smouldering out of the grate. She rose and replaced it with the tongs. After all the rows with David it was strange and comforting to be discussing him calmly, almost clinically, with her mother. She had not explained herself well, but could do no more. She waited for the diagnosis and prescribed treatment.

It was not what she expected. 'You'd better stay with him.'

'Stay?'

'I've been trying to imagine how you'd manage without him. Having listened to you, I don't think you could.' She paused. 'Sorry.'

'Sorry, indeed. That's not a cure you've given me, it's a sentence of death.' But Julia spoke calmly.

'Of imprisonment. Lock yourself up with him. Throw away the key. You'll get the worst of all worlds if you stay with David but are just passive and resentful. Go over to the attack. Marry him. Breed by him. Get into his life, politics and all. Find whatever there is, hidden in that rubbish. Bring it out, polish it, put it to use.'

'It's the strangest advice I've ever heard.'

But she took it. Or, rather, tried to take it.

Chapter 7

Sometimes a political crisis exploded out of the damp dreariness of some technical matter. By the time the Conservative Shadow Cabinet met on that Thursday afternoon fifteen months into Turnbull's Labour Government Peter Makewell could smell the trouble smouldering in the English Universities (Prohibition of Fees) Bill, which had received its third reading in the Commons the night before.

'The facts are clear. The Bill is illegitimate.' David Alcester, as Shadow Chancellor, had taken no part in the parliamentary debates on the Bill, but now he spoke with total confidence, a man on top of his brief. 'Universities are a devolved subject. English MPs have no say over Scottish universities; so Scots MPs can have no legitimate say over ours. Yet the third reading was carried only by Scottish Labour votes. Our senior universities propose to continue to charge the top-up fees prohibited in the Bill even after Royal Assent. They have senior counsel's opinion that any enforcement of the Bill against them would be struck down, if not in our courts then certainly

in the European Court of Human Rights. We've opposed the
Bill all the way. We can't let the universities down now. We
have to support them in disobeying it.'

The Shadow Minister for Education spoke next. 'I've led
the fight in the Commons. David wasn't there. I think I have
the feel of it. We argued well. The Lords were on our side. But
in the end we lost. The argument is over for the moment.
David wants us to play outside the rules and support disobedience of the law. The Tory Party has never done that.' Sarah
Tunstall, having backed Roger Courtauld in that distant leadership election, had been given the Education portfolio first in
the Makewell Cabinet, and now in the Shadow Cabinet to
represent the liberal wing of the Party. With her flowing hair,
West Country voice and incoherent clothes she looked like
the caricature of a progressive schoolmistress. In fact her policies had been steady and successful. But she retained from
her loyalty to Roger Courtauld an abiding dislike of David
Alcester.

'Sarah is not accurate. We have supported civil disobedience in the past,' he retorted. 'Over Northern Ireland. "Ulster
will fight, Ulster will be right." That was a great slogan.'

'Life is not all slogans,' said Peter Makewell from the chair,
showing his hand too soon. 'What does the Shadow Attorney
General think?'

But Sarah Tunstall butted in. 'It's a lousy slogan applied to
the universities,' she said. 'First, David is wrong. Only
Cambridge has come out definitely so far for defying the law
if necessary. The others are wavering. Much will hang on
what we decide this afternoon. Second, don't let's forget what
this is all about. These senior universities, the Russell Group,
want to charge our bright young men and women an extra

twenty or thirty per cent for their higher education. The students will resist ferociously. They are the strongest supporters of the Bill. The polls show the Bill is popular. I know all the arguments about quality and holding our own with the Americans. I've used them myself. But we'd be crazy to push this any further.'

Next, Peter Makewell called the Shadow Attorney General, which meant chief legal adviser to the Opposition. He saw at once that this was a tactical mistake. He would have had to call Clive Wilson into the discussion at some stage, but it would have been better later. Peter Makewell knew that he was making these tactical mistakes more often. He wished that there was a better clutch of lawyers in the Conservative Party from whom to choose. Clive Wilson had recently developed a lawyer's vocabulary, but that was different from legal wisdom.

He spoke at some length summarising both sides of the argument. He concluded that thirty years ago there would have been no doubt. 'Statute law was enacted by the Queen in Parliament and in those days that was that. The courts could interpret the law but not question it. If the Queen in Parliament enacted the slaughter of the first-born it would be illegal to prevent the killings – though I imagine there would be evidential problems as regards twins, the loss of birth certificates, and so forth.' He paused for the chuckle round the table, which did not come. 'But the position has now changed. What was certain has become uncertain. The Bill preventing the English universities from charging top-up fees is clearly unjust, as we have consistently argued. It restricts their independence and the independence of the parents and students who would pay these fees. Independence of education from political control is implicit in the clauses of the European Convention, which I have quoted. I cannot assert with confidence what would be the conclusion of any legal proceedings brought by the universities, but there must at least be reasonable doubt. I conclude that, the legal position being obscure, the issue for colleagues at this stage is essentially political.'

On that basis the discussion continued round the table. Some, like Clive Wilson, supported David Alcester because he was their man. Others supported him because it was the job of the Opposition to oppose, in and out of Parliament. Others knew that the universities were right, and the government blind with prejudice and the fear of seeming élitist. There was little doubt of the drift of the argument.

Peter Makewell took his decision without difficulty. It had been building up inside him for several days. He had told Louise in their pillow-talk that morning. 'You should know that I cannot lead a party that preaches disobedience to the law.' He did not elaborate, because there was no need.

Sarah Tunstall and four or five others followed him because they agreed with the principle, and liked people like Peter Makewell who were predictable and straightforward. But his qualities had been part of a chapter that had ended, as all political chapters do, in defeat. He had stayed on as Leader of the Party because enough people had asked him to, believing it was not wise to change leader in the immediate shock of defeat. But his time was over. It followed that the threat of resignation he had just made carried no weight. David Alcester spoke again. He wanted to defeat Sarah Tunstall but not antagonise her for ever.

'Sarah's quite right about the students. The polls show a lot of anxious parents too. But that is a short-term worry. The long-term gain is too big to throw away. We've got the Scots and the Scot-lickers on the run on this Bill, and we have to make that the issue. Look at this for a start.' He plunged into the case beside his chair and unrolled a poster. A kilted Scot with a beard and knobbly knees was crushing under huge boots two small models of academic buildings, labelled Oxford and Cambridge. Out of his sporran tumbled a scattering of euro notes. Two old men, one clad in stars and one in stripes, labelled Harvard and Yale, cackled happily in the background.

'My artist in the New England Movement dreamed this up. It'll be on all the hoardings next week if we can get the right caption.'

The Shadow Cabinet contemplated the future with mixed feelings and in silence.

'I shall not try to sum up,' Peter Makewell said. 'The points have been made clearly on both sides.' He paused. 'I think this is one of those occasions when it would be useful to take a vote. For the sake of future clarity.'

The vote was eleven in favour, six against, and gave public support to the universities in any decision to levy top-up fees even after the English Universities (Prohibition of Fees) Bill had received Royal Assent.

Peter Makewell resigned that evening. Within three weeks David Alcester had been elected Leader of the Conservative Party and the Leader of Her Majesty's Opposition, having defeated Sarah Tunstall by a substantial margin.

They hardly ever disagreed nowadays. Sometimes David regretted the early days with Julia when in between bouts of the other thing they had argued hammer and tongs night after night. But lately peace had come.

He did not quite understand how, but marriage and motherhood had proved a pacifier. In return he made love to Julia rather more often than he himself relished. He had a wife, he had a son; these necessary objectives had been obtained. Pumping himself into Julia once or twice a week had become in his mind the price he paid for these things. He had begun to feel a certain small fondness for her which had nothing to do with sex. He was even taking paternity leave from his duties as Leader of the Opposition, though his fatherly duties at home were hard to define. But all this was an appendage to the consuming interest of his steady political progress.

The baby had to have a name. The press would soon be restive.

'George is out,' said Julia. The object of the debate nuzzled at her breast, quiet after a stormy night. She, too, was exhausted. For the moment David slept in the spare room of the flat. He had to be protected against infant noise in order to keep up his strength. Even on leave, though, he coped with the usual flow of e-mail and meetings, the main difference being that the meetings now had to be held at home in the flat rather than at the Commons or Conservative Central Office.

'George would be hugely popular right across England.'

'The boy is a boy, a human being, not a political slogan.' Julia spoke quietly, but David saw that she would not budge. He had prepared an alternative.

'You're sure? It's a huge pity.'

'I'm sure.'

'Then it will have to be Simon.'

Julia stared at her husband, amazed.

'I always had a great respect for your father. I didn't agree with him about everything, but he was a great prime minister.'

And opinion research, as Julia well knew, showed that people still consistently rated Simon Russell high above anyone on the present political scène. 'You didn't know him, and what you knew you disliked. You're just cashing in on his popularity.' But she spoke without edge.

'That's an exaggeration. And it would delight your mother.'

Yes – Louise would make a sharp joke about it, but inside herself would be pleased.

'I can tell the press?'

'You can tell the press.' Julia sank back on the plumped-up pillows. Her inner resolution was that in no circumstance would the new Simon have anything to do with politics. But she knew it was a resolution that she had no power to deliver. Simon began to exact his breakfast.

It was a great relief to be out of the noise and muddle of the baby-dominated flat. David Alcester ran up the staircase of Conservative Central Office two steps at a time. The posters in the entrance hall showed him with Julia holding Simon, all three happy and smiling. That was more satisfactory than the reality of Cambridge Street, Julia tired and usually silent, Simon bawling, unhappy at the move from breast to bottle.

'You're nice and fit,' said an unknown lady from the research department passing her leader as she descended the wide Central Office staircase.

That was what he had hoped someone would say. In fact, he was puffing by the time he reached the landing and turned left towards the chairman's office.

He had never particularly liked Central Office, a stodgy great block in Smith Square, still too full of Makewell and Courtauld supporters. But Clive Wilson had started well as chairman. He had forced the party machine to let the New England leadership share their office space. This meant getting rid of some of the research department, including perhaps the lady with whom David had just exchanged smiles on the stairs. But neither David Alcester nor Clive Wilson thought much of academic contributions to political life. New England, not facts and figures about policy, held the key to success at the next election.

'Okay, what do we have this morning?'

The two men met each other alone each day, except for one small young assistant, wearing a New England tie, who sat in a corner adoring the two principals and taking notes of their decisions.

'Cambridge expect their verdict from the ECHR today or tomorrow.'

Cambridge University, having declared independence of government, was arguing before the European Court of Human Rights that the British government and Parliament had acted illegally in preventing them from charging higher fees for their tutorial systems.

'What do they expect?'

'To lose, unfortunately.'

'That's not what you advised Shadow Cabinet.'

Clive Wilson was nettled. 'Not at all, David, you remember perfectly well that I said it was an open question.'

'What happens after that?'

'Cambridge will obey. They'll refund the fees they've already levied. They're not the New England Movement.

They can't flout the law. They've come to the end of the legal process.'

'Bad headlines for us. We've invested a lot of political capital in this.'

'A setback, certainly.' But it got you the leadership, Clive Wilson added in his own mind.

'You can't stiffen the Vice-Chancellor?'

'No. They're not interested in our argument about England being run by Scottish votes. They just worry about the dumbing down of the university.'

'Most unreasonable. Cowardly, indeed.' David spoke without irony. The world of professional party politics, which had formed Clive Wilson and himself, no longer allowed any validity to argument outside its own concerns.

'We'll need to compensate. Something eye-catching over the weekend.'

They were back on territory in which Clive Wilson was expert.

'I think I have it. Flags.'

'Flags?'

'There are several places in London that fly the Scots flag, the blue and white cross.'

'St Andrew's.'

'That's it. St Columba's, Pont Street, that fat white church, is one. The Royal Bank of Scotland off Bishopsgate is another. I've got a list of a dozen. All on good sites for TV and press. We'll have New England pull them all down on Saturday morning. They'll put up St George instead.'

It was good, real politics.

'What do the lawyers say?' asked David, forgetting that Clive Wilson called himself a lawyer.

'Not breaking and entering if we do it from outside. Not criminal damage if we keep the flags intact. Not theft. New England would just fold the flags neatly and leave them on the pavement. A soundbite or two about freeing us from Scots rule. St George the champion of freedom, and that's it.'

'Fair enough.'

'Another thought. New England's got its own research team now. Quite unlike that useless bunch we're getting rid of from the old machine. They're coming up with some good material. Lots of quotes, of course, from Dr Johnson. God, that man despised the Scots. But earlier stuff as well.'

'Such as?'

'When the Scots King James succeeded Elizabeth, he brought a pack of Scottish courtiers down with him – 1603, I think. They had lice. They stank. The English courtiers wouldn't sit next to them. That's how the word "stinkers" came into the language.'

'Stinkers, wha hae wi' Wallace bled.'

'Precisely.'

The young man in the corner guffawed obsequiously.

'Race Relations Act, if we used it.'

'But we're going to repeal that. If anyone dared prosecute us, it would be a splendid case.'

But David still had some sense of reality, if not of taste. 'Leave it. Remember it if you like, store it away, but leave it for now. What next?'

Clive Wilson consulted the informal agenda on the laptop in front of him. 'That conference you want to go to in Cannes. It clashes with the rally New England are planning in Stratford-on-Avon Wednesday week. Anniversary of Shakespeare's marriage. Or so they say.'

'Can't be helped.'

'You really want to go to Cannes? What's it all about?'

But Clive Wilson was pushing too far.

'It's a Congress of the Majorities. Spaniards against the Basques, Frenchmen against the Corsicans, Germans against all those Turks in the Ruhr, Britain against the Scots. Majorities, too, have their rights, that's the message. I'm keen we should have an international dimension.'

Or rather, thought Clive Wilson, you're keen to show yourself on a wider stage. 'Sure you can get good publicity for it?'

'Certainly. I'm working on the speech and interviews. Good pictures, too. I'm taking Julia.'

'And little George?'

'My son's name is Simon.'

'Of course. Pity.' Central Office had argued strongly for George.

'No. We're leaving him with his grandmother.' And thereby getting for themselves a little peace and quiet in the sun.

The knock on the door was timid. The young man in the corner jumped up officiously to repel the intruder. It was a rule that the Chairman and the Leader of the Party were not to be disturbed. There was hurried muttering in the doorway, then a letter.

The young man gave it to Clive. 'A Scot apparently, though he tried to disguise the accent. Delivered by hand, insisting you got it at once. Said it was about something set to happen this morning.'

Clive Wilson extracted two papers from the long white envelope.

Conclusion of Minutes of the Council of the Scottish
Liberation Army, May 23.

After discussion the Council decided that the SLA
would move forthwith from the political to the revolu-
tionary phase of the independence struggle. Existing
plans for military mobilisation and consequent armed
action would be updated for implementation during
July, detailed operations to be subject to a further decision of the Council.

Meanwhile the Army Command was authorised to
proceed at once with Operation MONTROSE.

There was a separate letter. The Chairman of the Party
read it and handed it quickly to the Leader of the Party.

'Who's Hamish McGovern?' asked David.

'Labour Member for one of the Glasgow seats. He was my
pair in the Commons for a time. Reliable, never let me down.
Left the Party saying he now believed in full independence
because devolution had failed. Didn't stand at the last election, and I've not heard from him till now.'

Dear Clive,

Hope things go well with you. I don't miss the House
and all that useless blather. I'm glad Alcester had the
sense to make you party chairman. It's a job for a shit,
and I say that in the nicest possible way.

I'm in touch with the Scottish Liberation Army
here. Maybe you'll not have heard of them – yet.
Scotland will only be free through direct action, I see
that now. After I left Labour I joined the regular Scot
Nats, but they're all talk, the same as the rest of you,

no real blood in any of them. The SLA have what it takes.

They've asked me to send you this. They're keen it should reach you this Wednesday, not sooner, not later. This MONTROSE operation will be outside the law, that's for certain. But they told me at this stage no one will get hurt, if they're canny and behave themselves. I ken no more than that.

They want to get in touch with you. You Tories are enemies of Scotland, we all know that. But that's because you've persuaded the silly English that we're taking you over. Once Scotland's free we'll be out of your hair and you can have a Tory England for ever. Labour will never win again without their votes north of the border. So that's the shared interest between the Tories and the SLA. Can you work with them to get there? I don't know the answer to that. Their methods are different from yours. They'll make your old ladies of both sexes shiver. But they want to discuss it all with you, and if you've sense you'll listen.

All you have to do is to e-mail me the word aye. Then I'll fix time and place. It'll have to be you who sees them, not an underling. You'll come to no harm.

Yours,

Hamish McGovern

'Interesting?' asked Clive.

David said nothing.

'What shall I do?'

'Nothing. Nothing whatever.'

'But there's something in the argument.'

'No.' David gestured towards the young man in the corner. 'We can't discuss it. Nothing to discuss. Too dangerous. They're outlaws. The answer's no.'

'But . . .'

'No but.'

David Alcester had made Clive Wilson and could unmake him. Clive had already overstepped the mark that morning. Their discussion was not between equals.

Soon after, David Alcester left. The midday edition of the *Evening Standard* was on display outside St John's Church. The vendor was selling briskly to people going up the steps to the lunchtime concert.

SCOTS LAW CHIEF SNATCHED

James Cameron (45), Procurator Fiscal of Scotland, the country's chief law officer, was kidnapped by a group of armed men this morning as he fished the hill loch a mile from his home near Dumfries. His fourteen-year-old son, Archie, looked on helpless as the four men, wearing badges of the extreme Nationalist SLA, rushed at Cameron from a hiding place by the loch shore and after a brief struggle carried him off. The police . . .

'They'll frighten the fish. You won't catch a thing with the police around.' Louise was flinging every possible argument into the battle with her husband. She was losing, but had not yet given up. 'Who would want to kidnap you, for God's sake?' she went on. 'You're not Prime Minister now, you're not even the wretched Leader of the Opposition. You're a has-been, a nobody, you're finished with politics, thank God. These great hulking cops should be catching burglars in Perth and Dundee, not lounging around our salmon pool.'

Peter Makewell took all this calmly. He had been almost as dismayed as his wife when the superintendent had called, but his temperament, unlike hers, accepted the kind of authority that the superintendent represented. He continued to put on his boots. Rod and flies were already organised. Peter no longer employed a gillie and it would actually be quite agreeable to have the police sergeant for company as he fished. The sergeant seemed a decent enough lad. His grandfather had run the old bakery up the hill just this side of Pitlochry, so there would be plenty to talk about. For Peter now, most interesting conversation was about the past. Of course Louise was right – the SLA were most unlikely to have the slightest interest in him – but from long experience Peter knew that the police always insisted on slamming every possible stable door after one horse had bolted. He wondered where the SLA were holding poor James Cameron: a pompous fellow, a trimmer in politics, proper in his views and fond of his comforts. Peter could not imagine him dragged across the moors or nibbling biscuits in a cave.

'Anyway, there are no baps for the man's lunch. The last two are in your bag. I'm doing the shopping this morning.'

'The sergeant will certainly have brought his own.'

Peter Makewell was anxious to get out of the house. It had rained hard during the night. He could tell this from the noise of the burn as it tumbled towards the main river. The sky was happily overcast, the prospects good. Any minute now his step-grandson would start all over again. In theory Peter was devoted to little Simon Alcester and delighted that he had been brought to stay at Craigarran while his parents were at Cannes. In private he believed that his relationship with the

lad would start in about five years' time. Grandfathers, and
certainly step-grandfathers, had little in common with babies.
Meanwhile, what was required was endurance on his part and
perhaps on young Simon's as well. This was not easy in a
home largely built of wood where noise in one room was noise
everywhere. No doubt Simon would settle down nicely just
when it was time for him to leave.

Louise watched the two figures trudge beside the burn
towards the upper loch until they were lost behind a group of
rowans. On parting with her they had looked serious, even
downcast, but Louise knew enough about men to see enjoy-
ment in every sober step they took.

She had set aside this morning for the studio that she had
established in what used to be the head gardener's cottage
along one side of the walled gardens. The light was right in
the old parlour there, and the silence absolute. She would
certainly resist any suggestion that the police should take over
the cottage as a guard post. She was at work on a bust of Peter,
difficult at any time because he was a reluctant and fidgety
sitter, the more so now that the salmon were coming up the
river and little Simon was noisy in the home, distracting both
subject and artist.

But before she could settle down conscientiously in the
studio she had to do the shopping in Pitlochry. She had
thought of taking Simon in his carry-cot which converted
into a pram, but it might rain again, and the supermarket
would be crowded.

'Mrs Mackintosh, will you look after Simon for me for an
hour while I do the shopping? He's fast asleep. He kept us up
most of the night. The next bottle's made up in the fridge
when he wants it.'

Mrs Mackintosh had been with them as housekeeper for fifteen years. A grandmother herself, she had proved more adept
with the bottle than Louise. She smoothed her abundant grey
hair, a sure sign that she was pleased to be in charge. 'That's
fine, Lady Makewell, just fine. Here's the list for Tesco's, so far
as I've been able to do it. The oatcakes are better from
Andrew Dimmock's down by the post office, but you know
that already. He'll have a new batch baked yesterday. I'll just
hang out the washing, and then I'll sit here and do the beans
and sweep the place out till the bairn wakes. Never doubt,
he'll be fine with me.'

By nature Julia was restless, and she had organised her life
accordingly. A rebel at school, she had used her father's premiership as a battlefield for further rebellion at the same time
as she had grown to love him. She had allowed David to
seduce her as an act of defiance to her mother, but then
turned to defy David once she had put herself in his power.
She hopped into each cage in turn only to beat her wings
against its bars.

But this weekend in Cannes she was at ease, even happy. It
was strange to feel relaxed, surrounded by comfort, able to
enjoy that comfort without worrying about her husband, baby,
herself. She sat beneath a huge blue umbrella on the spotless
sand watching two attendants, in white T-shirts and sharp
blue shorts, erect similar umbrellas on the hotel jetty, which
ran a hundred metres out to sea. The early morning wind,
which had prevented them doing this sooner, had now died
down. To her left and right there were scuffling movements as
German and Italian women collected their belongings and
prepared to move to a more prestigious position on the jetty.

From there they would command a nobler view of sea and yachts and be more readily noticed themselves. Julia had no inclination to move. Pigeons strutted importantly on the sand close to her toes. That morning she felt the luxury of laziness for the first time since Simon was born.

The Congress of European Majorities was well funded, and had provided the head of each delegation with a high-ceilinged suite in the Hôtel Carlton overlooking the sea. There she and David had made love last night, for once in harmony with each other. This morning the press summary shoved under their door showed that his speech to the conference yesterday, 'England will stand up', had been excellently received at home. In high good humour he had taken her to swim before breakfast. They had run down the jetty in identical white hotel dressing-gowns, and raced each other to the small raft out at sea. For a few minutes he had stopped being a politician. She had caught her mother on the telephone just before she went off to shop, and established that Simon was happy and well. David had walked west along the promenade to the conclave of party leaders, relishing his reception for the first time as a party leader who was likely to win an election. The polls had turned heavily in favour of the Conservatives; all those present at the conclave lived on opinion polls. For the first time, too, she did not grudge David his coming success, even though she knew the tricks by which he had advanced this far. Louise had been right in her advice at Chequers – if she could not leave her strange marriage it was better to enjoy it. Perhaps, indeed probably, every marriage was strange.

She wondered whether to order another *citron*, weighing the pleasure against the effort. She wondered whether to spin out the latest Joanna Trollope novel which lay on the sand beside her, or whether it would be better to gallop through it and hope to find another in the hotel news-stand.

A tall African figure picked his way towards her, shining in white and gold robes. Across his shoulder he carried a light wooden yoke from which descended a glistening mass of jewellery – watches, sunglasses with sparkling frames, bracelets, rings threaded on silver cord, necklaces tangled in bright confusion. This cascade created the impression that the noble African was wearing a fantastic extra garment outside his robes. Despite herself Julia had picked up something from her mother, some knowledge of such matters. She saw to her surprise that the display was not rubbish. There were no price labels. The African, acknowledging her interest, came close to her deck-chair. With dignity he raised the yoke from his shoulders and held it before her. Forgetting the dilemma over the *citron* and Joanna Trollope, Julia spent ten minutes on a pleasure rare in her life. She supposed that when young her mother had enjoyed shopping, but by the time her own recollection began that phase had ended. Her father Simon Russell had always dressed decently. He bought about five books a year, and solid unimaginative presents for his wife and daughter at Christmas and when he remembered their birthdays. Louise herself spent a morning choosing clothes twice a year, and bought a picture occasionally from a small gallery in Highgate. Louise had left No. 10 Downing Street on memorable expeditions: when Simon died and, much more recently, when Peter Makewell lost the last election. Each time she had descended on Harrods and Peter Jones and, in a hurry, bought the furniture, carpets and curtains needed for the next chapter of her life. Julia had heard of these expeditions, which had been packed into two or three days, but had not been invited to take part. There had been no family tradition of enjoyable shopping. Her parents were not mean, but by the time she knew them well they had too many other things in their minds and diaries.

David, though, was mean by nature. Until recently he could reasonably defend meanness as necessary prudence. She had not forced the pace: she had simply noted that this was another underlying difference between them, a mine that might one day explode. Now, David was earning well from articles and speeches on top of his salary as Leader of the Opposition. Things were going better for him, though not to the point where he would go out and buy something useless and pretty for her. A fortnight ago he had forgotten their first wedding anniversary and had been ashamed for a minute. This was not a bad moment, Julia thought, to test the ground for a small move forward.

'C'est trois mille, Madame.'

The man spoke politely but with a firmness that, combined with his princely appearance, excluded bargaining. From his tone and the quality of his goods, Julia judged that he had some arrangement with the Carlton and its neighbours, allowing him to importune publicly the clientele of the main hotels of Cannes on their adjoining stretches of well-swept beach.

Julia still thought in pounds. She knew that almost all of her generation led their lives in euros, although David translated prices back into sterling for political reasons. She found herself doing the same, even though she thought his dislike of the euro absurd. And futile too, since even he did not believe that the Tories could bring back the pound. Once at Chequers she had pointed out this incongruity in a clever teenage way to her father. Simon Russell had said, 'It's quite normal, Julia. Scotland, and England too, are full of pine trees planted by sentimental Jacobites long after they were peaceful subjects of King George. They loved to drink to the King over the water and throw the glass to shatter in the fireplace. A cause lingers on in men's minds well after they have stopped doing anything about it. Women are less sentimental. Most men have a soft place somewhere.'

Julia still did not know if this was true of David. But she must decide quickly about the pearl and glass necklace, the coils of which were now frothing in her hand.

'*Permettez, Madame.*'

The African deftly loosened the clasp and fastened it round her neck, taking care that his long bony hands did not touch her warm flesh. He found a small mirror somewhere in his robes and held it to her.

It was pretty, at least out there in the open against her tanned skin. And, at just over a thousand pounds, more or less within the range that David in his present benign mood might tolerate. She had no intention of paying for it herself. He owed her something for Simon.

'*Les perles sont bonnes?*'

'*Les meilleures, de Bahrain.*'

The man did not plead his case, but stood before her patiently. Julia's courage carried her only a certain way.

'*Je dois les montrer à mon mari.*' A remark he must have heard many times.

'*Bien sûr, Madame. Je viendrai au Carlton à sept heures exacte. Si ça vous convient . . .*'

He left her with the necklace, knowing perhaps that his trust would strengthen her will to buy.

But David, when he returned to the hotel at about five, had something else on his mind. 'Damned nuisance, and all because of those bloody Scots.' But actually he sounded quite pleased.

'What exactly did the message say?'

'It was from one of the private secretaries at the Home Office. He just said that after the kidnapping of that man Cameron the Home Secretary had decided that all the politicians prominent in discussing Scotland must have full-time protection forthwith. A team of three are flying out to us from the Met this evening. The French have already been alerted. There's one of their policemen out in the corridor already.'

'You could refuse.' Julia felt a familiar grey cloud descend on her life. For years as a girl she had been used to protection, to the kindly intrusion of privacy carried out by large, friendly men. You could not possibly complain, even though from time to time you were driven mad by their proximity and the knowledge they had of you and yours. But that had all been to do with Ireland, and Ireland was now quiet. Were the Scots bringing the same cloud back to hang over them for ever?

'No, I couldn't. The Home Office was very clear. They rate the threat to me as substantial.'

Julia knew that David was not a physical coward. She saw that the thought of protection tickled his vanity, poor fool. He had never lived that life before. He saw only that he was entering a club of really important people.

'Are they sending a team to Craigarran?'

'I asked them that,' said David surprisingly. 'They've already got a sergeant up there looking after your step-father. Of course he'll keep an eye on Simon as well. But they say there's no threat so far as they can see to wives or children. Just to the principals.'

'Principals?'

'That's what the police call the VIPs they're protecting.'

In this self-important mood, David was quite pleased with the necklace, and hardly quibbled about the price. 'It's quite expensive. But I don't grudge it. It will be something to remember this conference by. It's really gone quite well. Von Blissach was particularly complimentary about my speech.'

'And Simon.'

'Simon?'

'Something to remind us of the summer he was born.'

David looked surprised, then said something which in turn surprised her. 'We shall remember Simon by bringing him up as a happy, successful child in a good family.' Pompous, of course, but she did not mind because he meant it.

They lay together, fully clothed and peaceful for half an hour on the wide double bed looking out through the skilfully placed windows on to the dancing sea. They watched the quality of the light change and sharpen as the sun began to set. The waves sounded faintly in rare intervals between the noise of cars along the promenade or the roar of a motorbike. From their pillows they could watch the evening breeze begin to agitate the top of the palm tree outside the hotel entrance.

Julia dozed. The telephone rang on her side of the bed. It was her mother, first composed, then, extraordinarily, in tears. Julia said, 'God, no,' then little else. Having put down the receiver, she shook David awake.

'It's Simon. He's disappeared. Kidnapped, they think. Mummy was shopping and—'

David sat bolt upright in bed. They gazed at each other as at strangers. Whatever happened from now on would be new for them both.

Having searched her own studio and the other rooms of the cottage by the garden wall, Louise walked up the path to the shed with the marble slab. Here, newly caught salmon spent the first hours of death before being cooked in the house or loaded into a car by grateful departing guests. Just one salmon lay there. Eleven or twelve pounds, she guessed, wearing much the same satisfied smile as Sergeant Fraser, who had caught it, had worn when he and Peter returned an hour ago. The police officer's smile had vanished at the news. Indeed it seemed possible that Sergeant Fraser would never smile again. Not that he could seriously be blamed. He had been sent to Craigarran to protect Peter Makewell, former prime minister and Anglo-Scot, thought to be particularly vulnerable to the new kidnapping campaign by the SLA. Fraser had been given no instruction as regards Lady Makewell or her grandson. He was concerned only with the principal. He had been clearly right to accompany Peter down the burn. It would have been quite wrong to stay in the house. It was less clear that he should have allowed himself to accept the loan of Peter's rod for half an hour. A glorious half-hour, one salmon hooked and lost in the swirl of the water under the falls, then within minutes the second salmon hooked and caught. He knew that Peter would do his best to protect him from any accusation on that score, which indeed seemed trivial compared to the disaster that had befallen while they were away.

The police had agreed to split into two teams, each team in turn searching every possible nook and hiding place in the home and garden, so that each possibility was examined twice.

Peter, the superintendent newly arrived from Perth and anxious Sergeant Fraser were now searching the main house. Louise and the two constables had already combed the garden and cottage. It was surprising how many small unnoticed spaces there were on the premises in which a baby might conceivably be hidden.

Louise could see that this was all nonsense. Simon was far too young to have crawled into any of them. He was a baby in a cot. It seemed certain that he had been taken away with Mrs Mackintosh or by Mrs Mackintosh, in her small Renault car. 'With' or 'by', that was the question. She fervently hoped that Mrs Mackintosh was a fellow victim with Simon of a kidnap organised by others. Over the years she had come to like and trust her housekeeper.

Dwarfing every other feeling was Louise's sense of shame and guilt. She could not prevent her clear mind from analysing this. A tiny grandson had moved into the centre of her life. She loved the little sprat for himself, but also because he was the future for Julia, whom she loved the more because of the years they had spent griping and squabbling with each other.

It had been perfectly reasonable to go shopping in Pitlochry, leaving Simon in the care of a trusted housekeeper. But it had turned out a disaster, for which somebody must be responsible, and that somebody could only be herself.

In the garden tool-shed, forks, hoes and spades of different sizes hung as they had always hung, each neatly in an appointed place, cleared of mud, witnesses of an order that human beings could impose on everything except their own lives. Louise thought about her telephone conversation with Julia. David had evidently been in the room. How would the disaster affect that shaky marriage? Not at all, if Simon were found quickly. But if not, if it dragged on . . .? Louise knew that David was cold and selfish. She was not sure whether under the surface he would be genuinely moved by Simon's disappearance. She hoped so, for Julia's sake. But whether he was moved or not, he would certainly regard it as a public-relations event, to be handled like other such events, professionally and with care. How Julia would react to this her mother could not guess.

The two constables, she could see, would go on searching the sheds and cottages over and over again, even though this was useless. Men, particularly men in uniform, fell back on routine when baffled, which put their minds into neutral gear. It was up to her to call a halt. 'There's nothing here,' she said. 'Back into the house.'

Both teams conferred in the ancient, somewhat grimy kitchen. There was nothing useful to be said. If Mrs Mackintosh had been there she would have made tea, with a clatter of friendly comment. Louise boiled a kettle on the Aga without speaking. Peter Makewell sat silent in a corner, exhausted.

The superintendent spoke to Sergeant Fraser and the constables. He at least had been thinking ahead. 'Next I'll get Forensics from Perth. They'll crawl inch by inch over the forecourt and the drive up from the road. There are places where the tarmac has broken up. After last night's rain the earth will have taken tyre marks. They'll want impressions from the vehicles we know have used the drive – the Range Rover Lady Makewell used for shopping, your car, Sergeant Fraser, the police car we came in, and—'

'Mrs Makewell's Renault,' said Louise.

'Yes. It's disappeared, but they'll know roughly what it would be like. Do you happen to know if the tyres were new?'

'She had two new tyres last year,' said Peter, from his corner. 'Can't remember whether they went on the front or back. The car was six or seven years old.' Mrs Mackintosh had not asked for a rise to meet the expense of the new tyres but, prompted by Louise, he had offered one.

'That's very helpful, sir. The real question is whether there is evidence of a fifth car using the drive since last night's rain.'

At least the superintendent was thinking. The mood in the kitchen lightened slightly. Louise had another idea. A broom cupboard off the kitchen had been appropriated many years ago for Mrs Mackintosh's personal use. There she kept an umbrella, an old raincoat, two aprons and a pair of smart shoes. Mrs Mackintosh arrived in these shoes each day. As the first act in her morning ritual she changed into flat slippers suitable for housework. Louise opened the cupboard door. Its normal contents were as familiar to her as anything in her own bedroom. It was bare except for two wire coat hangers. She summoned Peter. She did not need to say anything as they stared into the void. Mrs Mackintosh had not been kidnapped. Mrs Mackintosh had left in good order. Mrs Mackintosh was a traitor to them – and a servant to whom? For the first time in her life Louise felt a stranger in Scotland. She hurried out of the kitchen to master a second wave of tears.

They were booked on the first available flight from Nice, dislodging two other passengers. Air France was flexible in such matters. The French police would drive them to the airport from Cannes. Julia had packed quickly and wanted to leave at once. Cannes was already repulsive: she would prefer the isolation of a VIP lounge. But the police, so David told her, insisted they should stay in the hotel till the last possible minute. They were afraid that stringer journalists hanging around the airport would notice the now quite well-known British couple leaving prematurely and ask questions to which as yet there were no answers. They had an hour to wait.

'There's time to go back to the beach. Will you come?'

'Good heavens, no,' he said. It was as if they both realised that in this, the first disaster of their marriage, they had nothing to say to each other. 'I can't unpack my beach things again.'

But she gathered her bag, sunglasses and novel and left the room. She had learned, perhaps from her father, to put on a calm exterior over her jangling nerves. 'I'll be back in good time.'

Downstairs in the lobby the hotel bellmaster, greeting her, turned the circular swing door that led out on to the pavement, main road and beach. But Julia turned aside. She had to be active: the hours that morning when she had relaxed happily on the beach seemed infinitely distant. Moreover, two French police officers stood, dignified and silent, outside the main door, one of whom would almost certainly insist on coming with her to the beach. She had already noticed that past the hotel news-stand and leather shop a door led out on to a side-street.

Soon she was in the flower market, but its voluble brightness offended her almost as much as the beach would have done. She took out her mobile phone to ring her mother again. 'No network coverage,' its tiny screen read. Naturally.

The networks of the world had seized up. It was that sort of day. In the small church abutting on the market there would certainly be darkness and quiet. The church was indeed deserted; it offered nothing to tourists except the grace of God. In a side-chapel candles flickered round a blue and white Madonna with a crude gash of scarlet across her lips. Julia knelt but could not find anything to invest in prayer. She sat back and tried to think. At least it seemed certain that Mrs Mackintosh had gone with Simon, either willingly or by force. She had learned quickly how to feed him, run his routine, settle him when he cried, updating her own ancient experience. Julia did not care a damn about Mrs Mackintosh's political allegiance so long as she could change nappies and ply the bottle.

Julia's mind switched direction as an old man hobbled up the aisle and fumbled with money for a candle to light in front of the Virgin. It was impossible to guess how David would carry himself during this crisis. She felt as if she were assessing a stranger. At that moment she found no attraction to or affection for him. So far he had, like herself, seemed stunned. What would happen when the immediate shock wore off? Like her mother in Scotland at roughly the same moment, Julia realised that David would already be thinking of Simon's disappearance as a political event. He would be weighing up the timing and content of announcements and broadcasts. This did not necessarily mean that he had no inner feelings. But he would want, as far as possible, to be in charge of the world's searchlight as it fastened its clumsy beam on his own and Julia's drama.

Julia was not sure she could bear this side of the immediate future. She left the dark church abruptly, stood for a moment, dazzled in the contrasting glare, then walked back to the promenade. She turned east towards La Croisette, her back to the evening sun. She moved quickly, compensating with physical briskness for the emptiness of her mind. The boulevard led away from the fashionable part of Cannes. The shore to her right was no longer bright with umbrellas. The sand was unkempt, increasingly littered with cigarette packets and empty bottles. The craft in a small marina bobbed in a sea that seemed dirty: they lacked paint. Just short of the headland of La Croisette itself, a few square metres of trodden yellow grass surrounded the white bust of a writer, his nose chipped, his name obscured by graffiti in Arabic and what looked like a plea for help: *'liberate tutame ex feris'* – an echo of some incomprehensible feud, presumably in the Balkans. Children, gipsy or Balkan, ignored the faded instruction to keep off the grass. Julia kept moving. Her mind, too, had covered some distance from the comforts of the Hôtel Carlton and the highly organised political conclave at the other end of the bay. What would happen if she just kept walking? She had cash and credit cards in her bag. She could disappear into some cheap hotel along the coast, forget the puzzles of Simon and of David and sit out the next day or two by herself. By then Simon would have been found, alive or dead, and a new set of emotions would be required. Her present set had worn out. She was numb, not knowing how she felt.

A young man approached her. Julia realised that her hair was a mess.

'Cigarette?' he said, as if in English. He might be the elder brother of those children on the grass. He had learned a confident smile to go with his looks. Physically he was the exact opposite of David – a tall, well-shaped boy, about eighteen, long black eyelashes, his purple shirt wide open above tight grey shorts, which needed a wash. 'You have the time?' was his second gambit, pointing at his empty wrist. Julia kept moving. 'You like ice-cream?'

It was enough. If she went on east, that was the world she would enter. She must already look lost and dishevelled, available for a teenage grope. Julia turned back along the boulevard, walking even faster.

A black Mercedes was parked outside the main entrance of the Carlton. Just inside the swing doors a senior French police officer wearing white gloves was talking to the hotel manager. The two officers whom she had seen before stood behind them. Julia swept past; no one made a move to stop her.

Upstairs in the suite David, now dressed in a suit, sat on the bed, inclined over his mobile phone. Typically, she thought, his phone had coverage, where hers had failed. When he saw her, he took the phone from his ear as if to turn it off, then thought better of it. 'I must go now,' he said to the phone. 'At once. To sum up, then, I can look after the operation here. Just let the usual people know I'm available. Do that now. As soon as we finish. Then get hold of McGovern on the lines we discussed. At once. That's right. Goodbye. I'll ring again from Nice airport.'

'Who was that?'

'Only Clive Wilson.'

'Do you always give orders to the Chairman of the Party like that?'

'Yes.' But she could not hope to hold the initiative. David got up, and jammed the phone in his pocket. 'Where have you been? You look a mess. The police car's been waiting ten minutes at least. Your case is downstairs already.'

As they hurried through the lobby, the African chieftain came smiling towards Julia. 'Madame?'

She had forgotten him. The necklace was in her suitcase. She was confused. Their encounter on the beach that afternoon seemed months away.

David intervened. 'My wife liked the necklace. It seems expensive for what it is, but we will have it.' As was now quite usual David had formed the habit of carrying plenty of cash ever since the confusion over the future of MasterCard four years before. He began to count euro notes in large denominations.

'I don't want it,' said Julia, taut and unhappy at this diversion. 'It's rubbish, really. I can't think why . . .' She did not know what she wanted.

'We don't have time to argue. The necklace is yours.' He handed six 500-euro notes to the African.

'Merci, Excellence. J'espère que Madame—'

'We must go.'

They hurried through the suburbs of Cannes up into the hills, the police enjoying the need to move faster than the law allowed. Julia expected, from her earlier life as a protected person, that they would soon turn on the siren, and police happiness would then be complete.

Then David surprised her again. 'I spoke to you too roughly upstairs. You know why.' He took her hand and held it, for about half a minute. She noticed that, most unusually, one of his shirt buttons was undone, the third from the top.

In the intervals between thinking about Simon, she realised that, whatever else happened, her dealings with David would remain complicated. She wondered whether to fasten the button, but held back.

A few minutes later he brought their relationship back to the humdrum. 'I'm going to say a few words to the press at the airport. There'll just be time.'

'Words? About Simon?'

'Not about Simon. At least, not directly.' He paused.

Julia realised how difficult it was for her husband to speak directly about anything. Sometimes this made for slow speech. There were layers of calculation beneath most of his utterances. This could mean strenuous work for brain and tongue as they combined to make sentences. She interrupted his thought, impatient to push him on. 'Has anything come out yet about Simon disappearing? Who is McGovern?'

'Nothing yet. The Grampian police want to keep it quiet for as long as they can. They think publicity will confuse their investigations.'

'That won't be long. I've never known the police keep a secret more than an hour or two. There's always a sergeant somewhere with a hot line to the *News of the World*.'

'That's as may be.' David sounded disapproving. Julia remembered that, despite his hardness, David was inexperienced about some practicalities of life at the top, which she had known, willy-nilly, through all the years with her parents.

'And McGovern?'

That pause again. There was some justification since neither of them could be sure how much English was known by the driver or the inspector of police in the front seat of the car. David spoke in a low voice; now in the idiom of a lawyer presenting facts to a court. 'It's reasonable to assume, though not certain, that Simon has been kidnapped by the SLA, that's the far-out Nationalist group that snatched the lawyer, Cameron. McGovern is an old Labour MP who is in touch with these people. In turn Clive Wilson is in touch with McGovern. He has been for several weeks. Nothing to do with Simon, of course, or with Cameron, just politics. They've been in touch again today. McGovern believes the SLA want a political declaration out of me. I don't know what grounds he has for this. He's a foolish man, but well connected. Anyway, I've decided to make such a declaration. In five minutes, from Nice airport.'

The car was down from the hills now, and the signs directing to this or that outpost of the airport were multiplying along the roadside.

Julia was afraid that he would begin to tell her about the content of his coming declaration, a matter in which she had little interest compared with the main question. 'And if you do this they will let Simon go?'

'I can't tell. I really can't tell. But it's the only line we have. Do you know a better?'

'Of course not.' She subsided, dead tired at different levels from the sun on the beach, her flurried walk to La Croisette, and the crushing anxiety. She had no will to challenge her husband and, as he said, no alternative plan. She recognised in him the pleasure that comes to a man who has taken a difficult decision, a pleasure that provides able men with one of the main motives for entering politics. She hoped that beneath this she could find a real anxiety for Simon, and perhaps also, though of this she was less sure, a few particles of affection for herself.

Clive Wilson's telephone calls to London editors had produced only a scanty presence of reporters in the airport press room. The editors had done David proud with their coverage of his speech at the conclave in Cannes the day before. A couple of columnists in Conservative papers had, with insular exaggeration, described him as taking a lead for the first time in discussion among fellow party leaders.

But the indication, portentously conveyed from Conservative Central Office, that the leader of the Party wanted to impart an important modification of his policy on Scotland had created little excitement. Two men and a girl were present in the press room at the airport. They were stringers, who normally hung about the terminal for a lucky glimpse and quick, shouted interview with some Riviera celebrity: a plump divorced millionaire, a group of pop stars haggard with drugs, an ancient princess with her latest toy-boy. With these they were familiar. But to them David Alcester on a hot summer evening was a mystery and a bore, and as for his wife – she had a good figure but who was she and where on earth did she get her hair done?

'Thanks for coming,' said David. 'I apologise for the short notice.' His manners were always better in public than in private. He had done up the loose button. Air France would hold the flight a little longer, but he had to be quick. No time for elaborate introduction or explanation. 'I have decided to advance Conservative policy on Scotland in one important respect. We have been by tradition a Unionist party. We have always hoped that the majority of the Scottish people would stay loyal to the United Kingdom. We have not wished to desert those Scots who were genuinely loyal. We have wanted to redress the balance of the Union, to remove the obvious injustice to England of the existing system whether in money or in political power. As you know, that has been my main theme since I became leader. But there comes a time when one has to face facts, however unpalatable. The Union is no longer functioning in a manner acceptable to either English or Scots. It should therefore be brought to an end as soon as possible. I am calling a meeting of the Shadow Cabinet in London tomorrow and with their authority shall write to the Prime Minister Mr Turnbull demanding the immediate introduction before the summer recess of a Dissolution Bill conferring full independence on Scotland.'

This was big stuff. They realised it as soon as they heard him. But they did not know how to exploit their opportunity. There was a long pause.

'What has led you to make this U-turn?' was the best the old man from Reuters could manage.

'No U-turn. It's a development of policy. A fair deal for England – I've always stood for that. A fair deal for England now means independence for Scotland.'

A usable soundbite at last. They scribbled happily. An agitated Air France official appeared in the doorway. Within ten minutes David and Julia were airborne.

Despite herself she had been impressed by the size of the gamble.

'Colleagues?' she said. They had both refused the trays of plastic food. Why was the food in Air France, of all companies, noticeably nastier than anyone else's?

'The colleagues will follow. They have no one else.'

'Even when they discover . . . ?'

'Discover?'

'Your motive . . . Simon.'

'Particularly then.' For the first time David smiled. 'You'll see.' Then he slept.

*

'You'll see,' David had said, in the Air France plane. And what Julia saw in the days that followed was exactly what David had predicted. Not that this made them any easier to bear. They were the most unusual days of her life. A few hours after they reached the Cambridge Street flat on Monday night the chief constable of the Grampian police telephoned to say that the *Daily Record* had heard of Simon's disappearance and would publish next morning. The police were therefore making a simple announcement of the facts. When pressed by Julia on the progress of their investigations the chief constable proffered satisfaction. Mrs Mackintosh's Renault had been found in a pub car park at Musselburgh, just outside Edinburgh. Forensics had established that there had been a fifth car up the entrance to Craigarran that morning, probably a Japanese four-wheel drive. So now that the news was out, the police would smother Scotland with photographs of Simon and Mrs Mackintosh, using prints, if Julia agreed, which Louise had lent them from the sitting room at Craigarran.

'I'm hopeful, Mrs Alcester, very hopeful,' the chief constable had ended, without giving any grounds for that hope.

Julia feared that at this stage David might make her appear in some joint televised display of anxiety and appeal for help. Over the years she had seen so many couples, egged on by the cameras, sobbing and stuttering their fears for their vanished children. As the days passed the appearances would be repeated on evening bulletins, the sobs louder, the fears greater, until the moment when the little body was found in a gravel pit or lay-by, then a final explosion of grief and anger by parents for whom, after a week or a fortnight, the exploiting cameras had become a way of life. Julia, by views a democrat, by nature patrician, would have none of those awful platitudes of grief.

The hopeless twentieth century had opened everything up and spilled it on the ground, but that century had gone. People were rediscovering boxes and containers in their own minds. The colleges and courses for counsellors were closing one by one. People were reinventing the brake between mind and tongue. They were coming back to the belief, so Julia thought, that most suffering is best borne in private.

But, to her surprise, David never mentioned the idea of a joint appearance, and firmly turned down all bids from the media. She knew, however, that this was not because he shared her disgust. She had heard him answer one particularly insistent editor: 'Wait, wait. You'll see, it'll be much better later.'

So David and Julia simply issued through the Press Association a third-person statement expressing confidence in the police and requesting privacy. This led to the arrival of an army of press and cameras, which camped in the narrow Pimlico street on which they lived.

There was absolutely nothing to do. David cancelled his engagements, including the Shadow Cabinet meeting he had announced at Nice airport. He spent much time on the telephone, but receiving calls rather than making them. 'Some of the colleagues are being troublesome,' was all he reported to Julia, though she read in the newspapers the whole awkward argument in the Conservative Party as it built up over the week. She gave her Filipina cleaning lady the shopping list, and Rosetta, with her carrier-bag, smiled her way silently through the cameramen each day. It had not rained in London for a fortnight, and Julia busied herself watering the tubs of blue and white agapanthus that were the pride of the roof garden above the flat. She read novels, watched tennis and athletics on television, listened to *The Archers* on radio and talked to her mother on the telephone. Louise and Peter, also besieged by the media, had decided to stay at Craigarran for the time being. When he was not telephoning, David spent most of his time reading and writing in his study. He and Julia met for brief meals and sat together watching television in the evenings. There was neither tension between them nor communication, except on trivial questions of food, drink or television programmes. They were both waiting for an event that would change everything, including their marriage, but for which they did not know how to prepare.

WAITING FOR SIMON

By Alice Thomson, in the *Daily Telegraph*

More than a baby was kidnapped last Monday. We all wait to hear news of David Alcester's little son, Simon. But to an extraordinary extent his fate is now tangled up with the future of the United Kingdom. Rarely if ever have a private tragedy and public policy been so closely connected. This connection is acutely embarrassing for politicians of all parties, and indeed for commentators like myself. But I do not think it is right any longer to avoid the subject just because of its unique awkwardness.

This awkwardness arises because of the way in which David Alcester reacted to the news of Simon's kidnapping. He at once, even before the news broke, drove to Nice airport and announced a new Conservative policy, namely independence for Scotland. He must have done this for purely private reasons, judging that Simon, like James Cameron, had been kidnapped by extreme Scottish Nationalists who would be likely to relent and release him after this announcement. What evidence the Leader of the Opposition had for this judgement none of us knows. There are rumours of earlier abortive discussions between Central Office and the Scottish Liberation Army, but nothing definite.

While David Alcester himself remains wholly and understandably silent, some of his friends are arguing that he has not changed Conservative policy, just advanced it a step along the road the Party was travelling anyway. The Party, it is argued, has found no response from the Government or the official Scottish National Party to their plea for a just balance inside the Union for the English majority, by which they mean less tax money for Scotland and fewer Scottish MPs at Westminster. That being so, they say, it is entirely logical for the Party leader to press for the abolition of a Union which is so manifestly unfair. But the Shadow Cabinet has still not been consulted and at least four of them, led by the Education spokesperson Sarah Tunstall, disagree in private with the leap forward their leader announced at Nice airport. In private only, for none of them is ready to say anything in public that might endanger the life of baby Simon. The two grandees of the party outside the Shadow Cabinet, Roger Courtauld and Peter Makewell, are in the same position, made more poignant for Peter Makewell because he is married to the baby's grandmother. The Prime Minister and the Cabinet worry themselves sick about the effect of all this on English opinion, but they, too, are tongue-tied. Once the baby is found, whether happily or tragically, these arguments will break out into the open. We are used to debate how far politics should invade personal privacy. This will be a debate the other way round. How far should private happenings be exploited for political purposes? But that debate has not yet been joined. The crowd, gathered day and night, outside the Alcesters' flat in Cambridge Street remains silent.

Mrs Mackintosh took the shuttle tourist bus down from Waverley Bridge to Leith. It was a dour day, the euro was high against the dollar, and the bus was almost empty except for a group of Australian tourists who took no notice of the quiet grey-haired Scottish woman with the baby in her lap. The conductor warned all his passengers in turn not to dally on the foreshore because the sale of visitors' tickets to the former Royal Yacht *Britannia* terminated at 4.30 p.m. precisely. 'They're wanting their tea, and they don't hang around.' Mrs Mackintosh knew this already from the reconnaissance that two SLA members had undertaken three days earlier. It was obviously important that she should be almost the last visitor on board that day. But it was also important that she should leave the *Britannia* in a group of others so that she was as inconspicuous as possible. The reconnaissance team had established that there was no difficulty in bringing the baby aboard, but there was a risk of someone noticing that the woman who had boarded the Royal Yacht with a baby disembarked without one.

Mrs Mackintosh worried that Simon would wake during

the video show in the visitor centre, which included some
loud loyal moments from the band of the Royal Marines, but
she had given him his bottle with a mild sedative in the bus
and he lay in her arms as good as gold. Mrs Mackintosh
approved the style of the state apartments on *Britannia*, spa-
cious and comfortable in a chintzy way, old-fashioned without
being grand. Rather Scottish, she thought; it reminded her of
Craigarran. Mrs Mackintosh had no difficulty in reconciling
her fierce nationalism with affection for the Royal Family,
which she regarded as essentially Scots.

The Queen's cabin was particularly charming. She knew
that because of a glass partition she would not be able to leave
Simon and his bottle actually on the Queen's bed as had originally been intended. But there was a comfortable sofa nearby
in the equerries' sitting room. She imagined the courtiers
gathering there in the old days, ladies-in-waiting sipping a
cup of tea with a scone or slice of fruit cake, the equerries
poised for an early dram. Simon did not stir in these august
surroundings and she left him sound asleep on the sofa, a
second bottle ready prepared by his side, this one without the
sedative.

Mrs Mackintosh tagged on to a group of Scots ladies not
unlike herself and went down the gangway with them. The
car waiting for her beside the new Ocean Terminal was a different car with a different driver. The SLA liked knowledge to
be spread as thinly as possible. For a minute, unusually, Mrs
Mackintosh thought about the country for which she had just
taken such great personal risk. Around her she was vaguely
aware of a contrast with her own spotless cottage back in
Pitlochry. It being Saturday afternoon all the bleak little shops
of Leith were closed, with a smug 'I could have told you so'

expression on their shutters, except for a couple of news-
agents with Pakistanis standing in the entrance. The Ocean
Terminal was new and magnificent, but behind it Leith had
not renounced the ancient blight of paper bags blowing down
each street and litter everywhere. Willowherb and thistle, the
national emblem, flourished untidily where decades ago the
council had pulled down the traditional stone terraces but so
far built nothing. At present they were busy taking down the
street names and replacing them with new signs in Gaelic as
well as English. The man drove her fast into the centre of
Edinburgh, then out on the Glasgow road. Precisely ten minutes away from Leith she telephoned to report that everything
had gone to plan. The SLA official then made the calls to the
Lothian police and the BBC, which had been planned as the
culminating point of the operation.

Though they had talked of little during the awful cloistered
days of waiting in Cambridge Street, David Alcester had tried
to convince his wife of one thing, namely that the news of
Simon, good or bad, would reach them from the police or the
Scottish Executive rather than from the media. This assur-
ance proved accurate by a margin of about two minutes. That
Friday the seven o'clock morning bulletin led with the news
that Simon was safe in Leith police station, taking his bottle.
David was still on the telephone to the Lothian chief constable. He had given Julia a quick kiss when he passed on the
immediate message, but his priorities were elsewhere.

   'We are very grateful, Chief Constable. I will call Lady
Makewell at once. She will be with you within a couple of
hours. Can you guide her in from the southern exit of the
Forth Bridge? She may not know the exact geography and

every minute counts. Where exactly is the First Minister's
helicopter? . . . I really don't think you need confirm avail-
ability, I checked with him myself yesterday that it would be
available for my mother-in-law if necessary . . . Yes, I'll warn
the Battersea heliport. Please make sure the pilot communi-
cates with them direct before take-off . . . I'm sure you
understand we want no photographs, no interviews with any
of your officers, nothing whatever until my son is safe back
here. You'll understand our concern for privacy. My wife is
particularly insistent on that . . .' and then, quickly following
a call to Clive Wilson, 'Yes, indeed, excellent news. Your press
man should make it clear we are not making any statement or
giving any interviews until Simon is back under this roof.
Then, of course, plenty. Who's your best man now in the press
department? . . . Not him, he's hopeless. Who else? . . . Don't
know her but if she's good send her round at once, and I'll
brief her. She'll have to keep them in order and organise a
queue. But first we'll have a balcony photograph. It's a small
balcony, but it'll just take the four of us – parents, grandmother, Simon . . . Didn't I tell you? Louise is bringing the
baby down. A good touch that, I thought . . .'

Julia realised with a shock that David had been preparing
for this moment ever since they had got back from France. A
thorough detailed plan had been concocted in his study,
including her own mother, and all of this without consulting
her. She had been brooding all these hours about danger,
death, private bereavement while he had been rehearsing
safety, success, public rejoicing. Perhaps it was as well that
they had hardly conversed. She lay back on her pillow and
watched her husband as he made call after call. Enthusiasm
seemed to have knocked ten years off him. Lately he had

turned sallow. Lines now ran up diagonally inwards from the corners of his mouth, and a vein stood out on his neck. But for these moments, as David leaned forward, slightly flushed with excitement, cuddling the telephone as if it was his child, pyjama jacket open to the waist, lock of fair hair falling over his forehead, he seemed no older than the young man who had held her eye at the memorial service for her father in Westminster Abbey so long ago.

'Finished?' she asked, in a pause between conversations. She touched his forearm, but tentatively so that she need not feel rebuffed if nothing followed.

Nothing followed. David was back in the whirlwind of political planning and execution, which alone of all human activities he enjoyed wholeheartedly.

It was late afternoon before Louise and Simon arrived at Cambridge Street. The outriders who preceded the police car in which they travelled needed the help of a dozen constables on the ground to clear a path down the crowded street. The television companies had had time to build a stand of stepped benches on the opposite pavement, despite the protest of the residents who were thus virtually imprisoned in their homes. The cameras of a dozen nations swung this way and that as commentators set the scene, over and over again, searching for fresh phrases as bulletin succeeded bulletin. They were the warm-up act for the latest drama to capture the hearts of the world. While Julia was not looking the man from Conservative Central Office had removed three large terracotta pots of geraniums from the tiny balcony of the Alcester flat and swept it carefully. The spectators greeted him with the applause, half sardonic half affectionate, with which a waiting British crowd traditionally greets the mundane preparations for a royal ceremony. This crowd, growing fast and spilling round the corner into neighbouring streets, was made up partly of local residents and casual tourists, but increasingly of youths and girls wearing the New England T-shirt and carrying New England banners. When one of them, a handsome young Amazon, began to sing 'I Vow To Thee My Country' the response was at first ragged, then hearty. Most of the residents joined in; the tourists remained baffled.

The arrival of Louise in the police car was greeted with a huge cheer. The camera crews shouted to her to look this way and that and above all to hold up the baby. She hesitated on the doorstep, turned and gave a half-wave, then hurried in as the door opened.

'You'd have thought she'd have learned the trade by now,' said one disgusted commentator. 'She was a prime minister's wife twice, for God's sake.'

'She's had a rough week,' said his companion.

'No excuse . . .' then into the mike, 'And so, fighting back her tears, Louise Makewell, Simon's granny, takes Simon into the house for the reunion that means so much to them all. We can only imagine . . .'

Louise found herself manoeuvred expertly into the lift, then upstairs and into the small dining room, which had been converted into a campaign office. Julia gave her a long hug, and took Simon from her. They had managed to talk without David's participation on Louise's mobile while she and Simon were still at the police headquarters in Edinburgh, so there was no need for long explanations. This was just as well, for David was not losing a moment. A police officer, a doctor and two 'public relations' men were already seated at the dining-room table. He kissed Louise, kissed his son in Julia's arms, and spoke to both women as to a company board meeting. 'Louise,' he said, 'it's marvellous to see you. Julia and I owe you more than we can say.' A pause, as if for Julia to say, 'Hear, hear,' but she did not oblige. 'The first thing is the medical check-up, and here is Dr Saunders, whom Carlton Television have kindly sent round. I gather this need only take a couple of minutes.'

'The police doctor looked at Simon at the police station in Edinburgh,' said Louise. 'He's fine.' And indeed he looked entirely composed, indeed half-asleep as he made history.

'That's good, really good. But we shall certainly be asked about him ourselves and we need to have our own answer. Anyway, this small delay will give time for New England to pack the street tight full. Dr Saunders, Julia, if you don't mind . . .' The doctor and Julia left the room.

David resumed, talking fast to Louise. 'A glass of wine, or something soft? You must be exhausted . . . I've run through the procedure with Julia already. Sandy here has worked out a schedule, but it changes all the time as fresh media bids come in, so we must be flexible at every stage. First, of course, the balcony appearance. There's just room for the three of us. No need for you to say anything, Louise, and perhaps better not to answer any questions that may be shouted up from the street. Just smile. Julia will hold Simon. A couple of minutes will do initially, though we might need to go out again later. The stand they've constructed won't be big enough for all the camera teams we expect, so almost certainly there will be a second shift. After that, the interviews. Twelve arranged so far. They'll certainly want to see you alone, Louise, almost all of them I expect, but don't worry about that. We've sketched out something quite straightforward and factual . . .'

Louise, up to now bewildered and off balance, sipped a glass of Chablis and felt strength return. 'I'll go out on the balcony if you insist, David. Once only. But that's all. No interviews.'

David misunderstood. 'Don't worry, Louise. Of course you're concerned they'll ask about what happened at Craigarran. We'll head them off that before you see them. If they do slip in a question about Craigarran, Mrs Mackintosh and all that, you simply say all this is being investigated by the police and you've been advised to say nothing.'

'No, David.' Louise paused to sip again. 'I've brought little Simon back. I'm glad to do so, particularly as he was stolen when in my care. I want to talk through all that with Julia and yourself. But I didn't come here to take part in a political campaign.'

'There's nothing political.' For the first time David sat down. Louise could see that he was controlling a huge, stressful, pleasurable excitement. 'There's just great natural interest. Saturday evening's not ideal for the TV, but the football season hasn't started, and the test match is heading for a draw. The BBC have thought up something particular for you. Apparently there are three other ladies whose grandchildren are missing at the moment and they thought you might join a link-up and say something comforting to each of them. I told them to withdraw Joanna Letford's grandmother – she was the girl whose naked body was found yesterday on Romney Marsh – though I gather she was quite willing to take part with you. Perhaps not in the best of taste . . .'

'I think you must be quite mad,' said Louise, backing out of the room.

Somehow they got out on to the balcony, once, David leading the way. There was a great roar of greeting and approval from the street. As it died away the clicking of cameras continued, holding David in his place. 'That's enough.' Julia pulled at his sleeve. She had managed to keep a smile going, despite the fearful family argument that this appearance interrupted. Simon, reacting late to the quarrelling of adults, which he had just witnessed indoors, began to cry. Louise had no expression on her face at all – 'Evidently too deeply moved for any ordinary display of emotion' wrote the *Daily Telegraph* loyally the next day.

'Again, in a couple of minutes,' said David, still enthused.

'No,' said Louise. 'I'm going to lie down and rest in the spare room. As soon as this lunatic crowd has gone away I shall leave.'

David could see that she would not be persuaded. He turned to Julia. Unlike Louise, she and Simon were essential participants in his day – and, since this was a critical day for him, in his future.

'Your mother's tired,' he said. 'You and I will go out on the balcony for just another two minutes. It would be a mistake to overdo it. Then,' consulting the list in his hand, 'we have four joint TV interviews planned, five if we decide to do the Irish RTE, then I have three separate, and you two separate. We can do them all in the dining room. Sandy, the Central Office girl, will produce them in the right order. I'd thought we could use the spare room as a waiting room, but as it is . . .'

He had made the mistake of pressing on with these arrangements before Louise had left the room.

'Julia,' she said, 'I have one other thing to say to you before you go any further with this rigmarole.'

'There's no time for any more argument,' said David, pulling at Julia's elbow. They could hear the New Englanders outside shouting 'We want Simon.' But emotional exhaustion had robbed Julia of her usual decisiveness. Simon was quiet again in her arms. Her overwhelming concern was that he should remain there. Strong-minded husband and strong-minded mother were battling way above her head. She sat down on a hard chair.

'I believe,' said Louise to Julia, sparing her words to give them weight, 'that your husband David organised the whole thing.'

'Of course,' said David. 'Someone had to grip the arrangements once they let Simon go.'

'I don't mean just that. I mean the whole thing, kidnap and all. It is giving you publicity such as you have dreamed of. It is putting you on the path to win the next election. For this man here your son's safety, your own happiness are nothing in the scale compared to that.'

Julia was not taking this in. David gazed at his mother-in-law in amazement. 'Now, it's you who are mad. What possible evidence have you?'

'You and that louse Clive Wilson were in touch with the SLA weeks ago through some intermediary. The Scottish police know that, though they don't know what passed. Well, I could tell them. You were planning the whole thing together – kidnap, change of Tory policy, Simon's release, publicity. You and the SLA are the only ones who benefit from it all. You had the motive, you had the means, and you have no scruples to hold you back.'

David now took it all in. He had to move quickly and decisively.

'There is no proof, and it is nonsense,' he said to his wife, standing over her chair. He thought of putting his arm around her shoulders, but refrained. 'I swear to you solemnly that I had no hand in planning Simon's kidnap. It was as much of a shock and horror to me as to you. You could see that for yourself at Cannes.'

As he spoke Julia was already remembering Cannes, trying to sort out the jostling crowd of her memories, testing Louise's accusation against what she remembered of David's reaction to the kidnap.

'Time to go out.' Once again David mistimed his move. If he had ignored the growing invitation from the crowd and waited for two or three minutes, Julia's mind might have swung the other way.

There was a pause.

'No,' Julia said. 'Sorry, but no.'

The 'sorry' made the 'no' sound considered and final.

'You're letting me down,' said David, because he could not help it. Julia said nothing, but sat cradling Simon in her arms.

David thought of snatching the baby, but that would not work. He went out on to the balcony alone. Quickly there was a hush.

'You will understand that Julia and Simon are both very tired . . .'

Chapter 8

The Chairman of the Party stood up and clapped as soon as David Alcester, folder under his arm, entered the big room next to his own office in the House of Commons where the Shadow Cabinet met each week. It was a mistaken gesture. All the other colleagues felt bound to rise and do the same. David Alcester had not proposed this piece of theatre, but he knew that many of them would think that he had. Feigned loyalty had been one of the vices of the modern Tory Party, and David had no intention of being destroyed by it.

By contrast he had arranged what happened next. Lord Downbrook spoke. 'David, we are none of us clear as to why you have called this special meeting, though we can guess. But before you open the business, I would just like to say how greatly we welcome the news of your baby son's release. This was an atrocious crime, we have all felt that. We have shared with you and Mrs Alcester – Julia, if I may so presume – a small part of the anxiety with which you have lived during this last week. We can well imagine how drained and exhausted Julia and her mother must feel, indeed how you yourself must feel. Please convey to her our warm sympathy and congratulations – and all good wishes to the little lad.'

It was pleasantly done, and this time the murmur of support was genuine. Lord Downbrook had sat in every Cabinet and Shadow Cabinet for many years. Simon Russell had put him in charge of the annual public-spending review at a critical moment. He was not a well-known figure, and contributed little to discussion. Equally there was no harm in him, and when he became leader David Alcester had kept on the elderly peer in the Shadow Cabinet for the time being, until he decided which of his own intimates he wanted to promote. There were occasions like this when something empty had to be said in the right way. Lord Downbrook had been made a life peer at the time of the Blair reforms, but had earlier sat by right of inheritance. One of the things he had inherited was the right touch for such occasions from a long line of Whig ancestors – a touch that someone like Clive Wilson would never develop, however hard he tried.

'Thank you, thank you. Yes, Julia is exhausted, but Simon is fine. She'll be delighted to get your message.'

In fact the Sunday press had been pretty good. Even the Mondays, though they had had the whole of Sunday to sniff around, had not caught any hint of the flaming domestic row in Cambridge Street on Saturday night. Louise had said nothing to the few reporters still lingering at the time the taxi she had ordered came to take her away to King's Cross and Scotland. His improvisation from the balcony about exhaustion had played brilliantly, though he was conscious that the time gained was short. He had only two or three days to bring Julia round before her silence became noticeable. David

Alcester was free with lies when they served his purpose, but he found it monstrously unjust and wicked that when he told the truth, as he had to Julia, he should not be believed.

But the immediate problem before him was political. It had to be solved at this meeting. He was vexed that Alice Thomson, and following her, other commentators, had expounded the problem so clearly in public. His only hope, he had decided, was to ride the Shadow Cabinet with a high hand, but he began with an apology.

'In a way it is because of what happened to my family last week that I have called this special meeting at short notice. Indeed, I had meant to hold it last week, but you will understand the uncertainties through which I was living each day. I wanted to apologise to you all for doing something in extraordinary circumstances that I would normally have scrupulously avoided. At Nice airport I announced a significant development of Conservative policy, namely our support for Scottish independence, in advance of a decision by Shadow Cabinet. I apologise unreservedly for this. I hope you will agree that this development of policy had become inevitable. I had intended to bring it to you before the recess. Only the timing was in question. Ever since I became Leader we have told the government that the Union with Scotland as at present constituted was intolerably unfair to the English majority as regards revenue sharing, as regards representation at Westminster and in other ways. The government has refused to act. What I have long described as an unacceptable situation, namely the dominance of a Scottish minority over our affairs in the United Kingdom, has continued. In these circumstances the logical next step for us is to encourage the Scots to go their own way. Separation has become, unfortunately, the only cure for an unjust union. That, indeed, is the only basis on which I could continue as Leader. It is hard for a Unionist Party to be forced to this conclusion, but we have always fared best when we faced uncomfortable facts fairly and squarely.'

There were many holes in this argument, and no mention of its connection with the kidnap. David was keen to hang on and smother the meeting with detailed proposals, but he allowed a pause lasting about three seconds for an objection of principle, and even dared to look round the table. He was anxious that they should not be able to argue afterwards that they had been bounced. When he saw Sarah Tunstall staring at the shiny oak table in front of her he knew that he had won. She looked deeply unhappy but showed no sign of wanting to speak. He thanked God that it was not as it had been in the old days. Neither Peter Makewell, nor Roger Courtauld, let alone Joan Freetown or Simon Russell, would have accepted this sleight-of-hand for an instant. His colleagues were genuinely irritated by the Scots, and tempted by the glistening prospect of Tory dominance in a country without them. They were inhibited by the noisiness of New England, a body over which they had no control. They were embarrassed by the kidnap. They would all have noted the blackmail in what he had just said about his own future. It would be deeply damaging, indeed unthinkable, to promote another leadership crisis so soon after David had replaced Peter Makewell. All these thoughts were in their minds, as he had intended. He despised the lack of spunk among his colleagues which was giving him such an easy victory.

'I wonder if you have consulted any of the senior members of the Party on this? I am thinking of Peter Makewell and

Roger Courtauld in particular.' Lord Downbrook spoke mildly. He was not putting the point to oppose or even delay the change of policy. But the men he named were some of those who had guided his own views over many years and it seemed odd that they were no longer in conclave with the rest.

Indeed, it was a better point than he knew, because the media would certainly ask those two at an early stage for their comments. David intended to speak to both of them, but only after he was armed with a Shadow Cabinet decision. 'An excellent point,' he replied. 'Their support will be very valuable. But I think we need to take our own responsibilities first.'

Lord Downbrook always relished mention of 'responsibilities'. He nodded sagely.

'Now, as to implementation. As I see it, there are three separate stages after we announce this evening our endorsement of the new policy. First, we need to explain and proclaim it by every means on all possible occasions. It should take priority over all other issues. I shall lead this campaign. Its climax will be a motion and debate at the Party Conference in October. Incidentally, the Scottish Conservatives will still be invited to Bournemouth, but on the same basis as other like-minded sister parties, such as the German CDU and the French RPR. Second, shortly after that when the House gets back, we will table an amendment to the Queen's Speech regretting the absence from the government's programme of a Scotland Independence Bill. Arguably one of us should table such a Bill ourselves, but we need to examine the most promising parliamentary procedure. Third, in parallel with these orthodox political initiatives, we should launch an imaginative public campaign designed to stir up opinion on our side. The polls are already in our favour. But that's not enough. Public opinion has to be made furious. Its anger has not yet been brought to bear on the media and on Parliament, for example the Liberal Democrat MPs. To put it bluntly, we want to scare all such into supporting us. That campaign will be the responsibility of New England under my direction. They will remain within the law, but otherwise will use all their drive and energy in bringing the question to the boil during the holiday months. I want it to be a long hot summer, plenty of noisy fun. I give you some examples. New England will launch a boycott of Scottish-owned banks in England, in particular NatWest. They will deal with offensive monuments, for example the plaque to William Wallace in Smithfield Market. They will name and shame all government bodies operating in England which have more than one-fifth of their members who live or were born in Scotland, encouraging surplus Scots to resign, beginning, of course, with the Cabinet. They'll discourage English clubs from taking on Scottish footballers. They will keep up the campaign against the flying in England and Wales of St Andrew's cross or the red lion except on Scottish official buildings. Sympathetic local authorities will set up voluntary registers in each borough and county so that residents bearing Scottish names can make it clear that they regard themselves as English. This will prepare the ground for the nationality legislation, which we will need to introduce once Scotland is independent. These are just some of the ideas coming forward, but there are certainly others . . . Yes, Sarah.'

Sarah Tunstall spoke in the truculent voice of someone half ashamed of herself. 'In the *Mail* today they speak of a

possible boycott of Scottish produce – oatcakes, even whisky.
I doubt . . .'

'Of course you are right, Sarah.' David spoke with affection,
delighted that the silly woman had come in on a secondary
point. 'It wouldn't work – and, anyway, it's not in line with our
philosophy. We want Scotland to prosper, to sell us oatcakes
and whisky. Those of you who like them will be able to go
north and toss the caber and play the bagpipes. We'll propose
them for membership of the EU. NATO too, though they
may not want it. The UN certainly. What we don't want is
Scots domineering here in England, owning our banks, running the unions. Our natural allies now are the Scottish
Nationalists – not the puny Scotnats lot now sitting in the
executive in Leith, co-operating with Labour at every turn,
but the true Nationalists out in the streets campaigning for
independence now.'

'But not the kidnappers, presumably,' said Sarah.

It was an awkward remark, made too late. David hesitated,
but only for a second. 'Not, of course, the kidnappers. As I
said, everything must be within the law.'

Sitting in his deck-chair watching the polo Roger Courtauld
reviewed his life. It was a habit growing on him, perhaps
because he found the balance between regret and satisfaction
hard to strike. He had inherited a little money, put by a little
more during his years at the Bar, married more again, learned
as a politician to live within his means and was now coasting
quite comfortably into old age. By contrast his son, young
Roger, liked to contemplate a wide range of pleasures without
having to think how they might be paid for. Of these pleasures
polo was the latest and most expensive. Up to now Roger had

borrowed ponies from friends and a godfather. If he was to continue with the sport he would soon have to buy one, perhaps two.

From his chair Roger could just see Manston in the valley below him. It was not a big house, in fact three small cottages knocked together, but distinguishable by its thatched roof in a land of stone, and by its position on the bank of the Axwell. Odd that a slim thread of water could have cut such a wide valley through the heart of England. The polo field had been created on a ridge separating the sweep of the Cotswolds to the south from the softer more flexible Midlands to the north and east. Because the flat ground on the summit was a little narrower than the necessary measurement of the field, riders and ponies as viewed by the spectators would, from time to time, suddenly lose their legs, and continue the game with heads and legless bodies outlined against the woods and pastures of Northamptonshire verging towards the distant smudge of Birmingham. Then legs would be miraculously restored as the two teams returned up the incline and manoeuvred towards a goal mouth.

Today the silhouettes were solid and hard against a particularly hazy background. For a fortnight the sun had ruled England, providing the hottest and driest summer since 2005. The fields were parched and yellow. There had even been a question, quickly dismissed by eager competitors, as to whether the ground was too hard that day for the game to be safe. But the sun's reign was crumbling. Blunt, massive clouds, interleaved in a different shade of grey with touches of yellow, were accumulating and gradually thrashing forward from the west. Roger had already heard one distant rumble of dry thunder.

On the whole sitting in his chair, feeling a little younger than his sixty-seven years, Roger struck the balance in favour of contentment. It was six years since his disastrous leadership campaign, two years since separation from his wife Hélène. These events had built confining banks through which his life flowed more narrowly than before. More narrowly, and yet also more sluggishly, for the volume of his energy had lessened. His two non-executive directorships in London and a third in Bristol took up four or five days a month and kept him mildly in touch with the world of business. He chaired the governing body of a local school for those with learning difficulties, the fund-raising committee for the fabric of the cathedral, and the local branch of a national cancer charity. And he was still, of course, the Member of Parliament for South Northamptonshire. It was fashionable, indeed had been fashionable throughout his political career, to write about the formidable pressures of an MP's life. Roger, on the backbenches, had been surprised to find how easy it was, provided you knew your towns and villages, employed a good secretary and research assistant, and had said goodbye to political ambition. Faced with a Labour majority of over eighty in the Commons, the whips did not bother him much about voting. Every now and then the BBC or someone else invited him as a former Home Secretary to give an interview on some asylum case or prison escape; he almost always refused. Politics had lost its savour for Roger; he had never developed an appetite for finance or commerce; Hélène's decision to leave him had removed the attractions, never great, of social coming and going. A staid part-time housekeeper made his bed and cooked his supper. John, the pensioner down the road, mowed the lawn. What was left were books, a few friends, his interest in his children, the prospect of a week's fishing with old Peter Makewell in Scotland, the choice of wine for today's picnic, the decision whether his lavender hedge at Manston, now in full bloom, had grown too scraggy and needed replanting.

In a pause between young Roger's chukkas his father began to snooze. The sun shone hotter than ever, through a thickening haze.

'Sorry to interrupt, Sir Roger, but . . .'

He recognised the voice of the man who had been broadcasting an often inaccurate commentary on each chukka from the committee hut in the centre of the ridge, just his side of the ice-cream van. A somewhat patronising voice – what was the name? Martin Venables – but a good man. Venables ran the whole event almost single-handed, using the respect that he had earned locally fifteen years back by leading the Pytchley hunt down Whitehall at the height of the campaign to save fox-hunting.

Roger opened his eyes properly and found that Venables, having left the commentary in charge of a deputy, stood at his side. 'Weather's going to break.'

'We need the rain.'

'That's certain. I'll have to cancel the cross-country next week unless the ground softens.'

'Looks like thunder.'

'Might be rough on the partridges if it comes too hard. Chicks at their weakest just now.'

Roger's wife, being French, had often complained that in rural England this kind of conversation could go on for ever. Nothing so far explained why Martin Venables had deserted the commentary box to interrupt Roger's snooze. Roger decided on silence, and this unlocked the mystery.

'What do you make of young Alcester?' asked Venables.

Still baffled, Roger prepared to creak into his usual ambiguities about the leader of the Conservative Party. 'Plenty of good material there. Of course I don't know him well, just—'

'Have you seen the paper today?'

By 'paper' Martin would have meant the *Daily Telegraph*, or less probably the *Mail*.

'Not yet.' Roger felt no guilt. The *Telegraph* lay, still folded and unread, at the bottom of the canvas bag that had held their picnic baps and the bottle of Gewürztraminer. It had seemed more important to listen to young Roger talk about his ponies and their rivals than to read what had happened in the world yesterday.

'Alcester made a big speech. In Carlisle, I think. Somewhere in the north, anyway. Waving his arms at the Scots. Threatening to throw them out. And against Europe, too, of course. Thousands turned up. Arrests, mounted police, people knocked down. It was even worse on TV than in the paper.'

'Nothing new in any of that.'

Venables stood awkwardly in front of Roger's chair leaning on a stick. He was ill at ease except when handling horses and the affairs of horses.

'Have a glass of wine. Alsace. Plastic, I'm afraid, but it's still cold,' offered Roger.

'No, I must go back to the box. I just wanted to say—'

'There's nothing new about this. Alcester has been banging away against the Scots for many months now.'

'I know. Look.' Martin jabbed at the turf with his stick. 'Up to a point I'm with him. It's wrong that the Scots should

march all over us. I'm English to the bone. But he's stirring
things too far. The pot's beginning to boil. Too much noise, no
respect for the law. Pulling down that plaque in Smithfield for
example, the one to Whatsisname, Wallace – torn off the
hospital wall by a mob. It's not a proper way of doing things.
Not in this country, anyway. It's different abroad.'

Wearily Roger Courtauld turned his full mind back to politics. 'I agree, the young man goes too far. Always has, always
will. But he's got a case. Years ago, when William Hague ran
the Party, he had a sound plan for making sure that English
MPs could not be overruled on English matters. I looked it up
the other day. If only that had been carried through. Hague
proposed . . .'

But Roger had made the mistake of supposing that laymen
who protested about politics were interested in policies.
Martin Venables cut in. 'I don't know about the details.
Several of us talked over dinner last night. At the Lord
Lieutenant's actually, though of course he's non-political and
he kept quiet. We all thought that as our MP you ought to put
a stop to the Tory Party running amok like this. Many of us
have voted Conservative all our lives. We've put up with a lot
of nonsense from the leaders we voted for. But there's a limit
and Alcester has passed it.'

This, from Venables, was quite tough talk.

'You forget that I'm way back on the backbenches. No one's
going to take any interest in my meanderings.'

'I beg to differ. That's not so. Everyone knows you,
respects you. You've been quiet for a year or two. All the
more reason why people should listen if you found your
voice.' Venables paused, then ended abruptly. 'Sorry to break
into your afternoon. Wouldn't have done it if we hadn't

thought it important. Think about it, will you?' Another
pause. 'You owe it to us.'

That was nonsense, of course. He had worked hard,
deserved a rest, owed none of them anything. Roger settled
back into his chair, and tried to drive politics back into its
cage. But after a minute he delved into the blue canvas bag for
the *Telegraph*. David Alcester appeared in colour on the front
page, his fair hair somewhat dishevelled. He was behind a
cannon, a heap of cannon balls beside him. His youthful face
shone with excitement as he shouted against the Scots. He
was not in Carlisle, Venables had got that wrong, but Alnwick
in Northumberland, the ancient castle of the Percys, often
through the years besieged by successful Scots. Having served
as prison house and execution place for unsuccessful Scots, it
was civilised into Victorian Gothic, and yesterday had been
the scene of a huge Conservative rally.

'We have been patient, we English. I should say too patient.
We accepted a Scots Parliament. We accepted Scots equality.
We cannot accept Scots superiority. Five million cannot rule
over forty-six million. We suggested a fair solution at Westminster; that was rejected. Then we suggested an English
Parliament; that was refused. We have waited – and watched
our money and our power over ourselves, our life blood flow
north to Scotland, east to Brussels. But, my friends, enough is
enough. We have lost enough blood. On these historic
English battlements . . .'

And so on. The beer had flowed as copiously as the elo-
quence, the police had tried to prevent the burning of St
Andrew's cross, there had been scuffles, a dozen arrests, a leg
broken in a fall. It could all be looked at as a lighthearted frolic.
No need to take it as seriously as Martin Venables had done.

Anyway, it was not as if he, Roger Courtauld, could do much about it. True, in Northamptonshire they nodded at him in the street, asked him to plant trees and lay foundation stones. Walking down village streets at the last election he had begun to feel like a moving monument rather than an active politician. People had been glad to see him in their neighbourhood. Children had run giggling out of doors to touch his sleeve, their parents had talked to him briefly about their lives, the local golf tournament, about the weather, about everything, indeed, except politics. But no one recognised him nowadays in the streets of London or in other places where it mattered. People stared for a few seconds, then questioned one another as to whether sometime somewhere they might have seen him on television. There was no fuel to launch him as saviour of the nation or the Party. To suppose otherwise would be a futile pretence. Nor would he wish it otherwise. At sixty-seven he might live for another fifteen or twenty years. He knew how he wanted to handle these years, through the gradual and contented narrowing of horizons. If Hélène and he had remained together, this narrowing would have been more difficult since she had enjoyed Covent Garden, Ascot, political dinner parties, and even (though she pretended not) the Party Conference each October. He had been deeply sad when she left him. But the sadness was now lifting, and he was skilled in matching his energy each day to the small items of contentment which it might bring.

Young Roger's polo, for example. His team was now in the field, wearing the claret and blue of their pony club. Young Roger, large with a pink outdoor face, looked better on a pony than on two legs. At sixteen he possessed independent limbs rather than a single co-ordinated body. He showed no outward affection or gratitude to his father, but took the latter's kindness calmly for granted. Perhaps that was a genuine proof of intimacy.

Roger had taken the boy to *Antony and Cleopatra* at Stratford-on-Avon a week ago, just twenty minutes drive from Manston. Young Roger had been won over by the first half of the play, but his father had forgotten how long it took Antony and then Cleopatra to die. The unmatchable lines and half-lines floated over young Roger's head as he dozed; that afternoon's polo practice had been particularly strenuous.

Young Roger's team, the Pytchley, were now pressing hard. Just before lunch they had drawn one goal each against the Cottesmore; the deadlock now had to be broken. Anxious to make quick progress Venables, despite some mutterings from traditional colleagues, had decreed an Argentine run-down, a device that did not appear in the rules of the game. The first team to score a goal would win the match and, for this occasion only, the whole of each backline constituted the goal mouth. Both teams half disappeared down the slope at the far edge of the field. Young Roger reappeared in control of the ball, raising dust as he galloped. He wheeled to face the enemy's back line, hesitated, missed the ball.

Roger, though ignorant of the finer points of the game, enjoyed its sudden reversals of fortune, quicker even than politics. Long moments of static turning and thrusting in a confused mêlée without pattern or advantage to either side would suddenly resolve into a breakthrough. This match ended in smiles for the right side. The umpire gave a penalty against the Cottesmore, which young Roger took, and scored.

The hunting horn sounded the end of the chukka. Young Roger disengaged and rode up to his father.

'Well done, boy. That was dramatic.'

'Not too bad, I suppose. She's still pulling to the right.'

Their conversation rarely went deeper than this. Young Roger disappeared to unsaddle and sluice down his pony. Next year, no doubt, when he was heavier, he would need a second mount. Roger hired a groom to advise, to supervise the tack and drive the trailer, but insisted that young Roger do the main work of preparing and cleaning up after each mount. Roger did not wait for this, but drove his own Rover out towards the exit gate. The first heavy raindrops flopped against the windscreen, mixing with the dust of two weeks to create a few seconds of blurred vision. As the wipers washed the glass clear Roger saw Martin Venables wave him down. He had no wish to renew their discussion, but he could hardly ignore the outstretched hand. He braked, lowered the side window, took the initiative. 'Well done. A good day.'

'Thanks. That lad of yours is riding well. But did you get your letter?'

'Letter?'

'It was something urgent from Manston. Your gardener brought it up on his motorbike, looking for you. He saw young Roger first, gave it to him. I suppose the idle young sod forgot.'

Roger turned and found his son who, with a muttered apology, produced the envelope from the back pocket of his breeches. It was bent now and heavily smudged with sweat but the words 'Urgent' on the front and the red government crest on the back stood out. Inside was a regular Government Hospitality card.

The Prime Minister
requests the pleasure of the company
of
The Rt Hon. Sir Roger Courtauld, MP
at dinner
in honour of
His Excellency Mr Adi Husseni
Prime Minister of the Hashemite Kingdom of Jordan
at Chequers
on Thursday, 31st July

7.30 for 8 pm
Black Tie

Rather odd. True, Roger had once been involved with Jordan, in the days before he became Home Secretary when he was casting around as a backbencher for subjects of interest. He had visited the country twice and joined the Anglo-Jordanian Friendship Society. But that had been a long time ago. There was no reason why old Turnbull should ask him to Chequers to meet the visiting Prime Minister of Jordan, and certainly no reason why he should go to a dull official occasion in the middle of the polo season.

The stiff card did not slide easily back into its envelope. It had come up against a half sheet of notepaper. Roger recognised the Prime Minister's own hand: 'Please come if you can. It would be good to have a talk. Politics are in a dangerous state. I may need your help. I would count it as a favour if you would stay the night.'

Cryptic, but enough to draw Roger back into the world he thought he had left for good.

*

The Prime Minister of Jordan was an ideal guest for this occasion. Having passed out from Sandhurst thirty years earlier he knew the rudiments of an English official dinner. Under King Hussein, his grandfather had moved up the social scale from the merchant to the military, tendering stalwart service to the King when he led a battalion against Arafat's guerrillas up and down the hills of Amman in the autumn of 1970. Both his father and his uncle had served the Hashemites briefly as Prime Minister, a role into which he himself had slipped gracefully when the call came.

For an hour before dinner he had sat with his British counterpart John Turnbull in the study at Chequers, each of them with a private secretary scribbling at his elbow. The agenda was not exciting. The Jordanians were in the market for tanks again, but the credit being offered by the British export authorities struck them as mean. Without entering into detail (it was, after all, two generations since his family had bargained in public) the Prime Minister wished to make clear that they hoped for better. He needed EU support in a long-running argument with Israel over the costs of replenishing the Dead Sea, now so diminished and over-salted that the tourists were staying away. But none of these were testing matters. If the Jordanian really wanted to ask about the disturbed state of Britain, the flag-waving riots in the streets, the extraordinary virulence of the Conservative Opposition, he was far too polite to do so.

After the business talks, the two men joined the guests for dinner. The commandant of Sandhurst of course, a distinguished lady novelist, a bank chairman, a trade-union leader, a couple of Labour backbenchers, all in black tie – in this as in other matters John Turnbull followed traditional ways, the

Labour version, but without any hint of the raffish media-driven innovations of the Blair era. A large photograph of Clement Attlee, the Prime Minister Turnbull most admired, stood on the grand piano of the Great Hall, to which they adjourned for coffee. The Jordanian was not surprised to find two Conservative grandees at the table, Roger Courtauld and Peter Makewell, though he would have been more interested to meet David Alcester, whose name was in every headline. The Leader of the Opposition had refused his request for a meeting on the grounds of pressing work elsewhere. The Jordanian took a malt whisky with his coffee, more as a cultural statement than because he wanted to linger. By eleven o'clock he and the other guests had departed, except for Makewell and Courtauld. With a word of appreciation to Mrs Turnbull, they and the Prime Minister adjourned to the study and sat easily in the big armchairs before the log fire. For all three this was politics as they liked it. The Prime Minister lit a pipe. He believed in silence as a political tactic, but this evening he had to lead off.

'Thanks for staying,' he said. After a pause, 'Your party's leading us a fearful dance.' Another pause. He fished a folded piece of paper from his coat pocket. 'These will be tomorrow's headlines. A riot in York. Forty arrested. Scottish bus hijacked in the middle of Newcastle. SLA march through Perth; police use tear gas. The official Edinburgh Festival cancelled. The fringe festival may descend into anarchy, say organisers. Alcester at Nottingham calls for Parliament to sit into August to pass Tory Independence Bill. A load of nonsense, of course. All of it.' He puffed. 'But it's getting out of hand.'

'I don't think either of us has any control over Alcester,' said Roger.

'Nor influence,' added Peter Makewell.

'He's your son-in-law.' The pipe stem pointed at Peter.

'That makes it more difficult.'

'I see.' Pause. 'It's late. I won't beat about the bush. I have a plan, not put to Cabinet, just here in my head. I'll share it with you two if you answer one question correctly. A reasonable question. If either of you answers no, then we'll to bed.'

Roger Courtauld savoured the malt whisky. Some of the best moments in politics came in dialogue across the party boundary.

'What's the question?'

'Are you in principle willing to help me preserve the Union, even if it means breaking with Alcester?'

'That would be the end of him,' said Roger. 'And ensure that Labour won the next election. Why should we want that?'

'The first, yes,' said Turnbull. 'The second, who can tell? That's three years away.'

The two Conservatives could have asked for time to consult each other in private. They were not personally close enough for either to think of this.

'My answer to your question is yes,' said Roger. 'In principle.'

'So is mine,' said Peter Makewell. 'But, of course, it depends on what we make of your plan.'

'If Cabinet approves, I will write this week to Alcester, accepting that the House should sit into August, but not to consider Scottish independence – we will put forward a Bill for a referendum on the Union. To be held at the end of September. Not just in Scotland – everywhere. Do you support the continuance of the United Kingdom? Yes or no.'

'The polls are against you. In both Scotland and the rest. Consistently they favour separation.'

'So it's a gamble. But I believe Alcester has overreached himself. The heart of England and the heart of Scotland don't like all this shouting and violence. They don't like being ranted at day in day out by the tabloids that Alcester has in his pocket. That's not the way we take decisions in this country – and it still is one country. But I'd need your help. "Conservatives for the Union", something like that. Joint literature, joint platforms. Vote yes for the future.'

'We're old,' said Peter Makewell.

'So are most people,' said Turnbull sharply, as if he had argued this point before. 'I rescued the Labour Party from Youth with a capital Y. It did us a power of harm, that fashion. The fashionmongers forget that young people change their ideas as they grow old, get kids, settle down. They want a settled country too. That's why we still have a monarchy and something called the House of Lords. Now it's you Tories who've caught the disease. It'll do you no good either.'

'Nothing to do with the two of us,' said Roger.

You let him in, the Prime Minister almost said, but bit off the sentence before speaking. It was not that kind of conversation.

Roger thought of Turnbull's phrase 'the heart of England'. He had just come from the heart of England, the plateau looking north and south, sun and shadow chasing each other over soft green slopes and hedges, villages now friendly with roses, young men foolish on ponies, endless conversation about the weather. For Turnbull the heart of England must be something quite different, shirt-sleeved argument in a Huddersfield bar, the click of snooker in the Labour club, the roar of a football crowd on a November afternoon as the cold came down. Both out-of-date images of course, but compatible. They lingered on, both of them. Turnbull had dealt neatly with that point about youth and age.

'I'll do it,' he said.

'I need till breakfast,' said Peter.

The other two guessed that he needed to telephone Louise, and did not blame him.

Over the kedgeree at eight next morning Peter Makewell agreed. Roger had a condition to add. 'If we get a good yes vote, no snap election. We're saving the Union, not the Labour Party.'

Turnbull was ready. 'Agreed. No election for at least two years, unless I come to you in some emergency.'

The three shook hands, self-consciously. It was not really necessary. The long years of opposing each other had created mutual trust.

From the evening of the dinner at Chequers for the Prime Minister of Jordan events moved quickly, in a direction that, later, most people felt was profitable. It did not seem so at the time.

GAMBLE OF A WISE MAN

By Alice Thomson, in the *Daily Telegraph*

Sometimes it is a mistake to seize the initiative, as Lord Cardigan found at Balaclava. The Prime Minister has launched his Light Brigade down the valley at the Conservative guns. The odds are against him. For eight weeks now public opinion polls have shown big majorities across the United Kingdom in favour of

independence for Scotland, the policy that David
Alcester has enthusiastically embraced since the
kidnap of his son. The majority in favour of Scottish
independence is now actually larger in England than in
Scotland. Long-standing unease in England and Wales
about the privileged position of the Scots inside the
Union has been transformed this summer into active
resentment. The Conservative leadership has managed
to convert resentment into active anger, and its off-
shoot New England has loosed this anger into the
streets. A dangerous tactic is now running out of control, and it is not surprising that the Prime Minister
decided he must exert himself before the summer holidays. Characteristically his initiative announced
yesterday is an attempt to jerk the discussion back into
traditional channels, first Parliament, then a referendum.

The first key vote will come in the Commons next
week on the second reading of the Government's Bill
providing for a referendum. The Commons will certainly pass the Bill, as will the Lords, for there is no
serious dissent in the Parliamentary Labour Party.
What will count, however, is the size and quality of the
majority, which could powerfully affect the result of the
referendum in September.

Watch two factors in particular. Most important,
how much disagreement exists in the Conservative
Party? David Alcester has no deep claim on its allegiance. He fought his way to the top quite recently by
tactics that many disliked. He allowed his own personal
drama to affect at least the timing and probably the

substance of policy. He then bludgeoned a weak
Shadow Cabinet into accepting his decision. He has
established personal control over the New England
Movement, whose noisy tactics make many
Conservatives uneasy. Where does all this leave traditional Conservative stalwarts, such as Roger Courtauld
and Peter Makewell? It leaves them silent – not a peep
out of either of them, or out of the dozen or so other
backbenchers who would follow their lead. They will
have to make their position clear at the second reading
or before. In the constituencies the activists are still in
love with David Alcester's slashing style. But just
behind the activists in most Associations is a bigger
range of traditionalists, brought into the Party in the
time of Simon Russell, standing for sober orthodox politics in reaction originally to the shallowness of New
Labour. What do these Conservatives make of New
England and David Alcester? In London we can identify the question, but not the answer. Courtauld,
Makewell and others may give us their answer soon.

Finally, the Scots themselves. Holding office
demurely in Edinburgh, the First Minister Robert Fraser
is, of course, in favour of Scottish independence. He
leads the Scottish Nationalist Party, for whom independence has long been the main aim. But he is not
pressing for independence, immediately. 'Prepare to be
strong' has been his watchword ever since he became
First Minister. Canny lawyer that he is, he enjoys
squeezing money and even greater autonomy out of the
Labour Government in London. He may calculate that
he is in a stronger position now, forever manoeuvring

on the edge of independence, than he ever would be in
an independent Scotland. Yet the horrid prospect of
real independence now confronts him – independence
gained not by careful profitable negotiation clause by
clause with London, but forced by his own half-violent
rivals the SLA and by anti-Scottish feeling in England,
which must in the long run do Scotland real harm. The
SLA still hold hostage his personal friend and colleague
the Lord Advocate James Cameron. In his inner heart I
am sure Robert Fraser would like to vote yes. He would
like to preserve the Union a little longer for him to
criticise and exploit. There might be more support in
Scotland for such a stance than most commentators
realise. But how could he justify such a vote to his
party? Once again a question easy to pose, impossible to
answer. It will be an unsettled summer, south and north
of the Border.

Editorial in *Thunder*:
Monday, 1 July

STRAIGHT TALKS AT LAST

At last we have it straight. At last the Tory Party has a
leader worth the name. Russell, Makewell, Courtauld –
clever men, no doubt, but clever in spinning little webs
of mystery and deceit. My proudest moment as editor of
Thunder came when we exposed Roger Courtauld and
stopped his bid for Downing Street. We had to live
through the short reign of Peter Makewell ending in
Tory defeat. But that defeat was worth while. It brought
to the fore a brave young leader who prefers light to

darkness. David Alcester has shone his searchlight into the dark corners of the Union and found them full of deception and fraud. 'The Scots want to go: let them go. Get rid of them now.' That's the simple message. It comes from the streets. It comes from the opinion polls. It comes from our *Thunder* readers. David Alcester has heard it and agrees. John Turnbull had heard it and is trying to frustrate it.

Thunder stands four square for Freedom – Freedom for Scotland, Freedom for England. And we give a word of warning to any ancient Tories who might use this crisis to stab young David in the back. We won't stand for it. Go back to your country houses, your grouse moors and polo lawns. Your time has gone: David is here with his sling and stone, ready for Goliath.

Extract from record of Scottish Parliament debate, Holyrood, Thursday, 4 July, Statement after Questions:

Mr Robert Fraser (First Minister): In the Scottish National Party we aim for a legal independence achieved by detailed negotiation with a friendly England. We aim to prepare our economy and our infrastructure for that negotiation and that independence, so that when it comes Scotland can not only be free but strong. We have nothing to do with violence, with kidnapping, with riots, with anti-English prejudice. That would only lead to an impoverished, despised Scotland, unable to hold up its head among the nations of Europe.

So it follows that we cannot touch, can have no part

in, the manoeuvres of the SLA and the English Tories.
Theirs is not the path for us. We have made good
progress on our path, and shall make more. We have no
intention of throwing ourselves over a cliff. On the
second reading of the government's Bill in Westminster
next week our SNP members will abstain, explaining
our position as I have done today – a principled absten-
tion for a principled independence. As a party we will
not take part in the referendum on 21 September, neither in the speech-making nor in the actual vote. It is a
referendum that has nothing to do with the Scotland
in which we live and for which some of us have worked
all our lives.

Lead story in the *Daily Telegraph*:
Friday, 5 July

In a last-minute shift of tactics the government yesterday postponed the second reading of its Scotland
(Independent Referendum) Bill from Monday next
week until Thursday. No reason was officially given but
clearly the delay is intended to give maximum effect to
the mass meeting to be held on Monday in Central
Hall, Westminster, by supporters of the referendum and
a yes vote in favour of the Union. So far the only
speaker named for this meeting is the Prime Minister
himself, who will also, of course, lead the second reading debate on Thursday. There is talk of surprise
speakers. Certainly a big effort is being made to attract
a large audience with hundreds of police drafted in to
prevent any disruption by New England demonstrators.

This news came as ministers digested the news that Scottish SNP leaders were advising their supporters, who had been expected to poll a massive no vote in September, to boycott the vote entirely. On the whole this was good news for the government. The Mori poll published on page 2 suggests that the pro-independence vote in all parts of the UK has begun to soften. On 1 July, of 1500 electors sampled 48% would vote no, i.e. against the Union (down 14 points on the last poll), 30% yes (up 5), with the don't knows rising to 22% (up 9). Much will depend . . .'

Chapter 9

'It's all your fault,' said Sarah Tunstall. 'You should never have stood down in that leadership contest. You'd still be Prime Minister now, and everything run in its proper way.'

Roger Courtauld looked at her affectionately across the table. It had taken him longer than he had hoped to pin her down. She had just finished her constituency surgery at the West Ealing community centre. He remembered the last time he had felt a spark of affection for Sarah, that night in the Carlton Club when he had come straight back from seeing young Roger at Hillcrest and had ruined the dinner party she had organised to win support for him. She had pleaded with him to stick it out, and he had turned her down. She had been entitled to go off and join David Alcester's Shadow Cabinet, and she was entitled to remind him now. But she could not evade the present by debating the past.

The years had tidied her up a bit. Her hair, now grey and thinner, no longer flowed across her face, and her voice was quieter. She had tried, he thought, to look and sound as tough as Joan Freetown, but she had never succeeded, even in the days when she had attemped to harass him as Home Secretary for softness on crime. The dreary years in opposition had mellowed and disappointed her as she tried in vain to restrain her new leader. Roger found that he liked and respected her more than in the past, but he could not spare her a hard choice.

'I'm going to speak tomorrow in Central Hall.'

'For the government?' But she could hardly be surprised.

'Not for the government. For the referendum, and for a decent way of running the United Kingdom.'

She did not react. Her hands were clasped on the folder of constituency cases which she had just dealt with. He read something in the whiteness of the knuckles.

'You must pull David back. He's run out of control. His policy won't work.'

'Not his policy, ours. All of us in the Shadow Cabinet supported independence for Scotland, independence for England. So do the opinion polls.'

'The polls are shifting already. People see how David Alcester hijacked policy on the back of that kidnap. He exploited you all. I bet you opposed him at that special meeting of the Shadow Cabinet after he came back from Nice. He's a shit, Sarah, you know that now. Some people say he even organised the kidnap himself.'

'I don't believe that.'

'Nor, as a matter of fact, do I. But he certainly exploited it to the full.'

Sarah was not proud of her performance at that meeting of the Shadow Cabinet. She should have been quicker, spoken out more strongly. But she wouldn't give in to Roger, who had backed out of the struggle earlier and more completely.

'You don't understand about women in politics.'

'Don't change the subject, Sarah.'

'It *is* the subject. Or part of it, as it concerns me.'

'What do you mean?'

She tidied her hair with one hand. 'There are still too few of us. We still feel it's a world run by men, under the rules they made. Loyalty to party is one of them.'

'Rules are there to be broken, when necessary.'

'That's a silly remark, as you know. Frivolous, masculine. Women feel they must hold on to the rules even more tightly because they did not make them. Men can fool about with rebellion and disloyalty. We women can't afford that.' Another pause. 'In the end the Shadow Cabinet decided unanimously in favour of David's independence policy. I can't go back on that.'

Roger pointed to the bundle of papers on the desk. 'There are wider loyalties. You have them there under your hand, all those constituents you are helping. You didn't go into politics to serve David Alcester.'

'But that's where I've ended up. You bear some of the responsibility for that.'

It was true, of course. Roger now believed he could have won that leadership contest, and probably the election that followed. In that case Sarah would now be a successful Secretary of State for Education, not a wispy has-been dealing with the pension cases and traffic problems of Ealing West. But what a stubborn woman. 'I admire your stubbornness, Sarah.' Wrong tone. 'No, seriously, I respect what you say. I can't ask you to come on the platform with me tomorrow. But you can reopen the whole thing in Shadow Cabinet. You can force David Alcester to back down. You can.'

'I'll think about it, Roger.' Sarah stood up, as if dismissing a constituent at the end of his allotted time. 'Thank you for coming to see me. I have a Chamber of Commerce lunch round the corner and I need a few minutes to sort these papers.' She let him peck her cheek.

As he went down the stairs Roger was dissatisfied. Somehow he had let her take the initiative from him.

Sarah did not sort the papers, for they were already sorted. She sat at the table for some minutes staring at the row of photographs on the wall of past Town Clerks. Then a noise in the street outside disturbed her. She got up and opened the window. A small group of youths in balaclavas carrying New England banners had established themselves outside the NatWest Bank opposite the community centre. Two of them moved to fasten a big poster on one of the windows facing the street. A solitary policeman made no attempt to hinder them.

'England for the English. Boycott the Tartan bank. Send the thieves home across the border.'

Discordantly the small crowd began to sing 'There'll Always Be an England.' Somebody put a match to a kilt, but it would not burn. The youths who had fixed the poster began to tape up the slots in the outside cash machine. The police-man still made no move.

Sarah watched for a minute. The futility and small malice of what she saw changed her mind. On her laptop she summoned up David Alcester's home telephone number. She had never been good at remembering telephone numbers by heart.

'It would be marvellous if you could. People have a huge respect for you and for Simon in the background behind you. You just have to say a few words.'

Louise was attracted by the idea, but still amazed that her husband should suggest it. 'It would be such a final step. I'm not sure I could do it.'

'It would make my position easier. No, I didn't say that. It's quite easy for me, though I shall hate every minute of it. By contrast, once you get going you'll relish it. Hat?' he added.

'Hat?'

'Will you wear a hat?'

'God, no – or yes, perhaps I should.' Pause. 'Peter, you're trying to force the pace.'

'I think you should definitely wear a hat. Something formidable in straw.'

'I haven't decided whether to go at all.'

'When are you going to give us an answer? The Prime Minister rang me again this morning.'

'I can't until I've given myself an answer. I've married two prime ministers, no need to bother with a third.'

'But you're genuinely still thinking?'

'Still thinking.'

'Think hard.'

John Turnbull had disliked the cold, unfeeling pillars of Central Hall, Westminster, ever since as a young minister he had been heckled there by the massed ranks of the Metropolitan Police Federation. But it held a lot of people. Because it was just across Parliament Square from the House of Commons, its meetings seemed to radiate a special influence to the political world outside.

He could still hear shouts from Tothill Street, which the police had given over to the New England crowd as part of the bargain to keep Victoria Street open to traffic. The Home

Secretary had just passed him a note along the line of Cabinet ministers seated on the front of the stage. All well: some scuffles, a dozen arrests so far, no serious violence, fewer demonstrators than expected.

All reasonably well, too, he thought, inside the hall. His opening speech had been short and simple. He had not argued at all closely the case for the Union. The referendum, he had said, was in part a vote on the right way of doing things. Our forefathers and great-grandmothers had fought for the vote because it was a way of achieving change without bloodshed. There was another way that was always tempting for those who were impatient and intolerant. Then he had launched into an attack on New England, and on the SLA in Scotland. James Cameron had just been released by the SLA but in a bad way, bruised and beaten. Turnbull referred to those politicians, unnamed, who had taken no part in violence – indeed, had themselves with their families suffered from it (pause while this sank in) but who nevertheless were willing to benefit from it. None of this was particularly logical as a defence of the referendum, but it had gone down well, and if he was right about the quickly changing mood of the public, it would help.

Then the surprise speakers. Neither Peter Makewell nor Roger Courtauld were great orators, but both were in that stage of retirement where the controversies of their own pasts were forgotten, and it was remembered that they were decent people who had done their best. Decent people, decent methods, a decent country – every now and then this underlying decency had to be reasserted so that the practitioners could get back to the games, often silly games, of politics without doing any real harm to anyone. Turnbull, not used to articulating such thoughts even to himself, supposed this was why he, Courtauld and Makewell had agreed after dinner at Chequers.

The name of the final surprise was not announced. She simply walked from the wings up to the lectern. This, too, was a gamble. Would enough of the audience immediately recognise Louise and give her the necessary welcome? The answer was yes, after a pause of three seconds, and the applause was excited and tumultuous because of the surprise. She wore a black coat and skirt over a yellow blouse. No hat, her silver hair profuse but disciplined.

'Unlike the others who have spoken I have no knowledge of the ins and outs of the constitution.'

A noise of polite dissent.

'Well, perhaps you do pick up a bit late at night or across the breakfast table, though usually it's the last thing they want to talk about.'

Then back to her notes.

'I am here as a widow, as a wife, as a mother . . . as a grand-mother.'

A murmur of sympathy in the hall as they remembered little Simon's ordeal.

'From all these relationships I have watched and helped human beings who are deep in politics. After all these years I am not one of those who are cynical about politics and politicians. On the contrary, I have never known a set of people who work so hard for others, as well as for themselves. But I have learned about a right way of doing things in politics and a wrong way. The Prime Minister is trying to get the discussion about Scotland back into the right way of doing things. The Prime Minister belongs to the Labour Party. You have heard my Conservative husband, Peter Makewell, support him. I know I am absolutely certain that Simon Russell, whom I remember day and night, would have done the same. I hope that you will support him too. That is all I have to say.'

It was enough. It was all worth it for that. The standing ovation would throw Louise's words round the world again and again. They would stay in people's minds for the necessary weeks up to the referendum.

The organisers had hoped that Julia Alcester would follow Louise. On the whole, the Prime Minister was glad that she had refused. He was a conservative in some matters. Whatever their views (and they could only guess at Julia's) he thought that wives should stick with their husbands. And, anyway, it was enough. His new Conservative allies had given him an impetus that he knew was now unstoppable. Weeks of argument lay ahead. There was no doubt in his mind of the outcome.

'Well done, Prime Minister.' Peter Makewell and Roger Courtauld took leave of him rather formally, at the side door of Central Hall.

'Thank you. It's enough, I think.'

'It's enough,' said Roger Courtauld.

'I agree,' said Peter Makewell.

There was no need for any more making of history that day. The old man who was Prime Minister was ushered into his car. Peter Makewell waited for his wife, who was besieged by photographers. The third old man, Roger Courtauld, began to look for a taxi to take him back to Marylebone and Northamptonshire.

Four days later the Cambridge Street flat was very quiet. Even the baby rites of Simon's day seemed to be performed in half-silence. David Alcester closed the lift door gently as he returned home at mid-morning. Unusually, he sought out his wife. She was in the kitchen shelling broad beans. 'I've thrown it in.'

Julia said nothing.

'The referendum campaign. The lot.'

'Why?' she asked, no expression yet in her voice.

'It was hopeless. Everything has been running against us. We're down to thirty-five per cent no, against fifty-five for yes.'

'You've got three weeks to go. Clive Wilson was saying on TV last night . . .'

'Clive Wilson,' said David, as if passing some judgement.

'What does he advise?'

'To carry on. He said his job and mine depended on it.'

'Was he right?'

'He was certainly right. I shall give up the leadership as well.' A pause. 'I don't know what I'll live on.'

'What *you* will live on?'

They were at the heart of it.

'Thank you for not going to Central Hall that day.'

'How did you find out that I was asked?'

'These things do not stay hidden. Why did you refuse?'

'I didn't know what to wear.'

David gaped. The old Julia was in the kitchen with him, shelling beans. He was glad. But he needed to be sure.

'You don't believe what Louise believes about Simon's kidnap?'

'I don't believe it. I half believed it when she said it. But not now.'

'Then . . .'

'Then we have to consider what *we* will live on.'

David ran to the window where, unbelievably long ago, he had held up the rescued Simon to the crowd.

The *Evening Standard* headline was just legible from the stack of papers at the front of the newsagent opposite. 'David Loses All,' it said.

'Perhaps not quite everything,' said David to the empty street and hoped it was true.

THE SHAPE OF ICE

Douglas Hurd

Brilliantly conveying the unrelenting pressure of
political existence at the highest level, *The Shape of Ice*
shuttles the reader from routine parliamentary
procedure to a media-fuelled international military
crisis, from the G8 Summit to Prime Minister Simon
Russell's most private moments, in a novel of stark
authenticity and escalating tension.

'A consistent page-turner . . . What makes *The Shape
of Ice* so enjoyable is that you constantly feel you are
getting the inside info on what it is like to hold high
office in government. The writing is full of sharp
observation and fascinating detail'
Sunday Telegraph

'The pace of the novel and the interweaving of plot lines
are breathless . . . Hurd has done his old trade a service,
by painting so vivid a picture of muddled, thrilling,
frustrating, compulsive reality'
Max Hastings, *Evening Standard*

'Richly authentic . . . an intriguing, unusual and
ambitious consideration of the political life'
Mail on Sunday

VOTE TO KILL

Douglas Hurd

Sir James Percival is the world-weary veteran of Tory politics. When he becomes PM after seven years of Labour rule, he – and the rest of the country – feels justified in looking forward to a quiet time.

But life is not like that, and neither is politics. He must contend with a new wave of violence in Ireland and turmoil in his own party, in the form of maverick MP Jeremy Cornwall. And when the Government is betrayed from within, the new administration – and Percival himself – must fight for its life. Politics and personal relationships become irrevocably entwined and the sheer pace of events takes control. *Vote To Kill* is a dazzling portrait of politics as the most addictive of all drugs.

'Beautifully written, the atmosphere at No. 10 is well conveyed (and) amusingly topical. Once started it was impossible to put down and I finished it at a sitting'
Edward Heath

SCOTCH ON THE ROCKS

Douglas Hurd and Andrew Osmond

From the blackened, crumbling tenements of Glasgow
come ugly rumours . . .

An army of separatist fanatics, recruited from the
razor-gangs of Europe's most violent city and funded
and armed by an unknown power, are standing ready –
waiting for the moment to strike. Is the nationalist
tide about to turn? Will Prime Minister Harvey
avert catastrophe . . . ?

A stunning political thriller set in the world of Scottish
Nationalism, Douglas Hurd and Andrew Osmond's
classic novel remains as compelling and as timely as ever.

'Refreshingly original . . . an ingenious
and well-told tale'
Sunday Times

'Hurd and Osmond are a brilliantly
perceptive political team'
Economist

'The pace of the action never slackens
from beginning to end'
Daily Telegraph

TEN MINUTES TO TURN THE DEVIL

Douglas Hurd

In this, his first collection of short stories,
Douglas Hurd combines his political insight and
fictional finesse to provide ten tales of intrigue,
deception, war – and startling perception.

Delving where politicians are forbidden to go, he explores
the shadows behind the failures and fruits of diplomacy,
weaving fictional characters into factual backdrops.
Behind the killing machines of Bosnia and Serbia we
meet people whose lives have been destroyed by truths,
half-truths, heroism and lies. A journalist attempts
to rewrite the Falklands history – until he encounters
reality. And amidst the olive groves of Tuscany, shades
of Agatha Christie turn a house party into hell as
blackmail and the black past rear their heads . . .

Drawing on his own extensive experience as a
traveller, writer and politician, Douglas Hurd has
created a rich and unique cocktail of entertainment
and enlightenment; served with equal measures
of tension and tragedy, hope and humanity.

'Mr Hurd is at his strongest when he brings a light touch
to affairs of state. The juxtaposition of substance and
trivia in the lives of politicians provides a rich seam
which he mines to great advantage'
Country Life

Other bestselling Time Warner Paperback titles available by mail: